THE SECRET OF SPELLSHADOW MANOR

P9-DGW-165

Brainerd Memorial Library
920 Saybrook Road
Haddam, CT 06438

BELLA FORREST

NIGHTLIGHT PRESS

Copyright © 2017 by Bella Forrest

All rights reserved.

No part of this book may be reproduced in any form or by any electronic
or mechanical means, including information storage and retrieval systems,
without written permission from the author, except for the use of brief
quotations in a book review.

First Edition

"There is no exquisite beauty without some strangeness in the proportion."

—Edgar Alan Poe

THE SECRET OF SPELLSHADOW MANOR

CHAPTER I

A HARD KNOT FORMED IN ALEX'S STOMACH AS HE stared at his laptop screen. He'd hoped this would be the month he finally earned enough to provide a meaningful contribution toward his mother's bills—that all the sleep he'd sacrificed to hone his coding skills would pay off and he'd begin earning a real income.

Scrolling through his latest earnings report, disappointment swelled in him. He was on track to earn less this month than the last. Barely three hundred dollars. Most seventeen-year-olds in the sleepy town of Middledale, Iowa, would have been happy with that kind of side income, but most seventeen-year-olds in Middledale didn't have a mother with a serious heart ailment.

Alex ran a hand over his face, tracing the lines in his furrowed brow. Then he dimmed the screen and pushed back in his chair. He was being unreasonable. He'd started looking for a way to earn money from home only five months ago, after his mother had returned from a two-week stay in the hospital barely able to walk. Coding websites had seemed like a natural fit for him because of its linear and analytical nature, but he needed to get a lot better at monetizing them. Still, five months wasn't long in the grand scheme of things. He just had to keep working at it.

His eyes travelled to the clock on his bedroom wall which had just struck 2 a.m., then to the pile of neglected homework on the right side of his desk. He was glad that it was Friday—or Saturday, now. He'd make time to get through his school assignments over the weekend.

"Alex?" his mother's voice called softly from her room across the hallway. "I hope you're not *still* awake?"

He whispered a curse as he realized he'd forgotten to line the crack of his bedroom door with his jacket, to stifle the light from escaping under it. He'd promised his mom he'd stop staying up so late and get more sleep. She hated that he felt pressured to earn money, and worried he didn't *live* enough—go out and act like other boys his age. That would have been easier for Alex if his father hadn't left them before he was born. His mother's health had been deteriorating for the past three years, and he didn't like to leave her alone whenever he could help it.

He rose from his chair and moved to the door, opening it with a sigh. "No, I'm asleep," he said wryly, making his way to her room. He pushed her door, which was always left slightly ajar, fully open and stepped inside. She was sitting up in bed against a pillow, her dark hair in a braid, the TV playing on mute in the background.

Her blue eyes looked rheumy against the flashes of the TV—as they usually did when she was in pain—and became tinged with disapproval as she took him in.

"It's Friday night, I'll sleep in," he reassured her quickly, moving to the bed. Noticing that the bottle of medicine closest to her on her bedside table was pain medication, he felt a stab of worry. "Are you okay?"

She caught his hand and pulled him down to kiss his cheek. "I'm okay. Just a headache." She cupped his face in her hands and narrowed her eyes. "But you look like death warmed over."

Alex smirked, knowing it wasn't much of an exaggeration. He *felt* exhausted. Catching his reflection in the mirror above the bed's headboard, his eyelids looked heavy, his dark brown hair mussed, and the premature lines in his forehead deeper than usual. He'd always looked unusually old for his age—now closer to a man in his mid-twenties than late teens—which his mother worried was from stress, but tiredness made it more pronounced.

"Goodnight to you too, Mom," he said, stooping to kiss

her cheek before heading for the door.

"Goodnight, honey."

As he left, he caught her mumbling, "Good thing Natalie's getting a taxi here after all."

Alex stopped in the bathroom doorway. *Natalie Chevalier.* He'd almost forgotten about their guest tomorrow morning. It had been his mother's idea to volunteer as host for the French student who was supposed to be staying with his classmate Garth's family. Garth's parents had dropped out of the arrangement at the last minute due to a "family emergency", leaving Natalie with tickets booked but no place to stay.

Alex had a sneaking suspicion that the bit of extra money they'd earn from hosting her wasn't his mother's only reason for volunteering. Certainly the idea of having someone his age hanging around the house for two weeks wouldn't have slipped her mind—and a girl, at that…

A French girl.

As Alex brushed his teeth, he found himself pushing back his hair and glancing at his reflection again, a little more critically.

Then he shook his head and rolled his eyes at himself.

With his school and business schedule, he barely had time for the few guy friends he had. He *really* didn't have time for girls.

CHAPTER 2

ALEX AWOKE TO SUNLIGHT TRICKLING THROUGH his curtains and the aroma of fresh pancakes. The sound of an unfamiliar voice drifting up from downstairs quickly oriented him. It was light and had a pretty, almost musical tone.

He sat up, pushing off his covers and rubbing his eyes. He glanced at his closed pristine white laptop, and then toward his door. The pancake smell made his stomach grumble, reminding him that he'd skipped dinner last night.

He approached the door and opened it slowly. Now he could hear the French voice clearly.

"Oh, this is so very good, Mrs. Webber. These

strawberries are even better than I've had in my town."

"I'm glad you like them!"

Alex raised his eyebrows. He hadn't expected Natalie's English to sound quite so polished. As he slipped out into the hallway and crept to the bathroom to take a shower, his mind was conjuring up images of what she looked like.

After he had washed and dried, he pulled on a pair of jeans and a loose t-shirt—his usual attire—and, after giving his hair a quick comb, returned to the hallway. Before moving to the staircase, he poked his head into the spare bedroom he had cleared out a few days ago. A large suitcase rested on the bed and the room was suffused with a pleasant flowery scent Alex couldn't quite put a name on.

He turned and headed down the creaky stairs.

"Oh," his mom's voice announced, "I think somebody has woken up."

Alex reached the bottom of the stairs, now in clear view from the kitchen, whose door had been left open. His immediate view was his mother, but as he drew closer, he caught his first glimpse of Natalie Chevalier, sitting on the opposite end of the table.

Alex's first thought was that her voice perfectly matched her appearance. Her face was pretty and delicate, with large brown eyes, a pert nose, and framed by silky black bangs. Her skin was light tan and her build was slim and athletic. Although Alex couldn't gauge her height too well from her sitting position, he suspected she was at least five foot eight.

"Hi," he said, clearing his throat and entering the room.

"Hello, Alex," Natalie said brightly, rising from the table and holding out her hand. He shook it, unable to help but notice how nice her skin felt. "Your mother has been telling me about you!"

"Oh dear," Alex said with a small smile, before seating himself in one of the only two seats available, both—most likely strategically—positioned next to Natalie.

Natalie chuckled. "Only good things."

Alex moved to busy himself with the pancake container, but before he could, his mom rose, supporting herself against the table with one hand, and served him.

"I told her that you're a budding entrepreneur," his mom supplied, and Alex looked back at Natalie.

He smiled placidly. "Budding being the operative word."

"You know, I think that is so wonderful," Natalie announced, beaming at him with genuine enthusiasm. "I don't know anybody my age back home who is an entrepreneur. You make websites, yes?"

"Uh, yeah." Alex glanced swiftly at his mom, who gave him a knowing look. He was a little surprised that she would've told her this already, since she didn't usually encourage Alex's extreme work ethic.

Though, Alex supposed there wasn't much else to say

about him at the moment. Other than working on his business and playing the piano, he currently didn't have any extracurricular activities.

From Natalie's build, he wouldn't have been surprised if she was a member of a basketball team, or maybe a tennis player.

"Yes, websites," Alex confirmed in a louder voice. "It's not very interesting, though." He'd been experimenting with building sites around narrow audiences in order to avoid competition and make it easier to attract traffic, which had led him to some *very* "niche" subjects that weren't exactly sexy. From Halloween dog costumes to dating websites for farmers, Alex had probably thought of it.

"I find it very interesting," Natalie replied. "I would love to see them—oh." She paused, her eyes widening. "I completely forgot. I said that I would video-call my parents as soon as I arrived at your house."

"Why don't you go ahead and do that now?" Alex's mom suggested.

Natalie ducked beneath the table, reaching for a backpack she had resting by her feet. She resurfaced holding a small laptop. She started it up and the sound of dialing filled the sun-streaked kitchen.

"Bonjour!" enthused a voice that sounded almost identical to Natalie's, but older.

Natalie began speaking in rapid French, looking up constantly to Alex and his mom, smiling and flashing her pearly teeth.

Then she picked up the laptop and hurried to Alex, who had just been in the middle of his last mouthful of pancake. He quickly swallowed, managing not to choke as Natalie stood beside him, presenting him with the screen. Gazing back at him was clearly Natalie's mother, father, and a younger girl who must've been her sister—perhaps middle school-aged, he guessed.

"Hello Alex!" the three greeted at once.

"Hi," Alex replied, wiping his mouth with a tissue before giving a small wave.

"Thank you for having Natalie!" Mrs. Chevalier said. "I hope you both have a good time."

Before Alex could respond, the young girl fired a bout of French at him. He blinked, uncertain of what she'd said, when Mrs. Chevalier laughed and translated, "Elena says to promise to look after her sister!"

"Ah, right." Alex grinned. "We—I—promise. Don't worry."

Natalie chuckled and then moved on to Alex's mom, where they had a similar, slightly longer greeting.

Alex's mom eyed him with quiet amusement as Natalie ended the conversation with a flurry of air kisses. He averted his gaze to a strawberry.

"Now, have you had enough to eat, dear?" Alex's mom asked after Natalie ended the call.

"Oh yes, certainly." She leaned back in her chair and

rubbed her stomach.

"And you, Alex?" his mom asked.

Alex looked up, frowning. "Uh, yeah," he replied, unsure of where his mom was going with this.

"Well, I was going to suggest you take Natalie on a tour of the town while it's so bright and sunny outside."

Natalie sat forward. "That sounds perfect!"

He was an idiot to not have seen that coming. He thought of all the work he had planned to do this weekend, including that stack of homework, but he couldn't refuse without appearing extremely rude…and if he was honest with himself, he thought a break from his laptop screen might do him some good. It was a beautiful day, after all.

Pushing his plate and cutlery away from him, he glanced at Natalie and smiled. "Okay, let's go for a ride."

His mother winked at him as the two of them left the room.

"I'm gonna be honest, there's not a lot to see in Middledale," Alex said, as he opened the passenger door of his car for Natalie to slide in. She did so gracefully, pulling the small handbag she'd unpacked onto her lap. She had changed out of the clothes she had arrived in—leggings and a pullover—in favor of an outfit that oddly mirrored his; a casual t-shirt and jeans.

He moved around to the driver's seat and got in, scooping up a pair of sunglasses from the dashboard and donning them before starting the engine.

"I mean," he continued, pulling out of the driveway and swerving onto the road, "it's a nice place. Some beautiful scenery"—he gestured to the sprawl of fields that was already coming into view behind the row of houses on their left—"and a lot of peace and quiet. There's a mall in the center of town, which has a small movie theater, a bunch of shops, restaurants, a bowling alley..."

He trailed off as he caught a glance of Natalie. She sat stiffly, looking straight ahead and clutching her seat a little too tightly.

"Hey," he said, drawing her gaze to his, "are you okay?

"Yeah," she said quickly, offering him a smile. "You just, um, drive quite fast."

"Oh, sorry." Alex reminded himself what it must be like to be a first-time passenger in a vehicle he was commandeering. His style valued efficiency over leisure, as his mom would describe it. "I'll take it easier."

He slowed down, and Natalie instantly relaxed.

"I'll take you past the school, it's coming up just on our right," Alex informed her as they rounded the corner.

"How do you like school?" Natalie asked.

"It's fine," Alex replied. He couldn't really think of

a better adjective than that. He neither loved nor hated school, though recently, it was becoming more and more of a distraction from his entrepreneurial endeavors.

They arrived within view of Middledale High. It was a large, very boring rectangular building, its exterior in need of a renovation. But it was a decent school by most standards—average, but decent.

"Do you have many friends?" Natalie asked.

"Mmm, not many," Alex replied honestly, and decided not to embellish his answer. He tried to hide the fact from his mom that his social life had deteriorated along with her health. He was so busy these days and rarely saw friends outside of school hours, which resulted in him growing apart even from his best friend, Colin.

Natalie probably found his short answer a little odd but didn't press. Instead, she moved on to a topic that was much more interesting to Alex—herself. She began to talk about what it was like to grow up in France, and the differences between there and America. She said she'd visited New York before when she was younger, and this was her second time in the United States. Alex had never been abroad—heck, he'd hardly been out of Iowa—but hoped to someday. When his mother got better.

Natalie came to a pause as they neared the mall, and her face took on a thoughtful expression. She spoke again after a few minutes. "I suppose I don't have many friends either. I mean, there are people you see every day and are friendly with, but…real friends"—she smiled—"I think they are quite a rare species."

Alex wasn't sure if she was just saying this because she wanted to be companionable, or because she hadn't found his response to her earlier question strange after all. "I agree," he replied, in any case.

They were quiet again until they neared the mall's parking lot, when Alex suggested they stop for ice cream. Natalie expressed her strong agreement, so he parked up and led her into the mall.

As they neared the ice cream parlor, he spotted four guys from his class. Phil, a blond-haired giant of a seventeen-year-old, with his three hangers-on, David, Sam, and Josh.

Their eyes drew to Natalie as though she were a magnet. Alex rolled his eyes internally. He could practically see the lightbulbs sparking in their heads as they exchanged glances, and then Phil walked over.

"Hey, Alex!" he said, throwing him a smile. This was probably the first time Phil had spoken to him directly all year; Alex had never been close to Phil.

"This is your new girlfriend?" he asked.

"Nope," Alex replied.

"We're friends," Natalie added.

"A guest from France," Alex clarified. He moved around Phil and Natalie followed as they lined up at the ice cream store. He sensed all four boys' eyes on her.

"I'll take a double mint chocolate chip," Alex ordered. "And Natalie?"

"I'll take the same."

"Hey, Alex." Phil came at him again, leaning an elbow against the glass counter. "Did you hear about the party I'm throwing this evening?"

Alex saw where this was going.

"No, actually," he said. He paid, took a lick of his ice cream, and then turned away, Natalie walking beside him.

"Well, I wanted to invite you," Phil persisted, catching up with them and arriving on Natalie's side.

"You" meaning Natalie.

"Starts at eight p.m.," he said. "I've got a massive back yard with a pool."

"An American *pool party*?" Natalie breathed suddenly, as though the idea was almost sacred. Her eyes lit up as she turned to face Alex.

"It'll be cool," Phil jumped in, capitalizing on her interest.

Alex stopped walking and looked at him reluctantly.

"Lots of people are coming," he went on. "Even your pal Colin might show up."

Somehow, Alex doubted very much that Colin would be showing up.

Still, Natalie had gotten all excited about it now. She clearly wanted to go, and as her host, he figured he should probably acquiesce. It was her first day here, and it was unlikely that he was going to get any serious work done today anyway.

"Okay, Phil," Alex conceded with a sigh. "Count us in, I guess...Thanks."

"Awesome!" Phil slapped Alex on the back, before taking the liberty of giving Natalie's shoulder a quick squeeze.

"*Awesome!*" Natalie mimicked with a giggle as Phil left to return to his friends.

Alex smiled faintly as they took a seat on a bench in front of one of the indoor fountains. He watched the four boys retreating from the parlor deeper into the mall.

Digging back into his ice cream, he thought forward to this evening and realized he could barely remember the last time he'd been to a party...

Touché, Mom. Touché.

CHAPTER 3

S O, WHAT WAS HE GOING TO WEAR FOR THIS THING?

He and Natalie had returned from their tour just after 2 p.m. Natalie had been feeling tired by then from her long journey, so she'd decided to take a nap before the party. That was several hours ago—now he could hear her in the shower, getting ready for tonight. His mom, of course, was delighted to hear that he had accepted the invitation and had given him her blessing to stay out late.

He examined the clothes in his wardrobe and ultimately decided to wear a slightly smarter shirt, while keeping his jeans. Then, seeing that he had some downtime, he figured he'd put it to good use and started on his homework—until a knock came at his door.

"It's Natalie," came her voice.

"Come in," he said.

She pushed the door open and stepped inside, bringing with her that heady floral scent. She had changed into a red dress that went down to just above her knees, and she had done something to her hair to make it look curly. She looked stunning, Alex couldn't deny that.

He rose to his feet, realizing that this was the first time she had ventured into his room. She gazed around at his bare walls, her eyes traveling over his single bed, then to his desk, chair, and bookshelf—the only four pieces of furniture he kept in the room.

"Wow. Minimalist."

Alex smirked. "That's one way to put it." The truth was, he just didn't like any form of clutter. It crowded his brain, and he could think much more clearly without it.

"And your bookshelf"—she walked over to it—"is alphabetized."

"Yeah."

"Interesting," she remarked, pulling down a book on marine biology and flipping through the pages. Alex noticed her eyes glossing over the text completely and focusing on the vibrant pictures.

He let her continue perusing his books for another minute, and then since they were due to leave in only five minutes, he suggested they head down to the car.

His mom came to the door with her walking support and kissed them both goodbye on the cheek.

"Have fun!" she said as they closed the door.

"Will do," Alex murmured, sucking in a breath as he led his pretty French date to the car.

As Phil had promised, the party was packed. Natalie stuck close to Alex as they milled through the teeming living room toward the back garden. She turned almost every guy's head they passed, but seemed completely unfazed by it as she chatted away to Alex about how excited she was to be here.

Phil strode over as soon as he spotted them by the pool and, predictably, angled for a dance with Natalie. To Alex's surprise, she blew him off, albeit very politely—citing jet lag as an excuse.

"He's not my type," she informed Alex with a grin as he walked away. Which left Alex to wonder exactly what her type was. From his experience, most girls seemed to fall over themselves for butch guys like Phil.

Alex searched the crowd for Colin, or someone else he was close to at school, but couldn't spot anyone. So he and Natalie found themselves sitting together by the pool, continuing to snack and talk. He guessed that she would expect him to ask her to dance at some point, but she still seemed to be happy talking, so he decided to delay that thought a little longer. It had been a while since his last dance.

About two hours into the party, Natalie needed the bathroom. She claimed she could find it herself, which left him sitting alone for the first time.

He took a slow sip from his drink, feeling the cool crackle of carbonation trickle down his throat, then lowered the can to his knee again. He focused on the scene around him now that his attention wasn't consumed by Natalie.

He actually liked parties, in general, even when he found himself alone. There was something intriguing about the ways people let their guard down; he might see some of them every day at school, but at a party he got to see a completely different side of everyone. In the darkened room, with music blasting its throbbing bass through an expensive PA system and colorful lights pulsing rhythmically, dancers dropped their inhibitions and personas, becoming freer, wilder.

Though most likely nobody could tell from his relaxed demeanor, he found the room's energy engaging, observing the scene with bright, interested eyes.

His eyes fell on a girl named Sarah, who was glowering darkly on the sidelines of the pool. Not unusual for Sarah, but a little out of place amid the revelry surrounding her. He followed her gaze to Josh, who he was pretty sure was Sarah's boyfriend, dancing closely with another girl. Mindy, he thought, from the basketball team. He felt a jolt of sympathy for Sarah, but it quickly dissipated when she seized Terry, a small boy with thin brown curls and bad posture, and pulled his arms around her. *Hm.* Interesting.

Dull, ghostly light was filtering up from the splashing water, throwing shadows of the swimmers up across the house like contorting dancers. The air was hot with the last embers of summer, and it hung heavy and wet against his skin as the smell of smoke drifted into his nose. Alex closed his eyes for a moment, savoring the earthy night-time scent.

"Hey, Alex."

Alex turned to see Phil approaching him again, his face dappled with watery light. Alex raised an eyebrow, wondering what he wanted.

"So," Phil said, drawing close and putting an arm around Alex, turning him so they were both surveying the party. "Got your eye on anyone, seeing that Natalie is just a *friend*?"

"Uh, no, not so much. Just hanging out tonight. I'll bet you do, though."

"No, no, no. I'm here for you tonight, bro. Gonna show you how to live a little."

"Is that so?" Alex had to stifle a chuckle. He'd always

thought Phil something of a brute, and they had never been what he would call friends, but in this more liberated environment, he found his behavior amusing. "All right then, do your worst." He was actually morbidly curious to see who Phil thought was his match.

"Okay," said Phil. "Well..." His gaze swept the sea of figures, and he frowned a little as he tried to decide how, exactly, Alex should live a little. "All right," he declared after a moment. "There's your girl. Constance. She's smart, right? Like you." He boldly pointed straight at Constance, who was seated primly at the pool's edge, chatting to her friend Jamie in an undertone.

Alex was surprised. He'd expected a much less thoughtful match from Phil. Constance was indeed smart, and quiet, and pretty. But she was also terribly shy, even now keeping her arms close to her and talking only to Jamie. And she was a little odd, too. Alex doubted Phil had noticed, but Constance often wore tiny pentacle earrings and a leather hex bag, or something like one, around her neck. Someone like Constance was unlikely to appreciate being bothered by a guy like Phil, and Alex threw out an arm to stop Phil lurching over to her. Luckily, she was too absorbed in her conversation to notice.

"Woah, Phil." He clapped Phil companionably on the back and steered him around to face the Jacuzzi instead. "Constance is pretty great and all, but—"

"All right, all right," interrupted Phil. "Tough customer,

okay. Let's see…yeah! Check out Julia!"

Julia was sitting by the Jacuzzi, a towel drawn around her shoulders, bare legs glistening with pool water. Her laugh tinkled prettily, the noise clear and carrying, but Alex detected a note of insincerity. She was clever, friendly, and beautiful, yes, but a little self-absorbed. Nothing out of the ordinary for a girl her age, he supposed, watching the practiced way she flipped a shiny lock of golden hair.

He glanced at Phil again, noticing the way his eyes lingered on Julia's legs, the way his pupils dilated ever so slightly. He smiled to himself.

"Yeah, Phil, that's more like it. I think she's perfect for you."

"For me? Nah, I'm not—"

"She's looking over here! Go on, go talk to her!"

"What? Is she really?" She actually was, to Alex's delight. She flashed them a smile before turning back to her friends, chatting a little more animatedly than before.

"Yeah, go on, man. You got this."

Phil collected himself fairly quickly and started for Julia, but stopped mid-step, seeming to remember he was supposed to hook Alex up.

"Okay, buddy, but come on…You really are going out with the French girl, right?" He grinned widely and gave Alex what was probably meant to be a light nudge before squaring his shoulders and heading in Julia's direction. At least Julia could handle herself if she wasn't as interested as she seemed.

Alex recovered quickly from the "nudge" and, upon straightening, immediately scanned the crowd for Natalie. She'd been longer than he'd expected her to be.

He spotted her as she stepped out of the house, looking a little flushed. Just as she began making her way toward the pool, he noticed something behind her that made him do a double take.

In a sea of flashy colors and swirling lights, the figure behind Natalie was almost comically different. Dressed all in gray, tattered clothes, the man stood three full hands taller than the girl he followed, who was seemingly oblivious to his presence, though she turned in his direction. His long fingers clasped and unclasped in front of him, stretching out toward her, and his chin tilted out as his papery lips moved as if to whisper. He moved slowly, hunching over and then straightening, swiveling his head back and forth.

"What the...?" Alex breathed, and jolted forward—just in time to collide with two dancing couples who swerved in front of him, blocking Natalie from view. When he searched for her again, to his surprise, she was moving toward the opposite side of the pool.

The man was still following her.

Alex surged ahead, grabbing Phil as he passed by him. "Hey, who's that weird guy following Natalie?" he asked, pulling him along.

"Uh, what?" Phil said, blinking. He looked where Alex did. "You mean Ben? He's not following her, he's just—"

Alex shook his head. Ben was following her, using the pretense of walking over to the drink stand, but that was beside the point. "Not Ben. That tall man in rags!"

"Rags?" repeated Phil, now sounding utterly confused. "I don't see any…"

The figure was following Natalie along the side of the pool now. Nobody else seemed to be reacting to his presence.

Alex left Phil behind and continued pushing past people.

He had his answer: either nobody else could see the figure, or they were pretending they couldn't. Possible explanations flashed rapidly through his mind—it was a prank, it was a trick of the light, he'd been drugged—as he cut through the crowd, trying to keep Natalie in view. The worst-case scenario was that the girl had been in this country less than a day before managing to pick up a creepy stalker. And he'd promised to look out for her.

She was just around the pool's corner from him, just through another throng of people. He had almost reached her, but before he could push through, there came an enormous splash, followed by whoops of laughter. The crowd tightened around the pool, hollering and cheering, and he lost sight of Natalie once again. He craned his neck, but the teeming mass of people was now impossible to penetrate.

Panic rose in his throat, humming there like a swarm of bees.

Suddenly, Natalie slipped through the crowd, appearing quickly at his side with a look of concern on her face.

"Natalie!" Alex sighed, trying not to appear too relieved. There was no sign of a figure in rags anywhere around her. It must have been some bizarre hallucination after all.

"That poor boy!" she exclaimed anxiously. "Did you see? The big one, right there, he just threw him in."

She gestured beside them, where a fully clothed Terry floundered pathetically, presumably dumped there by Josh. His embarrassment would be all over social media within seconds, judging by the dozens of phones aiming their bright flashes at him.

Alex bent to the pool, offering Terry his hand. "Come on, I'll help you up. Just ignore these guys."

Terry clutched at him, trembling a little, and ended up half-soaking Alex, too. He hauled the bedraggled boy out of the pool, sitting him down away from the thinning crowd.

He stood up, and while Natalie made sure Terry was okay, he found himself looking around again for the apparition to make sure it hadn't reappeared. It hadn't, but the experience had left a queasy feeling in Alex's stomach he couldn't shake. What had *caused* the hallucination?

They'd been at the party for over two hours, and now

that Terry had managed to soak his clothes, Alex figured he had a legitimate excuse to suggest they head back now.

He'd expected Natalie to be disappointed by the prospect, but as she turned away from Terry to face him, her face was traced with exhaustion—a stark contrast to the bright, well-rested girl he'd arrived with.

"Shall we leave now?" she suggested. "I'm tired."

"Yes," Alex replied, already leading her back to the house. "Let's leave."

CHAPTER 4

NATALIE STAYED IN HER ROOM FOR ALMOST THE entire next day, chilling and trying to fight off jet lag, presumably. Alex's mom thought it was a wise use of the rest of the weekend and hoped she'd feel fresh for school on Monday.

Alex slept in later than usual too, and then took the opportunity to catch up on his homework and spend some time on his business. The apparition at the party still bothered him, but he figured that, whatever it was, it was unlikely to happen again so he should just forget about it.

On Monday morning, Natalie was looking sprightly again. He drove her to school and guided her to the reception, where he left her to have a meeting with the school's exchange program liaison.

Then he made his way to the classroom where his first lesson of the day—history—was due to be held, and found it empty. He sat down and pulled out a book on marketing, which he read while students trickled in, until Colin sat down next to him and started telling him about a surprise weekend camping trip his parents had taken him on.

When their teacher Mrs. Lambert arrived, she was followed by Natalie, who waved at him.

And then the gray thing in rags stepped in behind her.

Alex almost choked on his tongue.

It was the same as before. Its skin was still sickly gray beneath the bright, fluorescent glare, the rags hanging off it yellowing and frayed, fluttering in an unseen wind. Alex's eyes bulged as the claw-like hand raked slowly through the air, reaching for Natalie, clasping for the back of her head.

This can't be happening.

He glanced quickly around, but once again, nobody else seemed to notice anything was wrong, and the thing in rags slid into the room after Natalie. Mrs. Lambert tied her graying shoulder-length hair back in a ponytail, introduced Natalie to the class, and then grabbed a marker. Alex gaped as she calmly wrote out the day's lesson plan on the whiteboard, then quickly looked back to see the thing shuffling along in Natalie's wake, following her to an open desk before hunching to whisper in her ear.

Somehow, seeing this creature here, in a perfectly ordinary classroom he visited every day, right in front of Mrs. Lambert, unnerved him even more than seeing it at the party. He must be out of his mind. Hallucinating—definitely, yes, but why was his hallucination so…specific? So focused on Natalie?

Mrs. Lambert began the lesson, oblivious to the corpse-like figure whispering into her pupil's ear. Alex, mind whirling, did his best to follow her lecture, but couldn't refrain from shooting his eyes over to Natalie every few seconds.

The thing didn't move much, save for its lips. It crouched now, rags spilling out around its feet like a pool of gray liquid, jagged hands grasping the sides of Natalie's desk. It was whispering incessantly, almost feverishly, into Natalie's ear, and caressing the desk as it spoke.

"Alex?"

Alex blinked, looking up. Mrs. Lambert was smiling at him expectantly, her marker held between two fingers.

"Yes?"

She looked a little surprised. "I was just asking," she said, "if you could explain to the class what the Hobbesian state of nature is?"

In the corner of Alex's eye, the thing's lips were fluttering as it whispered, as distracting as the buzzing of a fly. He answered Mrs. Lambert absentmindedly, his attention on the apparition.

"Hobbesian…yes." He ran a hand through his hair, trying not to look at Natalie. "Ah, philosopher Thomas Hobbes deduced in the seventeenth century that man's natural state is one of equality, but believed this equality to take the form of…of continuous warfare. Since man is naturally pitted against his fellows, Hobbes argued in favor of embracing a strong sovereign, with absolute… power"—he cut his eyes at the ragged thing—"seeing this as the only possible way to avoid constant bloodshed and, um, civil war. Though it seems extreme, one must remember that he wrote Leviathan, in which this theory is expressed, during…during the English Civil War, a particularly bloody time in England's history."

Mrs. Lambert beamed. "Excellent, Alex. Very well put. Would anyone like to expand on Alex's answer?"

Chris, a ginger-haired boy with a slash of freckles across the bridge of his nose, eagerly raised his hand. Alex glanced back to Natalie, unable to push the hallucination from his mind. He heard a bunch of girls whispering and giggling behind him, clearly thinking their conversation private. They seemed highly interested in the attention he was paying Natalie, but he ignored them, gritting his teeth, refusing to look at the hallucination again, trying to focus solely on the lesson.

Chris was just finishing his answer. "Therefore," he said, voice whistling out through his teeth, "when lived alone, life is nasty, brutish, and short."

Mrs. Lambert nodded, turning back to the board and writing the three words: Nasty. Brutish. Short.

"And, can anyone tell me the Latin phrase Hobbes used to describe this? Alex, I'm sure you know it; go ahead."

Alex paused a moment. Natalie was starting to lean listlessly to the side, head drooping toward the figure beside her. It tensed, flexing its long, pale fingers.

"Bellum omnium contra omnes," he answered, not taking his eyes from Natalie.

Mrs. Lambert made some exclamation of praise, but Alex wasn't listening. He knew the figure wasn't real, wasn't anything, but he felt chilled to the bone nonetheless. It was cradling her head now, pulling her close to its chest, running its hands over her as if excited.

Natalie raised a limp hand. "Excuse me, I…I don't think I'm feeling well," she said, her voice oddly toneless. "Is there a nurse?"

"Why, yes, Natalie," Mrs. Lambert replied, looking concerned. "You do look a bit unwell. Her office is just at the end of this hallway—turn left and it's only six doors along."

Alex shot to his feet, shoving his books into his bag and saying, "Mrs. Lambert, I should probably go with her."

"Oh, I think Natalie can find her way," the teacher replied with a knowing smile, and Alex stopped.

He stared as Natalie left without glancing back at him,

and the dread hallucination trailed after her, still whispering, its hands now at her forehead, stroking down her spine.

The giggles that broke out behind him sounded manic in comparison, making the scene even more surreal.

Of course, he told himself firmly, Natalie didn't need help finding the nurse's office. She was probably just still tired, her body adjusting to the new environment. Maybe she'd even caught a mild bug. There was nothing to worry about.

And, for some reason, I'm just still hallucinating.

He set his bag down and dropped back into his seat, watching as the door closed through the end of the thing's rags. Class continued as normal, though without further involvement from him.

CHAPTER 5

ALEX MADE HIS WAY QUICKLY BETWEEN THE ROWS of lockers that made up the halls of Middledale High. The other students bustled around him, chattering loudly as they grabbed books from their lockers and made their way to their next classes.

But Alex had no intention of going to his next class. He was heading straight to the nurse's office to see if Natalie was still there. It was an irrational thing to do, checking on Natalie. He was obviously having profound mental issues, and it could prove drastic to involve some-one else.

But as much as he'd tried to reassure himself that this

was all in his head, he just couldn't rid himself of the feeling that something horrible was happening to her, right now. Mrs. Lambert had seen Natalie was unwell too, when earlier this morning she'd looked fine. That wasn't just his imagination.

He found himself speeding to a trot, and soon approached the door to the nurse's office, which was shut. He remembered just in time that he should knock, and rapped quickly before bursting into the small room.

The creature in rags was standing less than two feet from him, with one hand at the small of Natalie's back. Alex sucked in a sharp breath, and with it came the vague taste of dirt, and something wet. He almost gagged, staring. He'd never been this close to the thing before. Seeing it now, he could tell just how dilapidated its clothes were. They weren't just tattered, but filthy. Streaks of dirt, and something dark and red, slashed along the back, and the loose sleeves were heavy with rot. Blue veins wrapped around the tendons in its wrists, standing out starkly through its papery skin, and it kept up an incessant, hissing whisper.

It was extraordinarily visceral for a hallucination.

Natalie didn't even seem to have noticed him enter the room, sitting in the nurse's chair with her head buried in her hands. Her glossy black hair spilled out between her fingers, cascading down about her knees. The thing stood as still as death, its torn gray clothes fluttering lightly around it.

"Natalie?"

Her head jerked up, eyes wide and staring, and she forced a weak smile.

"Hi. Alex." Her voice sounded remote.

"I just wanted to check on you," he said uncertainly. "How are you feeling?"

"Oh. Not well. I…can't be…here anymore." Her speech was oddly staggered, coming out in short bursts. Very unlike the exuberant, talkative girl he knew her to be.

If he had hoped seeing her would reassure him, he was sorely disappointed. She seemed worse than ever, worn down, drained of all personality. At her side, the thing turned in Alex's direction and shifted slightly beneath its rags.

"Do you think you're sick?" Alex pressed, keeping an eye on the hallucination.

"I think I'm…sick," she said lifelessly.

The thing stopped its indecipherable whispering and abruptly took a step toward Alex, removing its hand from Natalie's back to shuffle over to him. It moved its head back and forth, as if searching him out. Alex took an involuntary step back, horrified despite himself, his heart beating faster.

"Alex?" said Natalie, in a voice that was suddenly more her own. "Are you okay?"

"Y-Yes, I'm fine," he managed. *Act natural. She doesn't*

know you're hallucinating.

It drew closer, but didn't seem to see him, apparently staring right through him to the door at his back. For the first time, Alex could fully make out its face. The glassy eyes were like the night sky, black and full of stars. Its hollow cheeks were dusted with a short, bristling beard, and its patchy gray hair hung down in lank locks. There was a soft noise as its fetid clothes dragged upon the ground behind it.

"Okay." Natalie gave a weak laugh. "The nurse just had to take a phone call, but she'll be back in a minute. So… what are you doing in here? Are you feeling sick too?" She tilted her head a little. "And what are you staring at?"

"N-Nothing," he said. He forced his eyes back to her and saw a little more color in her cheeks. "And yes—I mean, no, I'm feeling fine. I just wanted to check on you."

"You shouldn't be here," rasped the hallucination with a soft sound of irritation.

That was the final straw for Alex. "*What?*" he snapped, turning on the thing.

"Huh?" Natalie frowned.

He whirled on her, running both hands quickly through his hair.

"Alex," she said cautiously, "are you sure you're feeling okay? You're acting…quite insane."

Yes, he was acting insane. He felt insane.

"Natalie, don't you see this man?" he finally burst out.

He jumped forward and pointed at the figure, now moving slowly back to her side. She recoiled a little and looked blankly where he indicated.

"*Man?*"

"He's standing right next to you. He's reaching toward you. Right there."

Natalie looked alarmed, even a little afraid. She grew very still as the thing replaced its hand at her back, the energy seeming to fade from her limbs again.

"Alex…" Her lifeless tone returned. "I…I think I have to go. Home." She rose gracefully and walked to the door. "I…hope you feel better." Alex gaped as the thing followed her out, one hand at her back again.

"Don't interfere," hissed the hallucination before continuing its low whisper.

"Home?" Alex exclaimed, rushing after them into the crowded hallway. "We can't go home without permission, I'll need to—"

Two things happened at once: the gray man disappeared, and Natalie—as if struck by a bolt of electricity—lurched forward into a swarm of students, vanishing from Alex's view.

"Natalie!" Alex called, his voice drowned out by the loud chattering. He pushed past students to chase after her, but when he got through the crowd and reached the other, sparser end of the hallway, she was nowhere in sight. Alex felt a breeze and looked to his left.

The side door was open.

He sprinted to it and slipped out, emerging in the parking lot at the front of the school. He looked around for Natalie, but still couldn't see her. She must have left the compound already.

What in the world was going through her head? Alex couldn't even begin to fathom it.

He hurried through the parking lot exit and scanned the adjoining road. He figured, if she really did remember the way back to his house, she would have taken the first left down Jamesdon Street, so he dashed directly to it.

His instinct had been correct. He spotted her about halfway down, though she had slowed to a walk and appeared to be moving with purpose toward Ellis Street, which ran perpendicular to Jamesdon Street.

The gray thing was with her.

Everything about it clashed with the placid, beautiful street. Amid the suburban houses, its eerie aura seemed almost to glow, warping the features around him into strange mockeries of their original forms. Trees seemed to loom, branches looked more like claws, and houses that had felt normal moments before now seemed to contain eerie lights.

Alex swallowed, rallying himself before rushing forward.

"Natalie!" he shouted. "Wait!"

She ignored him. She had stopped at the beginning of

the road that…should have been Ellis Street. When Alex looked for the sign, however, he found only a rusting iron guidepost pointing in the direction Natalie was looking. Upon it, a single word was written: Spellshadow.

"Natalie!" he urged.

Once again, it was as though she couldn't hear him. The emotion was gone from her face, her cheeks slack. She stepped forward, and the man behind her nodded, pushing her lightly. When she continued to walk, he let out a deep, throaty sigh.

Alex caught up, grabbing Natalie's arm.

"Where are you—"

She shook him off with such alarming force that Alex went sprawling to the cement. He shouted in shock, leaping back to his feet just in time to see her and her gray companion strolling away down the lane.

"What?" he gasped. He had known she was fit, but that was just insane.

He tried again, rushing forward and calling her name, ignoring the gray, tattered thing and grasping her shoulder. Again, she threw him off easily, and he landed hard in a scratchy bush. He rose, staring as she made her way.

Alex surged after her, but the second he stepped onto the lane, he felt something come over him. A sensation that was almost indescribable. Like he had just stepped into a dream.

The air suddenly became soft and sweet, filled with the

smells of strange flowers and hot sand. Where the houses had just been tall, proud structures with columns and rolling lawns, they became eerie things, all turrets and twisting staircases, some of them bent in improbable ways. Alex stared around, stunned for a moment, before realizing that Natalie and the gray figure were far ahead of him.

"Natalie!" he bellowed, and sprinted as fast as he could down the lane. Still she was ahead of him, and would not turn around, though he called for her again. How could she be so far ahead? She and the figure were walking at a measured pace, while he was running hard, feeling a stitch in his side. He stopped for breath, his hands on his knees. He was no closer to her than when he had begun. It was like a nightmare.

Then darkness fell abruptly. As if it had run out of energy, the sun froze overhead, and slid down off the horizon to the south. The moon, fat with light, burgeoned atop distant mountains, seeming to cover half the skyline with its girth, spreading a wave of resplendent light out over the houses, which continued to grow stranger.

Alex saw a building shaped like a coiled snake, wrapping around and around until it reared up into a tall tower, with window eyes and a long, crimson flag for a tongue. Crows were clustered upon its roof, screeching into the twisted night. Another house was built like a tree, little colored lights winking out at him from between the branches and leaves.

Each home he passed, however, was more derelict than the last. They crumbled, consumed by ivy and moss, their walls collapsing inward like punctured balloons. Indeed, Alex saw no sign that anyone had lived in any of these fantastical houses for generations, or even longer. There was something in the stillness of this place that reminded him of a graveyard.

Up ahead, the lane had reached its end, and finally he seemed able to catch up. He ran the remainder of the path, stopping just short of the pair.

"Natalie!" he gasped, moving to grab her hand. "Natalie, WAIT!"

Once more she brushed him away with unnatural force, and he crashed heavily to the path. He raised his head, the breath knocked out of him, to see the man standing next to a pair of massive iron gates with Natalie at his side. The gates were wreathed in ashen, gray ivy that completely obscured whatever lay beyond.

The ragged man reached out and, with an almost delicate touch, pushed one gate open. There was a protesting scream of rusted hinges as it swung inward.

A sinking, queasy feeling came over Alex where he lay, panting. He didn't know what the hell was happening, but there was one certainty he couldn't shake: She should not pass through these gates, should not go anywhere with this man.

Alex leapt to his feet just as Natalie slipped through,

following the man as the gate began to close behind them.

Alex cursed. Rushing up to the closing gate, his heart was in his throat. He gazed at the strange, twisting patterns that were etched into the bars. For several seconds, he stood there, his hand closing over the cool metal. Barely twenty minutes ago, he'd been standing in the sun on a suburban road.

Either he had really and truly lost his mind, or he was venturing blindly into an utterly unheard of realm.

He looked up at the gray ivy that hung down in curtains before him. Whatever lay beyond, Natalie had gone ahead, and Alex couldn't bring himself to turn away now. If nobody but him could see the gray man, there was no guarantee that anybody else would see what he saw now, here at the end of this impossible lane. He couldn't rely on recruiting help.

Swallowing hard, Alex set his jaw and pushed.

The gate began to open.

CHAPTER 6

THE FIRST THING ALEX NOTICED AS HE PASSED through the gates was the cold. It blossomed within him, even as the wind blew warm against his skin, and he shivered as the gate swung shut behind him, the sheet of ivy swinging into place over it like a wall.

He found himself standing before what could only be described as a mansion. It towered above him, windows flickering with uncertain light, red bricks almost entirely hidden by great swaths of the same gray plant that hung over the gates. The stuff was everywhere, covering the high wall that ringed the perimeter of the house's expansive gardens, and there was even a thin layer that crept over the ground. It seemed to drain the color from everything it touched. He shuddered and tried not to brush against it.

Gritting his teeth, Alex moved toward the manor. He didn't see Natalie or the man in rags anywhere, but there was only one place they could have gone.

Gravel crunched loudly under his feet as he walked, though he tried his best to walk lightly. He had the feeling he did not want to be detected here.

He tried to focus his mind solely on what he was here to achieve: Go in, get Natalie, get out. *Quick and simple.*

As he drew nearer, the manor came into sharper detail. Burns and scars streaked the bricks of the silent structure. It looked deserted, like it had been abandoned decades before. Maybe the man in rags would be the only inhabitant.

He shuddered at the thought of facing him, but braced himself for the likelihood.

Before he knew it, Alex was standing before the doors. They were strange things, and looked more like trees than anything else. Gnarled branches stuck out of them at odd angles, and twists of age mottled their surface. From each hung a heavy golden ring, shaped like a snake twisting to bite its own tail.

Ouroboros, Alex thought. The infinite cycle of creation and destruction, each eternally leading to the other. Not necessarily a bad sign.

He grabbed the handle and pulled the door open, slipping inside.

Whatever he had been expecting, it certainly wasn't what greeted him. Bright light blasted his face, and he raised a hand, abruptly realizing how dark the night outside had been. Alex stared around in shock at the opulent entryway surrounding him; at the long hall, at least twenty feet across, that plunged deeper into the manor; at the high ceiling hung with a series of crystal chandeliers that shone with hundreds of candles. Dozens of paintings of dour-faced men in black robes lined the walls, and suits of ancient-looking armor stood sentry on either side.

"Two?"

Alex spun in alarm.

A prim woman of middle age sat before him behind a desk, adjusting a pair of horn-rimmed glasses. She was wearing a rather incredible amount of blush and lipstick, and the impression it created was of a swollen red toad glowering at him from her seat. She held a pen poised over a large stack of papers.

"I haven't even finished the intake forms for the last one," she said, her voice sharp and exasperated. "He never brings *two* at a time."

"I'm sorry—*what?*" Alex blurted.

"Yes, yes," said the woman, "you're very confused. I know. The young woman is already off to her orientation, but I can show you the way. The Head will explain everything."

"No, I—"

"Ah, where are my manners?" the woman continued, ignoring Alex. "My name is Siren Mave. I look after the newcomers, make sure everybody is settling in, that sort of thing. If you've got any concerns, you can always come to me!" She licked her lips, smiling impishly before bustling out from behind her desk, grabbing Alex by the sleeve as she passed him.

"Wait—what is—"

"Yes, yes, yes," she said. "I know, I know. Very confused. Rest assured, you'll be okay! This is a good place." She let out a tittering laugh that could suggest either sinister glee or reassurance; Alex was completely unsure as to which it was.

This bizarre woman had, however, said something important. *The young woman is already off to her orientation, but I can show you the way.* Whatever "orientation" meant didn't matter at this point—Alex's mind already felt blown to a million shards—but it sounded like this woman would show him to Natalie, which was all his brain needed to focus on. He'd have a chance to get her out. So instead of continuing to ask questions to which he received only nonsensical answers, he should just hold his tongue.

The hallway seemed even longer than Alex had assumed, drifting on and on until he didn't think it was possible that they hadn't hit the back end of the building yet. They passed a window showing a sunlit garden, and another—to his bewilderment—that looked out onto a moon-drenched lake, sparkling with ice.

Once, through an open doorway, Alex glimpsed a group of young people sitting around a table, their heads bent together. They turned, quieting as he passed, their faces dark and unreadable.

How many others are in this place?

The end of the hallway they had come from seemed to have been swallowed up behind them, yet the rest stretched out before them, out of sight, seemingly infinite.

Siren Mave looked around, as if to get her bearings in the perfectly straight hallway, then picked out a door with a little black knob. She placed one hand on the knob, then paused and turned to Alex, looking him up and down.

"You look a bit like you've been *fighting*, dear," she said disapprovingly.

He glanced down at himself. His clothes were rumpled, smudged with dirt, and torn in places, and he had light scratches all over his hands. He noticed suddenly that they stung a bit—he was so distracted he hadn't noticed before. He imagined he must have gotten the injuries when Natalie had flung him away.

"Actually—" he began, but Siren Mave held up her hands in exasperation.

"Not much to be done for it, I suppose," she sighed. Her face grew stern, and she reached out a small hand and jabbed him in the chest with it. The blow was unexpectedly hard—just like Natalie's had been—and drove him back a step, leaving a stinging welt.

"Ow!" he spat, but she interrupted him yet again, as though he had not spoken at all. She was relentless, impossible.

"Remember," the plump little woman said in a humorless voice. "You will keep your manners about you and be polite when in the Head's company. He is a busy man, with many commitments, and he does not have much time for students. He does, however, make the time to meet with new arrivals, and you ought to be very grateful for that opportunity."

New arrivals.

Students.

He cocked his head, straining to make sense of the nonsensical, but Siren Mave was already turning the black knob. As it rotated, something beyond the door stirred. It was as though the dark that had been held inside grew eager to slide out, and began to bleed in thick, questing tendrils from the frame. Siren Mave swatted it away as it looped down toward her, then yanked the door open.

A black pit yawned there. It was full of little noises, like cat's paws padding over packed dirt. A ripple of cold broke over Alex's skin as a smell seemed to sweep up to envelop him. It was like a forest after rain, all wet grass and dripping trees, with just the faintest musk of something animal waiting nearby.

Was Natalie somewhere in there? In the feral

darkness? He peered at it, his heart hammering against his ribcage, and opened his mouth to speak.

Siren Mave, however, planted her strong little hand in the square of his back and shoved him in. He toppled forward, his head breaking through the layer of dark like he was falling through a sheet of suspended water.

He coughed, shivering as he staggered into the room beyond. It was small, stone, its only adornment a wooden bench along one wall. It looked like a prison cell.

Natalie sat on the bench, her eyes cast down toward the ground, her hands folded in her lap. He rushed forward, relieved to see her in one piece—and unaccompanied by the man.

"Natalie! God. Are you okay? Can you hear me?" He held her shoulders and looked into her face, but her head lolled to the side, as if she were unconscious.

"Hey! Natalie, wake up! We need to get out of here!" He snapped his fingers in front of her, then gave her a shake. She swayed back and forth, completely unresponsive, then rolled slowly to her original position, once more staring blankly at her feet.

He stepped back from her, feeling frantic, trying to assess the situation.

"Okay," he spoke aloud to himself, pulling at his hair. "Okay. It's fine. She can't be too heavy. I can carry her..."

Alex turned back to look the way he had come, and blinked. Whatever door he had entered through, it was now concealed. Only a flat mass of stone stood at his back now. A torch upon the wall flickered with dancing light, sending the smell of oil and smoke into the air. Siren Mave was nowhere to be seen.

He whirled back around, eyes darting from blank wall to blank wall, breathing ragged.

There were no doors or windows at all. *It makes no sense!*

He scanned the stone walls, running his fingers over them, looking for irregularities. There *had* to be something that might indicate a hidden panel or a secret lever that would spring back to reveal the exit, but there was nothing. He noticed that his hands were shaking.

Stepping back to the middle of the cell, Alex tried to steady his breathing. He had to at least attempt to stay rational, even in an utterly irrational situation. He folded his arms and turned again to Natalie, studying her nervously.

Her condition was unchanged, but at least she didn't seem injured. Just mentally *gone*.

He began to pace, slowly, going through the things he knew for certain.

Assuming he hadn't simply lost his mind, he knew he was trapped in a bare cell, somewhere unknown. He had not been harmed—at least, not much. Natalie was here with him, sort of. They appeared to be out of options, just stuck here, waiting.

The "Head" the absurd woman had mentioned must

be pulling the strings here. Yeah, meeting with him was something to think about. He thought quickly, trying to plan a course of action. When he was let out of this room, he should find a weapon, defend himself and Natalie, carry her to safety. And it was of vital importance that he not let her out of his sight again.

Alex sat beside her on the bench and leaned forward. In the dim, flickering light, her features looked softer, her tan skin warmer. Her slack expression made her seem childlike in her helplessness, and he felt more worried about her than ever.

"Natalie," he rasped. "Natalie, if you can hear me, I want you to know it's going to be okay. I'm going to get us out of here. We'll be home soon. Okay?"

For the first time, Natalie seemed to hear him. Her head tilted, her blank stare sweeping over to where he sat. She blinked, and it was as though her eyes were furiously trying to come into focus.

"Natalie!" he urged hopefully. "Natalie, it's Alex! We're—"

But then she shivered, and collapsed back into the same position she had occupied before.

Alex tried to speak to her again, but she was back to being unresponsive. Soon he too fell silent. He twiddled his thumbs, mind racing. He wanted to pace again, but was loathe to leave her side.

Alex lost track of time as the only sound that filled

the room became the crackling torchlight and his sharp breathing.

Then came a noise like a key turning in a door, and the far wall swung open in a splash of golden light, as though the door had been there the entire time.

Siren Mave stood silhouetted in radiance, looking down at a sheaf of papers.

"Young lady," she announced, "you'll be up first. If you'll follow me…"

Alex's eyes shot to Natalie—who had miraculously jolted upright, though seemed to still be in a daze. She rose and walked to the woman.

Alex swung out to catch Natalie's arm. "No!" he snapped, fixing Siren Mave with what he hoped was a blazing, determined gaze. "She's not going anywhere without me. Where are you taking us?"

Siren Mave's glasses flashed in the torchlight.

"I am taking her to her orientation, dear," she said with an exasperated roll of her neck. "Why can't you just behave yourself like this young lady?" She gave Natalie a firm pat on the shoulder, then gripped it hard, yanking the girl easily away from Alex. He didn't waste time feeling shocked at the small woman's inhuman strength, but rushed at her immediately, thoughtlessly, intent only on staying with Natalie, whatever it took.

She put out one thick-fingered hand, pushing him hard in the chest. It was like running into a solid wall, and he collapsed heavily to the floor. Before he could move again, or even breathe again, Siren Mave had whisked Natalie through the bright doorway, and it had closed up into a blank wall once more.

"No!" he hissed, leaping up to run his hands urgently over the spot where Natalie had disappeared.

He cursed, kicking the wall in frustration. If Siren Mave was that strong, escaping this place wouldn't be as simple as just finding a weapon and getting past her—even if he could get out of this cell at the same time as Natalie. He didn't know what to expect from the Head, but it would not be unreasonable to assume more of the same. Somehow, he needed to be smarter about this.

The chill in his bones continued to radiate outwards, and his breath came out in little white puffs, splashing against the wall before him. He turned away, jamming his hands into his pockets, when something caught his eye.

A shadow beneath the bench slipped out along the floor.

It flowed up the wall, then trickled down over the bench, pooling into the form of...a small black cat. The apparition yawned as if content, its mouth bristling with black fangs, and lashed its tail.

Alex stared at it with no idea what to think or how to react to this new development. His eyes felt like they had taken in so much in the last hour—or had it been longer?—that if they witnessed much more of this fantasy, they would burst.

He stepped forward cautiously, but the cat did not move. He crept closer, until he was looming over it. There it sat, just like a cat, pointedly ignoring him.

Was it, in fact, a cat?

Had he imagined it forming from pure shadow?

He reached out a hand as if to stroke it, and the cat's shadowy head swiveled to look up at him.

"Did I give you permission to touch me?" it demanded, in a voice that was deep for so small a creature.

Alex leapt back with a shout.

It was not a cat.

But what was it?

He circled it warily, looking at it out of the corner of his eye. He paced back and forth before it. He stood stock still, legs together, one loose fist over his mouth, regarding it sternly. All the while it stared right at him, exactly like a cat.

All this told him very little. But it was clearly some kind of shadow-being, and it must be here for a reason. It didn't seem hostile, at least not yet.

He cleared his throat and began carefully.

"I apologize for attempting to touch you," he ventured, feeling crazy for talking to this thing.

"Thank you," replied the cat, looking steadily back at him. "But I don't mind. As long as you ask."

Alex didn't exactly feel like petting it now. He

hesitated. "How are you holding that shadow around yourself? Making yourself look like a cat?"

The cat let out a throaty laugh. "How are you holding all those guts and skin around yourself? Yes, it is a choice to appear as a cat. It is an easy choice. But why should that mean I am not, as you suggest, actually a cat?"

Alex's jaw slackened. "What?"

"I doubt you would understand," the cat replied loftily, swishing its tail. "You're new here. New, and more than a touch disbelieving, aren't you?"

"There's a fair chance I've gone insane, yes," Alex said, rubbing slowly at his temple. "More than a fair chance, I'd say."

"Nonsense," scoffed the cat. "You haven't gone insane, you fool boy. You have no idea what's going to happen to you, do you?"

Alex felt a chill run through him at the words. Was that a threat?

"Please, enlighten me," he said.

The cat rose, stretching languorously, its whole body extending as it did so until one leg was stretched all the way to the end of the bench.

"Oh, but the Head will fill you in. Didn't that bizarre puff of a woman tell you?"

"No, not exact—"

The cat cut him off. "Just be patient. What's the rush?"

Alex fell silent, frowning at the cat.

The rush? The rush was that Natalie was lost some-where in this impossible place, that he was trapped in this prison of a waiting room, unable to get to her, un-able to escape, unable to even figure out what the hell was happening.

The cat, as if sensing his frustration, sighed. "Child," it said, hopping down off the bench to stand at his feet, "you've got all the time in your short, miserable life to fig-ure this out. I will tell you, though, as you will find it out eventually and to your detriment: you are here now. Here is where you are. Here is where, I'm afraid, you will stay."

It brushed against his leg as if to comfort him—or rather, brushed through his leg, the shadows lingering about his foot. He had the brief sensation of something that was like fur, but not fur—something soft and fathom-less and strange.

Then there was a click, and the door swung open again. For a moment, the light splashed all around the cat, which seemed to shrink back, hissing, little twists of vapor-ous shadow curling up where the light bit into its form.

Then it melted into a pool of blackness and slithered away into the corner.

Siren Mave stalked into the room, staring blankly at where the cat had disappeared. She looked back to Alex, one eyebrow rising.

"What manner of devil was that?" she asked, bemused. It was as if she had forgotten that she'd thrown him to the floor during their last encounter, behaving now like this was just business as usual. Alex fumed at the sight of her, but tried hard to hide it. He needed her now, had to use her to find Natalie.

He glanced at where the shadows still hung heavy with the memory of the cat. "Devil?"

Siren Mave stared at him for a moment, then burst into peals of high-pitched laughter. She staggered forward, patting Alex's shoulder and putting one hand on her knee as she tried to catch her breath.

"Oh," she gasped. "Oh my sweet, dear boy. It's a figure of speech, you silly thing."

He stared at her. Of course it was a figure of speech. He drew himself up, easily towering over the diminutive Siren Mave. She did not seem to notice, just lifted her glasses, wiping tears from her eyes.

"Devils," she said through her chuckles. "Oh goodness."

"As delighted as I am to amuse," he retorted, "I insist you tell me what is going on here immediately."

Siren Mave's mirth subsided slightly, but a smile continued to tweak at the edges of her lips.

"Do you?" she asked mildly, planting a hand in the small of his back and steering him toward the door. "Come, the Head is anxious to meet with you."

The Head.

The man in charge of all this.

Yes, he was anxious to meet with the Head as well.

For the moment, he should play along. He would gather more information, then decide on a course of action.

Even so, as he was forced out into yet another seemingly endless hallway, Alex wondered if he should just make a break for it. Bolt away, find an exit, inform the police. Yes, he could tell them he had gone down a street that didn't exist and into a mansion with talking shadows. Then he could explain to his mom why the police had been questioning him about his drug habits, and face the grief of Natalie's family when they discovered she was gone. The perfect plan.

Scowling, he followed the woman down the hallway, matching her pace. He hated feeling so disoriented.

The warm glow of the candlelit chandeliers slowly gave way to more torches. Alex and Siren Mave walked between patches of light and dark, and each time they stepped into a new patch of firelight, the world had changed. The walls grew older, more decayed, the wooden paneling peeling away to reveal a façade of stone and brick beyond. The gray ivy came back, piercing its way through the stones and spilling like frozen waterfalls to the ground, where it rustled against their feet.

The decor was changing as well. Where once there had been paintings of dignified men in fine suits, Alex began to see other things. Depictions of black-robed forms standing around a fire. A griffon, beak plunging down to meet a great serpent that rose up from the sea. Strangest still, a painting of nothing but an open mouth, filled with an unnatural number of teeth.

"I keep asking him to spruce the place up," Siren Mave explained as she kicked a line of ivy from her path. "But the master is old-fashioned and stubborn. He'll never adapt to modern times, I fear."

Alex wouldn't have called his surroundings "old-fashioned," exactly. Old-fashioned was a blue Mustang blaring the Beetles, not an eerie, chilly, haunted tomb of a place.

Siren Mave grabbed Alex by the hand, pulling him up short as he made to move past a large pair of double doors, and letting out a little cough. She spun him around, looking him up and down once more, just as she had when he'd first entered the building.

"All right," she said, beaming at him. "Now, just remember: manners!"

"Manners," he repeated coldly, crossing his arms over his chest and glancing toward the door. He was out of patience for the stupid woman, who pushed him around and spoke to him like he was a child.

"Young man." Siren Mave's voice changed suddenly. It cut through him like a cleaver, nearly making him flinch. The jaunty, cheerful nature had vanished clean out of it. "Do be careful," she said. "The Head has his rules. It won't do to break them."

Then she reached out and rapped twice upon the door. It groaned and creaked open.

"In you go," Siren Mave said, and shoved him inside.

Barely breathing, Alex blinked as the light shifted once again. The room was twilit, and smelled strongly of old books and freshly turned dirt. He examined his surroundings for a few seconds, trying to gather his bearings. Bookshelves lined one wall, windows the other. He stood upon a carpet of what looked like gray grass and by the far wall a great...*tree* grew, from the shattered remains of a fireplace and chimney. Its branches and roots coiled out from the masonry, adorned with gray leaves. If there was a ceiling, it was high up, hidden in the dusk that seemed to gather itself above the tops of the bookshelves. All across the room, fireflies flickered in and out of life.

It was, or should have been, impossible.

It took Alex a moment to spot the desk that sat against the far wall. It was made of stone, piled with books and pieces of paper, inkwells lying willy-nilly, some with their contents spilling out to drip from the edge of the desk.

And behind it there was a chair, occupied by the strangest man Alex had ever seen.

He seemed to melt into his surroundings, the ashen ivy wrapping around his wrists and legs until it was impossible to tell where man ended and manor began. His face was hidden in the shadows of an ancient hooded robe, fingers protruding from his sleeves like the tips of roots, searching for something to pierce and consume.

As he spoke, his voice was like the rasp of a clock's gears sliding into midnight:

"Welcome," he said, "to Spellshadow Manor."

CHAPTER 7

"THANK YOU," ALEX MANAGED AFTER A SPAN OF silence, staring numbly.

He worked to reorganize his thoughts. He had not been sure what to expect from this man, but he had at least assumed he would be dealing with a human. Now he was not so certain. It was more important now than ever to proceed with caution.

The man leaned forward, and, from under his hood, a pair of eyes glimmered.

"Do you know why you are here?" he asked.

"I, uh, I'm afraid I have no idea," Alex replied. Should he ask about Natalie? Would they be kept apart if it seemed like he cared about her? With no clue what the man wanted from him, he was unsure. "But hey, did a girl come through here not too long ago?" he asked, attempting to sound casual.

A glimmer of teeth bloomed in the darkness. It was disconcerting—Alex could see no lips or chin, only a neat slash of white.

"She's gone on ahead," said the Head. "I am told she was not *amenable* to being brought to the institute, and had to be persuaded. The process is exhausting. She will be resting in the girls' dormitory."

Not amenable.

In the girls' dormitory.

Alex swallowed, praying that Natalie was all right. She had certainly seemed amenable enough to him, far too amenable, and he wondered what could have happened during her own *orientation*. At least he had a vague idea where she was now.

"Oh, I see. Yes."

"You do not," replied the Head. "But no matter."

He spread his arms, and the gesture seemed to take in more than the room around them. For an insane moment, Alex thought he could see visions of the whole world—the plains of distant Africa, the crashing waves of a great ocean, the snow-gripped peaks of the Himalayas—all encompassed within this old man's hands.

His heart beat harder.

"You have been selected," the man said. "Chosen by our Finder to study magic. You have no doubt noticed oddities in your day-to-day life. Things that weren't quite right. Manifestations, as we call them. They are latent signs of your magical prowess, and we intend to hone that gift here."

Alex thought quickly. Finder—that might be the gray man in rags. That was a manifestation, and certainly "not quite right". But it was the only hint of anything magical about him, and he had not exactly been "chosen". No, he had snuck in.

And now he had to attempt to blend in, penetrate farther, to wherever Natalie was being held.

"Ah, yes," Alex replied. "That makes perfect sense."

The Head seemed momentarily perplexed, as though he had expected Alex to be more uncertain. His hands settled onto his desk. "Yes. Quite."

"But what would happen if I declined your offer?" Alex dared to ask. "If I chose to return to my home?"

Almost before the words left Alex's mouth, he knew he had made a mistake.

A coolness settled over the figure opposite him, and the man's mood seemed to manifest itself on the air. A page on the desk crawled with sudden blooms of frost, the icy tendrils spreading until the paper cracked and fell in two pieces.

"You do not leave this place," replied the man. "That is

our first, and most important, rule."

Alex wet his lips, staring at the shards of ice. "May I ask *why not?*"

Little flakes of snow were gathering around the old man, seeming to writhe out of the air itself, while the Head's withered hands formed a steeple in front of him.

"Magical talent," he said in a brittle voice, "must be honed. It must be crafted and molded and formed until it is safe. If you were unleashed upon the world, you would be a danger not only to others, not only to yourself, but to the fabric of reality around you. There is more at stake here than life, my young student."

Alex found himself unable to reply. There was something about the room's atmosphere that suddenly seemed to be pressing him down, clenching in on him from all sides. A cold, dark energy that demanded silence and absolute obedience.

The Head had been watching Alex for a reply, then nodded when he saw that he had gained the young man's silence.

The pressing weight Alex felt around him began to lift.

"You will be placed within the boys' dormitory," the Head said. "We have few students these days; I think you will find that there is plenty of space for you. Your classes will start tomorrow. Until then, I recommend that you acquaint yourself with your new home."

Your new home.

Faced with more of the same disregard Siren Mave had shown him, anger bubbled up in Alex again. Nobody in this absurd place was taking him seriously, or being remotely reasonable. Who was this man to tell him what to do? Alex wasn't some idiot schoolboy to be bossed around, to be shut up and made to fall in line.

"The thing is, though," he began, against his better judgment, "what you're talking about—magic or whatever—it isn't real."

The Head seemed to mull the words over for a minute.

"Do you truly believe that?" he asked, finally.

"Yeah, I'm afraid I do."

The older man went silent again. Then he reached forward, shoving aside a stack of papers and placing one hand palm down on the table. His veins and tendons stood out like pulled stitches against the papery skin, and the stone under his hand rippled. It pulsed once, a heartbeat quivering through the table, shaking straight into the ground.

Everything went black.

Alex flailed as it felt like the ground had vanished from under him, then he froze. All around him, stars began to spark into existence, cool crystals framed against an inky black void. They grew larger, and he could see spheres of flame, planes of ice, boundless crushing voids of energy and power. He felt the heat of them against his skin, felt the chill in his bones, smelled something clogging his nose, like rosemary and thyme and earthworms. He choked, attempting to thrash his arms, but his body was gone. He was gone. His whole existence had melted away, leaving only those spinning stars of power.

And then he was lying on the cool, strangely grassy floor of the Head's office.

The man was still watching him, in the same exact position, his frail hand planted on the firm, unmoving stone of his desk.

"And now?" he asked.

Alex, completely stunned, could only stare. All mundane explanations—drugs, lights, trickery, even madness—were gone from his mind. He felt the truth of his experience all the way to his core, knowing, without doubt, what had just happened to him.

"I-I see," he choked out.

The Head's smile was back. He nodded, and once again Alex caught sight of those eyes. Eyes like stars of ice and fire. He felt himself trembling involuntarily, and could not rise.

"Mave," the Head called.

The door opened, and Siren Mave bustled into the room.

"All done?" she asked in her cheerful voice. It seemed out of place here, like a child laughing in a cathedral.

"All done," the Head replied. "Take—I'm sorry, I forgot to ask your name. Who are you, young man?"

"Alex Webber," Alex whispered without thought, his

breath still short.

The Head nodded, then looked back to Siren Mave. "Take Alex to the boys' dormitory. I think he'll be needing to rest up before he starts classes in the morning."

Siren Mave gave a tittering laugh, then gripped Alex under the arm. He hadn't the strength or the power of mind to protest as she lifted him to his feet and shoved him back out into the hallway. He felt drained of all energy, exhausted beyond belief.

At some point, he was directed to a bed, and Alex fell into it, his mind blank.

All he could see was that endless expanse of power. He was blind to everything else, not even struggling yet to come back to himself, still lost in that unfathomable void.

He was asleep almost before his head hit the pillow.

CHAPTER 8

"**C**OME ON, YOU CAN'T TELL ME THAT NOSE ISN'T the most perfect nose you've ever seen."

"I, for one, do not spend much time looking at noses."

"Was that meant as an insult?"

"Just an observation."

Alex didn't open his eyes. He was struggling back to wakefulness, still feeling like a part of him was spinning eternally in the void. Overhead, the voices continued.

"Observations can be insults, you know."

"Facts are only facts, Jari."

"See, this is why you have no friends."

A snort. "Because *you* have so many friends."

Alex felt a weight on his chest now, felt it shift forward a little. It wasn't uncomfortable, and actually seemed to help him come back to reality, grounding him. Despite having some sort of cover over him, he felt cold.

"I do too have friends."

"Name one."

"You."

Alex could now identify two speakers. One of them spoke with a high, excitable voice, and seemed to be coming from directly above him. The other had a dourer cadence, laden with a heavy accent that reminded him of cinnamon and allspice.

Alex groaned, cracking open one eye. He was greeted by the sight of a short, freckled young man—perhaps around Alex's age, despite his immature manner—with a scruff of blond hair. The boy was partially sitting on top of him, leaning over to look at his face. When Alex opened his eyes, a bright grin flashed into life, spreading across the boy's face and lighting up his wide eyes.

"You're up!"

"What are you doing?" Alex grunted, clearing the sleep from his eyes.

"Oh, sorry!" The boy abruptly leapt off him, just about ricocheting into a chair nearby.

Alex sat up on his elbows, blinking around him. He was in a bedroom furnished with three beds and three desks, all of gleaming dark wood. It was virtually undeco-rated, quite small, and clearly a dormitory.

His eyes fell on an older boy, perhaps nineteen, with coppery skin and an untidy mess of black curls adorning his head like a crown. He sat at a desk across the room, straight-backed and proud, an ancient-looking book held in one hand. When he saw Alex looking at him, he offered a small wave.

"Since my friend has no manners—"

"See? Friends. I have them."

"—and apparently doesn't understand that in order to have *friends* he must have more than one, allow me to in-troduce myself. My name is Aamir Nagi." Aamir glanced at where the blond boy continued to loom over Alex. "The grossly oversized puppy that was attempting to climb into your bed is Jari."

Jari beamed at Alex. "Jari Petra," he supplied.

"I-I'm Alex," he said.

"Oh, we know!" replied Jari.

Aamir sighed. "Don't be creepy," he muttered. He nod-ded toward Alex's bed. "It's on the frame, though. That's how he knows."

Alex sat up slowly, remembering the previous day's events with mounting horror. He had chased Natalie down an ever-shifting lane of eerie, derelict houses. Had not saved her from the horrible ragged thing. Entered the manor wreathed in gray ivy. Found Natalie. Lost Natalie.

Met the Head, and then…No, he should not think of that.

But he had not left the manor.

Natalie was here somewhere, though, and he could get to her and find some way to escape this place. He felt a little sharper now, a little more himself, but he did not notice he was clutching the bedsheets tightly in his fists until the older boy spoke, bringing his attention back to his surroundings.

"How did you like your orientation? Informative, wasn't it?" The young man regarded him serenely.

Alex snorted. "Oh yes, it was brilliant. Really cleared things up."

Jari laughed. "More like a *dis*orientation, right?"

"Don't worry," Aamir said. "We'll help you get settled in here. It is this way for everyone." He cast Alex a small smile, which Alex couldn't help but notice looked more rueful than reassuring.

"Yup!" Jari stuck his hand out for an emphatic shake that jolted Alex really, fully awake.

Alex turned and saw that his name had indeed been engraved into the wood.

Alex Webber, it read, with sinking finality.

"To hell with that," he breathed, indignation rising in his chest. He rose briskly from the bed. "Well, it's been lovely chatting, but I won't be staying. If you could just point me to the girls' dormitories, I'll be on my way."

They stared at him, Jari looking taken aback, Aamir a little sad.

"You can't *go*," exclaimed Jari.

"Sorry, but I have to. I really didn't sign up for all this. It seems like a"—he eyed the two young men, who were apparently students here—"really interesting place, but it's not for me. The girls' dormitories are which way again?"

"Alex," said Aamir seriously, "you truly cannot leave. The Head informed you of this, did he not?"

"He certainly seemed opposed to the idea. But what he doesn't know won't hurt him, right? I'll find a way out."

"There is no way out, I'm afraid," Aamir countered gravely. "For any of us. There are enchantments in place, strong, old enchantments, that prevent any student's departure. Like it or not, you are now a student here, Alex Webber. The only way to leave is to graduate."

Alex stopped just short of the door. "Graduate," he repeated. "And what does that entail?"

Aamir's lips tightened. "We do not know until it is upon us."

Alex raised his eyebrows. That sounded ominous.

"But you really don't want to leave anyway," interjected Jari. "It can be dangerous out there for people like us. And we're supposed to learn control here, so we don't, you know, blow stuff up. By accident, anyway." He grinned. "And hey—it can be fun, too. I like learning new stuff."

Alex very much doubted he would encounter any fun here, or any trouble back at home. But the two young men seemed utterly opposed to him attempting to leave, and he certainly didn't want them telling anyone—the Head, for example—that he was planning escape immediately upon arrival.

"So what happens if you try to leave, anyway?" he asked.

Jari opened his mouth to answer, but Aamir spoke over him.

"It is extremely dangerous. Do not attempt it."

Alex looked between the two, wondering if this was true. As much as he hated the idea, maybe he would have no choice but to bide his time a little, acquaint himself with the place and its guardians on his own. In any case, he should be wary of letting them in on his plans.

He exhaled and ruffled his hair. "Okay. I guess I'm... uh, staying. But I still need to get to the girls' dorms. Do you know the way?"

Jari laughed dismissively. "Oh, you can't get in *there*— not without a girl to lead you. Believe me," he whispered loudly, "*I've tried.*"

"It's true," agreed Aamir. "You may want to refer to your rulebook before running off on your own. The punishments here are severe." He gestured to the nightstand by Alex's bed. "You'll find it in the drawer there."

Alex eyed the nightstand warily. He didn't want to read any kind of rulebook for this absurd place—what was the point, when he was going to escape anyway? Reading their rules would feel like one step closer to submitting to them.

The punishments, though. He felt he'd already gotten something of a taste of how 'severe' they could be.

He let out a breath. Well, Natalie would have to leave her dorm at some point. He would just have to find her as soon as he could.

"So," said Jari, "when did you realize you were a wizard?"

Aamir groaned. "Please, call us 'arcanologists'," he said. "'Wizard' sounds so…fantastical."

"And *arcanologist* sounds like someone with his head in a book," Jari retorted.

Alex frowned. "I am not a *wizard*, or an *arcanologist*."

Jari stared at him. "Huh?"

"You heard me," Alex replied.

"You're saying you didn't cause any magical events? No buildings catching fire, or luck turning miraculously in your favor?"

"Nothing like that whatsoever," Alex declared. "Unless you count seeing strange figures nobody else can see, I guess," he added.

Jari's eyes widened. Aamir's head tilted ever so slightly as he leaned in.

"Seeing strange figures?" he said in his rich voice. "That's a new one."

"Aptitude for summoning, maybe?" Jari said speculatively.

"That or necromancy," Aamir replied.

Jari looked horrified.

"Regardless," Alex interjected, as this conversation was flying over his head, "I think I would have noticed if I were a wizard or an arcanologist. I'm just a senior at Middledale High. Nothing fantastical."

Jari bounced to his feet with a bright smile. "Well, not anymore, you're not. Come on, you should get washed and then we'll show you around before class."

Aamir nodded. "That would be a good idea."

Damn it. Of course, Alex would be expected to go to class. He could try to skip it, but that would be more than a little suspicious for a student on his first day. He'd have to figure out a way to explore later, without attracting blatant attention.

Noticing Alex's hesitance, Aamir reached out and patted his shoulder lightly. "Don't worry. You've got a few hours, and you won't be asked to perform magic for the first few weeks." Aamir ducked down beneath his own bed and pulled out a plain dark outfit—cotton pants, a shirt, and a sweater. "You'll get your own set of clothes made to measure soon," he added, "but for now you can borrow one of mine."

"Perform magic," Alex repeated slowly as he accepted the clothes, his brain still coming to terms with the fact that magic even existed.

Jari chuckled. Grabbing Alex by the wrist, he dragged him out the door and into a hallway hung with gray ivy.

"You'll be fine!" he said. "The basics are easier than breathing. If you were chosen and brought here, you can do it."

But Alex hadn't been brought here.

What would that mean for him?

CHAPTER 9

JARI AND AAMIR SHOWED ALEX TO A BARE COMMUNAL bathroom lined with individual cubicles down the hallway, where he took a shower. He couldn't stop shivering as he stepped beneath the water, even though it was warm, and he didn't feel any better when he was dry and in his new change of clothes. The sweater felt fairly thick to the touch, but his bones still ached from the cold. *What is it with this place?*

Once he reunited with the boys, who'd waited in the hallway for him, the first room Jari showed Alex was a small study chamber, complete with bookshelves and a fireplace. Several other students sat in chairs around the mostly empty tables, some reading books, others just staring into space. Alex noticed one bored-looking boy spinning a tiny loop of flames around his finger.

"This is the study hall," explained Jari. "It's where you come to read books and generally be uninteresting."

Aamir made an irritated noise.

They stepped back out into the hallway, and Alex paused. The hallway was different than it had been a minute ago. The lights on the walls had a pinkish glow now, flickering slightly as dawn's first smear of red light pressed itself against windows overlooking a great lawn below.

"Did we come out a different door?" he asked, feeling disoriented.

Jari cackled in glee. Aamir sighed and put his hand to his brow, looking exasperated.

"The hallways take some getting used to," he said to Alex. "They shift on you a little."

Alex stared out at the grass. "Shift? They move?"

"No, no," replied Aamir hastily. "They don't move, not in terms of the manor itself. The doors will always be in the same places, and look the same. The hallways themselves, though, they don't seem to have any sense of where in the building they are located, or, for that matter, where in the world...The manor's surroundings change, you see—the view from the windows can look as though we were located in any number of places, or countries."

Like the Head's hands.

Apparently the whole world was out there, but in here was madness.

So the first step to escaping would be to figure out how to navigate the manor.

Jari looked down at a shining watch affixed to his wrist. He adjusted a few knobs on it, and it whirred, clicking and snapping until it let out a little chime.

"Looks like this hallway is somewhere in Southeast Asia," he said brightly.

Alex raised an eyebrow, but Aamir just clapped him on the back.

"Jari is much more adept than he may at first seem," he explained. "I keep him around for a reason, you know."

Jari tutted.

With a curious eye on Jari's watch, Alex followed them onward.

The dining room was an intimate place, with a few dozen little round tables spread out over a shag carpet, walls hung with hides of strange creatures that reminded Alex of the griffons in books of mythology, and lizards of improbable sizes.

The alchemy labs, located behind a small door with a crystalline knob, were filled to the brim with blue-green smoke when the group entered, only to be hastily shoved out again by a student with a panicked expression on her face.

Alex was still wiping at his stinging eyes when they

reached their next destination. Jari drew up at a door of dark wood, embellished with swirls of golden paint. Alex noticed that Aamir stood up a little taller at this one, his hands fidgeting at his sides.

Before Alex could ask what the new room was, Jari pushed the door open with a flourish, and a wave of musty air poured out over them, washing Alex with the familiar smell of books. Silence came with it, settling like fresh snow into his ears and dampening all sounds.

"This," Jari said, his voice sounding strangely distant and muted, "is the library."

The room inside was almost beyond comprehension. Three giant pillars rose up to the ceiling at the room's center, each lined with shelves and shelves of books. Iron walkways crisscrossed the pillars' surface in a lattice of stairs and ladders, and paper lanterns hung from above. Alex stared in awe as a student pulled out a book halfway up one of the great pillars, then vaulted the railing, flipping the tome open in his hands as he fell, his feet tapping against the floor as lightly as if he were a feather.

"Marvelous, isn't it?" Aamir said, reverence in his voice.

It was. Alex filled his eyes with the magnificent room, feeling a buzz of excitement.

There must have been hundreds of thousands of books here, framed by a great wall of glass that overlooked the front gates of the school. And surely one of them would be helpful in his escape.

"Bit stuffy," said Jari absently. "And the noise-dampening magic is a real killjoy."

Aamir grimaced. "I've been trying to figure out how to permanently apply it to Jari," he said to Alex. "But so far, no luck."

While the two descended into bickering, Alex continued to look at the books. Yes, there must be answers to many of his questions here. He could learn what this place was, hopefully what its weaknesses were. He scanned the shelves with wide eyes, thinking ahead to when he and Natalie would return home.

His gut twisted painfully as he thought of his mother. She would know they were missing by now. He imagined her alone in the house. It had been months since her hospitalization, and she could manage on her own, but it killed him to think of the stress his absence would be putting on her heart.

He had to hurry.

Jari broke through his thoughts as he grabbed him by the arm again with a smile.

"We're out of time," he said. "Come on. We've got class."

Alex swallowed and strode along, trying to push thoughts about his mother from his head. They wouldn't help him now; only crush him with worry at a time when his mind needed to be open and sharp.

The richly patterned black door shut, and noise came rushing back. They were standing in a hallway, and the view through this window was a great cave, the roof glittering with glowworms, twinkling like tiny stars.

CHAPTER 10

THEY REACHED A CLASSROOM—A PLAIN BOX OF A room with no windows and a large set of desks arranged before a blackboard.

Aamir showed Alex to an empty seat, then settled down next to him. Jari plopped down in front.

"You two aren't the same age, but you share classes?" asked Alex.

Aamir's lips tightened. "Doesn't make a lot of sense, does it?"

Jari jumped in to clarify. "The classes are more about strengthening and controlling your magic," he said with a shrug. "The teachers will show techniques for reining in your power, and ways to draw it out. To hear them talk about it, it takes about four years to cover all the material. During that time, we're encouraged to study specializations on our own, and are tested on our progress."

"It's utter nonsense," muttered Aamir testily. "It's like they intentionally teach us as little as possible."

"Not everybody can have my *prodigious* levels of control," Jari said offhandedly.

Alex was about to reply when the door opened and Natalie entered. His eyes widened as he saw her, her hair appearing freshly washed, braided, and tucked over one shoulder. A few other girls were walking with her, and one pointed to a seat, leading her farther toward the back of the room.

He hurried over to her immediately, trying not to make a scene but feeling indescribably relieved. There was no ragged figure near her, and she seemed bright-eyed.

"Alex!" she gasped as he approached. "Alex, you are here? But how?" She embraced him quickly, and the girls she had entered with started to whisper around them.

"I followed you," he said in a hushed tone, bending to talk closer and putting a hand on her shoulder. She touched it lightly as she listened with bulging eyes. "I had to make sure you were okay. That gray, ragged man that was following you—it didn't hurt you, did it?"

She looked confused, shaking her head a little and wrinkling her brow. "Gray, ragged man? No, there was no gray man. I'm not hurt. But Alex, *I want to get out of this place!*" She hissed the last part in a vehement whisper, her nails digging into his hand.

"Me too," he replied, feeling confused as to why, even now, she was oblivious to the gray man. Maybe he'd cast some sort of spell on her? That still didn't explain why *Alex* had been able to see him. "We will get out," he continued, forcing his focus back to the conversation. "But—we can't talk now. Later, okay?"

"Yes," she replied, glancing at the students seated all around them. "Yes, later." Still clinging to him, she followed him back to Aamir and Jari, who looked extremely surprised. They introduced themselves a little hesitantly, and shot him curious glances.

"You two know each other, I take it?" Aamir asked slowly, evaluating them.

"Yeah," replied Alex, his voice low.

"We were at the same school," Natalie added.

Aamir eyed them. "That is quite rare," he said, and Alex wasn't sure Natalie should have offered that information.

She stared as Aamir pulled a stack of papers, an inkpot, and three books out of his trim-fitting jacket, where they could not possibly have fit.

"Magic," she mouthed at Alex, and he gave her a thin smile. Clearly she was still coming to terms with it herself.

At that moment, the door opened once more, and a reedy man with a stooped back and a wiry pair of spectacles shuffled in. He had a stack of papers shoved under one arm, and held a glass jar of fireflies in the other hand. The class quieted instantly. Alex, assuming this man was the instructor, watched with wary interest as he made his way toward the desk.

He felt a little more at ease with Natalie at his side. At least he had accomplished the first two steps of his simple plan from the night before.

Go in. Get Natalie.

Next would be: *Get out.*

Maybe this teacher would teach him about the powers the manor and its people owned, help him figure out how to thwart or avoid them.

The teacher tripped suddenly, falling forward onto his face. He somehow managed to twist, keeping the jar of fireflies held away from the ground, but the papers flared out into the air around him. He stayed like that for a moment, frozen in place, one leg up in the air and twitching. Then he scrambled to his feet, wiping at a line of blood dribbling from his nose and smiling sheepishly.

Aamir let out an exasperated sigh.

"That," he explained, "is Professor Derhin. He's one of the five instructors at Spellshadow."

At the front of the room, Professor Derhin was waving his arms. The papers all across the floor lurched into the air, then flung themselves into an untidy pile upon the desk. Derhin hurried after them like a nanny chasing unruly children, tidying them into a neat stack before turning to face his class.

He squinted through his glasses, regarding the room. "Are there…more of you than there were?" he asked.

Aamir shot to his feet. "We have two new students, Professor."

Derhin's eyes widened, flicking about until they found Natalie. He smiled faintly. "Young lady. Stand and tell the class your name."

Natalie rose, her chin held high.

"My name is Natalie Chevalier," she said, her voice soft but clear.

Professor Derhin wet his lips. "And, um, is there anything you'd like us to know about you?"

She paused, shooting Alex a nervous glance, then answered, "No, I think not."

"Oh," said Professor Derhin. "All right, then." He nodded once, then turned to the board, apparently satisfied. "Today, we'll be learning about—"

"Sir."

Derhin looked back at Aamir with a weary expression. "Yes, Nagi?"

"I said there are *two* new students, sir."

Derhin's jaw dropped. He looked about, then finally spotted Alex.

"Oh my," he said, softly. "Yes. Quite so. Two."

Alex rose, feeling Natalie's eyes on him.

"Alex Webber," he said shortly, looking the man in the eyes. "That's about it."

"Very well, then," replied the instructor. "Thank you, uh…Alex. Now, let's see…"

Aamir leaned over. "Perhaps you have noticed already, but Derhin is completely *inept*." He threw an irritated look at the man's back as he wrote on the blackboard.

"At least he doesn't have a drinking problem like Lintz," Jari whispered with a quiet laugh.

"Lintz is a good enough fellow," Aamir retorted. At the front of the room, Derhin delicately cleared his throat, staring pointedly at them.

They hushed, and Derhin continued writing on the board. The topic of the day's lecture was *Alaman's Inner Enlightenment and Fire*, a strange process that originated in Papua New Guinea and appeared to involve a lot of gesturing and *feeling*. Derhin, staring intensely at his notes, seemed to want to copy the entire process, word for word, onto the board.

The man wasn't even a fast writer, taking his time covering the blackboard in tiny marks and diagrams. Aamir glared at their teacher's hand as if the intensity of his irritation could speed the man along his way, and Jari slumped lower and lower into his chair.

But to Alex, it was too surreal to be dull, sitting here in this cell of a classroom, learning about magical processes against his will.

CHAPTER 11

AFTER CLASS, ALEX WAS DETERMINED TO DASH OFF to the library immediately, to discuss escape plans with Natalie under the protection of the quieting charm. But Aamir, perhaps sensing that Alex was likely to take action he considered foolish, had other ideas.

"There is something I think you need to see," he said to Alex, stepping in front of him. "Both of you," he added, observing how close to Alex Natalie was standing. She was just as reluctant to leave Alex as he was to leave her, so Alex was glad Aamir had included her.

"What kind of something?" she asked.

"There are lines you should know not to cross," was

Aamir's vague reply.

Curious and wary, they followed him.

Aamir led them down a hallway lined with lanterns hung from iron spikes. Alex didn't recognize his surroundings, but tried to make a mental note. He was doing his best to create an internal map by which he would be able to navigate on his own. Without this, escape would be nearly impossible.

Once they had made it all the way down the hallway, Aamir held out a hand, indicating for Alex and Natalie to stop. They did so, glancing at each other uncertainly, and Aamir pointed to where a sapphire-blue line glimmered against the stone floor. It looped all the way up to the ceiling, forming a complete barrier through which one would have to walk if they wanted to proceed.

"Teacher's line," Aamir said authoritatively. "If you find one of these, don't cross it unless you want an irritated member of staff to hunt you down within a few minutes. It's strictly off limits to go past one of these."

Alex nodded, looking at the line. He could feel an intense coldness wafting from it, brushing against his skin.

Glancing beyond the line, he saw a turn in the hallway a few yards farther down, shadows stretching out from the corridor beyond. Gray ivy hung heavily from the walls at that turning point, pooling in dark corners and filling gaps between bricks.

"Got it," he said. "This line will call a teacher."

"And it's off limits," Natalie added, glancing at him.

"Right," said Alex. "Off limits." He wondered how much time he would have if he did cross this line. Probably not long enough to go far.

Aamir looked sidelong at him, then led them away, down another set of hallways. The bricks faded away, replaced by rough, battered stones the size of Alex's head, with deep gouges and scars from where something had torn at them.

This time, the line that Aamir showed them was made of gold. The older student licked his lips. "*Really* don't cross this one."

Alex tilted his head. "What do you mean, *really*?"

Aamir made a vexed noise. "This one won't bring a teacher down on you. It'll hurt you."

Alex could feel it now. A biting, wintry cold. If the blue line had been like snow, this one was like ice. It was all sharp, angry edges.

"What's behind it?" he asked.

Aamir didn't bother looking this time. He held Alex's gaze, his face serious and set.

"The Head's domain."

Aamir then escorted them directly to their next class, with Professor Lintz, whom Aamir described as his favorite teacher. Alex settled into his chair beside Natalie with a buzz of irritation, shivering in the chilly classroom air. He needed to get outside, to try the gates. He couldn't trust Aamir or Jari, but if he could just get some time alone, he was sure he could figure out this damn manor without their help.

He felt a hand on his arm and looked up to see Natalie gazing at him.

"We'll make it out, Alex," she whispered. "We have to keep up hope. If anyone can find the way home, it's probably the guy who can make sense of Jacques Lacan."

"How did you know I've read Lacan?" he whispered back, frowning.

She smiled faintly. "I saw *The Seminar* on your bookshelf."

"Oh, right," he muttered. He could hardly believe that had just been a few nights ago.

Alex looked up just in time to see Professor Lintz loping into the room.

For an overweight man, Lintz moved with a feline grace, his feet whispering across the floor as his thick-fingered hands floated along at his sides. He had a round, perspiring face, adorned with an impressive mustache that bobbed over sagging jowls.

The class fell silent as he entered, and his wolfish gaze

spread out over the classroom.

"New students," he barked, and Alex stood, sensing the command in the man's voice. Beside him, Natalie scrambled to her feet too.

"Mm," said Lintz, stepping forward. He moved straight past Alex, who turned to see the man eyeing Natalie up and down. "Can you produce an aura yet?" he asked, his voice skeptical.

"I…I don't know, sir," she replied. "I haven't tried."

"Go on, then," he said sharply. "Try now."

Natalie closed her eyes, drawing in her breath. Lintz stood still in front of her, staring at her with beady eyes. He let out a grunt of satisfaction when a burst of golden light rippled from her, tracing her form like ethereal fire. She looked utterly surprised.

"Good," he said. "Unformed, but strong. Very good." He looked her up and down again as she beamed. "Keep your back straight," he said, and her smile slipped a little. "Magic is about form and function. You must be iron. Do not forget that."

Natalie bobbed her head, and Lintz turned his gaze on Alex.

"You!" he said. "Can you produce anything?"

"I don't think so, sir. I'm not as fast on the uptake as Natalie, and Professor Derhin focused more on style and history," Alex replied calmly.

Lintz chuckled. "He's like that," he said, a note of

fondness in his voice. *So he and Derhin are friends, then.* "But my classes will be a bit different. You don't need to make a form or anything. Just let out some energy."

Alex hesitated. "Could you elaborate, sir?"

Lintz paused, flapping his hands at his sides. "Just... let it out," he said doubtfully. "Honestly, it's not something most students have any trouble with."

As stupid as this felt, Alex supposed it was worth a try. He reached inside himself, searching for some magic that he could unleash. He tried to imagine it, warm and golden inside him, but there was nothing. He just felt emptiness. He shivered, the cold running through his bones, looking uneasily up at Professor Lintz. The man regarded him with a critical eye, then let out a huff.

"Well, for every prodigy, I suppose we need a problem child," he mumbled.

The class laughed, and Alex sat down.

What would be done with him if it became obvious he was non-magical?

"Did you see me?" whispered Natalie excitedly. "I did it! I didn't know I could!"

"Yes, that was beautiful," he replied, quite stunned at her ability, but also sinking deeper into worry at the expectation everyone seemed to have of him.

Professor Esmerelda, a beautiful woman with raven-black hair and an apparent love of glittery dresses, held their next class. Although her lesson lapsed in and out of stories about her youth, she still had a commanding grasp of magic. She, too, commended Natalie for her powerful aura, and looked on in some shock as Alex failed to conjure so much as a spark.

"I have never met someone with so little magical energy," she mused, looking him up and down with her eerie blue eyes. "How very odd that Finder would bring us such a unique individual. We shall have to be tender in your raising, lest we break you." She had not made that last comment sound reassuring in the least.

Alex left her class with a dry mouth, a worried Jari at his side telling him it took time, Aamir quietly gazing down at his feet, Natalie frowning at him.

"What if I am simply not magical?" Alex asked, and Aamir patted him brusquely on the shoulder.

"I wouldn't worry about that," he said. "It is extremely unlikely."

"Yes, but what if?"

The older boy looked him in the eye. "I shouldn't like to think," he said seriously.

At least Natalie didn't have to worry about that. He glanced at her. Maybe tonight he would finally be able to sneak away, spend the evening exploring, plan an escape route…

"You go on ahead," he called to Aamir and Jari, hanging back with Natalie. "We'll catch up."

Aamir regarded him levelly. "We will wait for you at the end of this hallway," he said.

"Huh? Why?" asked Jari, but Aamir put one firm hand to his back, guiding him away, out of earshot. Alex was glad Aamir accepted his desire for a private conversation, and turned quickly to Natalie.

"Okay," he said in a hushed voice. "So you still want to get out of here, right?"

"Of course!" she hissed. "Why on earth would you think I wouldn't?"

Alex hadn't expected a different answer. "Just that you seem really good at this…magic stuff," he murmured.

She shook her head vigorously. "Perhaps I am good at it. Perhaps it's even fun. But I…" she hesitated, searching for the right words. "Even aside from the fact that I need to return to my family, I do not like this place. There is something seriously wrong with it."

Alex exhaled. *Tell me about it.* "Okay," he whispered, "so I'm thinking…" He glanced at Aamir and Jari, who were several yards away. "I'm thinking the best plan is to wait a little longer." She started to protest, but he quickly explained, "Right now I don't even know how to get out of here. The hallways in this place…It's confusing. We'll need a little time to figure it out."

She drooped, tears brimming in her eyes. "I guess that makes sense. I'll try to understand too. I want to help."

He nodded, refraining from telling her he didn't want to get her in trouble. It didn't make any sense for the two of them to risk being caught.

"In the meantime, let's play along, okay? I don't know what to expect from any of these people. Go to classes… stay safe."

"Yes, Alex," she whispered with intensity, holding his hand between both of hers. "Stay safe."

CHAPTER 12

ALEX AWOKE THE NEXT DAY TO THE UNPLEASANT sight of Siren Mave, who bustled in brandishing a measuring tape and jerked him rudely from sleep. He bristled, but put up no resistance as she spun him around like a top before bustling off again. It wouldn't be smart to antagonize her, he figured, gritting his teeth. She soon returned bearing a freshly tailored set of clothes in Alex's size, dropping them on the bed and dusting her hands off on her gown.

"Thank you," he grated out.

Siren Mave beamed. "Oh, don't mention it, darling," she said. "I'm here to look after you little rascals, after all. If you need anything, let me know, okay?"

Alex waited for her to leave, then stripped out of Aamir's clothes and pulled on the new set while Aamir and Jari faced the opposite wall. The new clothes fit more perfectly than anything Alex had ever worn, though they felt alien, and still insufficient against the cold.

Jari seemed to think they looked fantastic, clapping his hands at the sight of him. Aamir approved as well, giving Alex a critical onceover and saying these clothes fit a good deal better than his ones.

"So who is Siren Mave, anyway? What does she do here?" Alex asked, pulling his coat around him.

The smaller boy spun around and flopped down to land cross-legged on the edge of his bed, facing Alex.

"Well, she's certainly not here to be our friend," Aamir said. "Her goal is to make sure we don't die."

Alex frowned. "So she's a nurse?"

Jari laughed. "Magical folk have a hard time getting sick," he said. "And when they do, it's…dramatic. She can't help; she's pretty much just here to make sure we don't starve or freeze."

"Well, she's not doing a great job there. Aren't you two freezing?"

Jari looked puzzled. "Nope. Just you." Then he brightened. "Let's go get some breakfast! I'm starving."

After breakfast, Alex found himself alone in the dorm with Aamir for a while. The older boy had picked up a book to read and, seizing the opportunity to gather information, Alex began by asking him what he was reading.

"*Terothype's Discourse of Anima Arcana*," Aamir said, absently turning the page. By his side, a little puff of golden light flared to life, then warped. Alex watched, highly intrigued, as the magic molded itself into the form of a single, green leaf.

Reaching out, Alex took it just as it began to flutter down, running his fingers over it before turning it over. It felt so real. He could see the veins, feel the waxy surface.

"Is this…permanent?" he asked. "Or will it eventually disappear?"

Aamir lowered his book. "Anima magic focuses on severance," he said. "You create something, then sever your bond with the magic, simultaneously instilling it with purpose. Intent."

"Purpose. That sounds complicated. How could you identify something's purpose that way? Or hold it in your mind?"

"With plants, it is not too difficult. The purpose of a plant is relatively simple. Survive. Drink the light, set down roots. For an animal, however, it becomes more complicated."

"But a plant is part of a larger system, isn't it? Even a leaf, pretty simple on its own, must connect to the entire organism. And that organism must connect to its environment, and the organisms that environment contains. How do you hold all that in your mind?"

Aamir smiled, shutting his book and finally looking up at Alex.

"You are overthinking it. Magic is largely based on estimation, on feeling your way. One leaf is not as difficult as you imagine."

Alex thought for a moment. "A person must be extremely difficult, though," he mused.

"Well, a homunculus is not too hard," said Aamir. "However, to impart a complete, functioning mind upon something made of magic? That is beyond difficult: it is unheard of. When creating it, you would need to encapsulate all the thought processes of an entire individual. It would be the supreme act of magic."

Alex nodded slowly. "I see. Interesting. Is all magic like this?" He held up the leaf. "How does it work?"

Aamir seemed to think about that. "Well," he said, "those stupid exercises they have us do in class aren't entirely without merit. Each one teaches a different way of molding your energy. This most recent one, *Alaman's*, creates a spout of energy that bursts from the hand, for example. Once you know how to mold it, it's all about knowing how to hold each piece in your mind and bring it into the form and essence you desire."

"I see," Alex said slowly, considering this. "So, I would assume, the more detailed the spell, the more difficult it is. And magic could take the form of anything—physical, visual, auditory, depending on your intent?"

Aamir gave him an appraising look, a flicker of excitement dancing in his eyes. "Essentially, yes. You are grasping the concept quickly. Once you master summoning and molding your magic, I have some books you should read. They'll really explain all this better than I can."

There was a moment of silence in which a couple more leaves snapped into existence, drifting lazily to the floor.

"So, what about the other instructors here?" Alex continued. "I've only met three of them, and they seemed, uh, peculiar."

"Well, you won't have much to do with them for a while yet. Renmark and Gaze are senior instructors and only hold classes where the students are in their second year and up."

"What are they like?" he asked, disappointed he wouldn't be able to gauge them for himself.

"Renmark is *stern*. And Gaze is very strange."

Alex made a mental note, then led up his next question carefully, trying to sound casual.

"What about the manor? How do the hallways work?

How would you get outside, for example?"

Aamir looked at him for a long moment, eyes slightly narrowed, and Alex knew he had sounded too eager.

"The hallways just require memorization; they are pretty simple." Then he picked up his book again, leaving Alex's real question unanswered.

CHAPTER 13

I T TOOK PROFESSOR DERHIN TWO DAYS TO FINISH explaining what he insisted were the very basics of *Alaman's Inner Enlightenment and Fire*, and even after that, he was leery about letting them practice it. He eventually agreed to oversee the process as his students sat upon their desks and lifted one hand to the air as though they were "holding up invisible pineapples," as Derhin put it. The other hand they placed over their hearts.

"Now, eyes closed," Derhin said, in a voice one might use on an easily startled horse, "and breathe in through the nose, out through the mouth. Cycle the energy between the brain and the chest. Stoke it into a whirlpool."

Alex sat upon his desk, giving it a try. He closed his eyes, breathing in, then breathing out. He tried to visualize chakras moving within him alongside the air in his lungs, but nothing happened. He only felt the familiar cold, pressing against his gut. He sighed. If he couldn't figure this out, they would realize he had snuck in.

Seated in his usual spot in front of Alex, Jari had started to glow faintly. Little lines of fiery golden energy raced up and down his upheld wrist, and his hair was standing up. Shooting a sidelong look at Aamir, Alex almost groaned. The older boy was engulfed in little spouts and lashes of power, his whole body shining like some kind of great statue.

At an exclamation, Alex turned to survey the back of the class and was surprised to see Natalie similarly ablaze. She sat, eyes closed, a serene expression on her face as she billowed with radiance. The girls around her had opened their eyes and were uttering exclamations of surprise and awe. At the front of the room, Professor Derhin looked up from where he had been writing upon a sheet.

"Lovely aura, Chevalier," he said, though he didn't sound particularly pleased—almost put out. "You too, Nagi."

Alex was satisfied to see her succeeding. With a smile at him, she had chosen to sit with the girls from her dormitory today, which was a good sign. She was blending in well.

Professor Derhin's eyes swept the room and found Alex, sitting on his desk, his hand stuck in the air, looking firmly non-magical. "Webber," he said, rubbing at his temples, "while I have been told by your other teachers that you have…difficulties, in these matters, I do insist that you at least try."

A titter of laughter ran through the classroom. He shut his eyes once more, refocusing, making a stronger attempt.

Come on, he thought.

Nothing happened.

What will they do to me if they find out?

What will happen to Natalie if I'm sent away?

Still nothing.

Sitting in the dining room after class, Alex was again absorbed in thoughts of escape. Trying the gates was still the only idea he had, but he had not yet been able to master the hallways. Aamir was clearly unwilling to help, but perhaps Jari would know the way…The question was how to convince the boy to show him and Natalie. He would need to be more careful when broaching the question this time, as he didn't want a repeat of Aamir's reaction.

"It's all right," said Aamir suddenly, clapping him on the back. "You've still got a little time before your first examination. I'm sure you're just nervous."

"What?" said Alex. "Oh. Yes, I'm sure that's it." Aamir must have mistook his look of concentration for one of dismay.

"I'd be nervous," said Jari. "I don't think I've ever heard of someone failing their first examination. Do you think they'd kill him?"

Alex looked up sharply, and Aamir glared at Jari. "They would *not* kill him," he said. "Alex isn't non-magical. He's just having a hard time focusing his energy."

"Is that what happens to non-magical people here?" They hadn't harmed him yet, but he wouldn't put it past them.

Jari laughed, speaking around a mouthful of bread that sent crumbs scattering over the tabletop. "Non-magical people *don't* come here," he said. "There are barriers. Spells and stuff that keep them out. Anyway, I don't think that's Alex's problem. I think his problem runs a little deeper." His eyes twinkled mischievously.

Aamir turned with an expression of academic interest, his arms folding.

"Oh? What do you know?"

"I know Alex's little secret," said Jari.

Alex's mouth went dry. "You do?"

Jari grinned. "He can't do magic because he's got

something else on his mind. Or more specifically"—he leaned in conspiratorially—"someone else?"

"Oh, Jari..." sighed Aamir.

"Hey, it's valid!" said Jari as he held up his hands. "When I had that crush on Ellabell Magri last year, I could barely muster any magic for a week, remember?"

"But you could at least produce *something*, even if it was pitiful," said Aamir.

"I'm just saying," replied Jari. "I think our boy's problem isn't of the mind. It's of the heart." He tapped his chest meaningfully.

Thinking quickly, Alex jumped on the opportunity.

"I think you're right," he said, and Aamir and Jari both turned to him in surprise. "I've been thinking a lot about someone—Natalie—but it's hard to find somewhere to talk alone. If there were somewhere, maybe somewhere outside the manor, we could go..."

Aamir's expression darkened instantly, but Jari's face lit up like a Christmas tree.

"I know a place," he said. "I can get you some time with her alone, away from prying eyes."

Alex looked up at him, trying to keep the relief off his face. "I think that would be really helpful."

"Great!" said Jari. "Tonight work for you two?"

Alex was about to reply in the affirmative when Aamir suddenly interjected.

"I will bring Alex to your romantic getaway, Jari." He

held Alex's gaze for a long moment, his stare penetrating. "You can bring Natalie."

Jari looked quizzically between Aamir and Alex, but then shrugged unconcernedly.

"Okay," Jari said. "Let's meet there after dinner."

CHAPTER 14

THE WALK TO THE GARDENS WAS A STRANGE AND uncomfortable process for Alex. For one thing, he felt a little guilty for lying about his reasons for wanting to get outside. He still didn't trust Jari or Aamir quite enough to confide in them, but he found himself wishing he hadn't needed to fabricate a reason.

For another, the tall, severe boy at his side walked quickly and in complete silence, his disapproval coming off him in waves. He clearly had not believed Alex's lie, and Alex had no idea why he had insisted on accompanying him. He didn't even know if Aamir was really taking him to Jari's "romantic getaway". For all he knew, he was taking him straight to the Head's office, though he felt that was in a different direction.

The hallways of the manor didn't give any indication of what floor they were on, or which direction they were facing, so Alex found himself being led up a flight of stairs when he had thought they were already on the top floor of the manor, then down a flight of stairs from a hallway that looked like it was on the ground floor. Had he been trying to find the place on his own, it might have taken months of trial and error, opening doors until he finally found the one that led to where he wanted to go. They had likely been designed that way, intended to keep students trapped inside. The hallways didn't move, but the illusions they created formed as good a maze as any he had ever known.

He focused hard on memorizing all the manor's twists and turns, determined to remember the way out, but he was finding it far more difficult than he had imagined, and Aamir's quick pace gave him little time to commit much to memory.

Finally, after several minutes of nothing but the sound of their footsteps walking down the long, empty hallways, and the stern gazes of the rows of painted wizards upon the walls, Aamir stopped before a door.

"The gardens," he said dryly, throwing the door open.

Alex stepped outside for the first time in what felt like weeks, the fresh night air invigorating against his face. He breathed deeply, savoring the moment, feeling like liberation was just around the corner.

"Coming?" came Aamir's voice, and Alex quickly descended a short flight of weathered stone steps to join him in the moonlight.

Glancing around, Alex soon realized "the gardens" must be an ironic term for this desolate place. If there had ever been proper greenery here, it had been long neglected. Untended trees grew wild, clawing at the sky with untamed branches that played host to the same gray ivy that seemed to blanket everything in the manor. Barren heaps of dirt might have once been flowerbeds, and what looked like old gravel paths now lay as flurries of scattered stones, as if they had been struck by a windstorm. Beyond the distant wall, the sky seemed to flicker, moonlight spinning out into a silvery cord that blended into sunlight in a sudden spray of gold.

Alex followed Aamir past blackened trees and benches reduced to shards of stone, over split, rotting logs, and around tangles of dry, thorny brambles. Aamir seemed to know exactly where they were headed, never slackening his pace, never glancing back to make sure Alex was keeping up. At least he really had taken him where he'd said he would, but it was far from what Alex had imagined. He observed his surroundings with mounting trepidation, sticking close to the older boy.

At last, Aamir stopped atop a small mound of earth overlooking a great field. In the middle of the field was a clearing, and Alex could see swirls of ash curling lightly in the breeze. Skeletons of toppled trees surrounded the place, looking as though they had all fallen outward, away from the clearing's center. The moon's pale light had a stark effect on the withered, upturned roots and the flat expanse alike, the shadows long and deep, the moonlit spots cold and still. Alex found himself shivering against the area's hollow, haunted feel just as much as he did against the chill that had not yet left his bones.

After giving him a moment to take in the scene, Aamir spoke, his voice low and serious. He sounded strangely muted by the eerie landscape's pressing atmosphere.

"What do you think happened here, Alex?"

Alex thought for a moment, his silence hanging in the chilly air as thickly as his breath did.

"It looks like something happened in the middle there, something devastating."

Aamir nodded. "It does indeed look like that. Any theories?"

"Magic?" Alex suggested.

"Yes," said Aamir, a hard edge to his voice now. "I think so too."

"Why are you showing me this?" On the strange breeze, his own voice sounded thin and alien.

Aamir exhaled slowly and set his chin. "I do not think you take magic seriously, Alex Webber. It is not all conjuring leaves and glowing with pretty golden light. We can create marvels, yes. But there are those who also wield magic to destroy, and to destroy utterly." His words drifted into the deadened landscape.

"I do take magic seriously," Alex retorted. "Of course I do. I've seen how powerful it is. I saw what the Head can do."

The older boy turned to face him and looked him deliberately in the eye, the moonlight casting half his face in darkest shadow.

"No, Alex. I do not believe you did."

Alex paused. Had he been rushing headlong into a dangerous situation without considering the consequences? He didn't think so. He felt he had played it pretty safe so far, and acknowledged that the manor was likely rife with unknown dangers. But he could see how Aamir could have gotten that impression. He had been secretive, and probably seemed reckless and desperate to the oddly rigid boy.

Aamir's shoulders relaxed a little, his voice softening. "I don't mean to frighten you. In fact, I completely understand. If you think you are the first student here to think of escape, you are mistaken." He paused, gazing into the bleak distance. "I merely wanted to impress upon you the gravity of our situation, the power of the forces you contend with when you push too far."

"What happened to the people who have tried in the past?"

Aamir shrugged. "Some never even find their way out here."

"And those who do?"

"They fail." He looked down. "I cannot stop you from trying, Alex. But please, tread carefully. I should not like to see harm befall you."

A silence settled between them, interrupted only by the sound of dry branches rubbing against each other in the wind.

"You mentioned graduation earlier," Alex said eventually, thinking of the only certain way out of Spellshadow.

Aamir stood a little straighter. "So I did."

"What does that word mean here?"

"That," said Aamir, "is the right question."

"And that's not an answer," replied Alex.

A strange look stole over Aamir's face. "All we know is that those who graduate vanish completely. We never hear from them again, and they are never spoken of."

Alex wet his lip. "And you don't think they're just off making their way in the world?"

Aamir scoffed. "Wouldn't we have heard of them? Wouldn't one of them slip up somehow, lose control? Wouldn't the professors boast of their favorite students' success? Wouldn't we have role models, positions to which we should aspire? Wouldn't their names at least be spoken?" His eyes flashed in the moonlight, his expression grim and tight, carefully controlled. "No. I do not think they are off making their way in the world."

And suddenly Aamir's odd vehemence when discouraging Alex from finding trouble, from pushing boundaries, made perfect sense.

Aamir was afraid.

CHAPTER 15

AMIR LED ALEX THROUGH THE GARDENS ONCE again, stopping near a tree that looked like it had been ripped in half. He bent down, wiping some gravel and dirt away from a patch at his feet, and Alex saw a small wooden door there. Aamir eased it up, and they gazed down a wooden ladder into the darkness below.

"This place is secret, as far as we know," said Aamir. "But let me go before you, just in case."

He lowered himself carefully down the ladder, disappearing into what looked to be a dirt cave. Alex stood alone in the garden for a moment, the silence and the moonlight beating down upon him, their conversation reverberating in his mind. Musty smells of wet wood and dust drifted up through the hole to him.

"Come on," Aamir called. "It is empty."

Alex turned, grabbing the ladder and descending slowly.

By the light trickling in through the hole, he could see Aamir squinting as he examined the dark. Then, Aamir made two swift gestures. A pair of torches at the far end of the room burst into flames, crackling happily, and the room came into focus.

It was a wine cellar. Or at least, it had been. Like everything in the manor, it seemed to have fallen into disuse, the great wooden racks now covered in cobwebs and dust, housing only a few bottles of wine now. The dirt ceiling was held up by wooden frames at regular intervals. Aamir looked around the empty space once more before moving toward the ladder.

"Jari and Natalie should be here momentarily. You are fine alone?" He paused, one foot on the bottom rung, waiting for Alex's answer.

"Yeah," said Alex, looking around him. "I'm fine alone."

"Good." Aamir left without a backward glance, leaving the door above open.

Alex stood in the empty cellar, thinking of Aamir's warning. Maybe he should proceed with greater caution, be more fearful of punishment. But failure to escape

Spellshadow was not an option. What else did Aamir know that he wasn't saying? Alex had the impression that the older boy was holding back quite a bit.

He wandered over to one of the remaining bottles on the wine rack and idly tugged it free of the cobwebs and clinging dirt, trying to remember the way through the maze of hallways. The bottle fell into his hands with a puff of dust, and he turned it over to read the label.

Fields of Sorrow, 1908.

"Hello."

Alex jumped and looked up. Sitting in one of the slots meant for a bottle of wine was the small black cat. Its shadowy head was turned away from him, and as he watched, it let out a mighty yawn.

Alex stared at the shadow creature, replacing the bottle. So much for being in here alone, or this place being secret. He was getting the unnerving impression that you couldn't really be alone at Spellshadow, no matter where you went.

"You have calmed a great deal," the cat remarked.

Wondering whether it was wise to engage with the thing, Alex just put his hands in his pockets and narrowed his eyes at it. He was no less wary of it now than he had been at their first meeting. Perhaps even more so.

"Too good to talk to me," said the cat, sounding hurt. "And here I came all this way just to give you a warning."

"What?" asked Alex, too apprehensive to resist. "I've

already had a warning tonight."

"Oh yes, I know," it purred lowly, flicking its tail. "And very interesting it was. But did it occur to you that there are many things in this place, seen and unseen, of which you should be warned?" A laugh that didn't fit the little animal burbled out into the room, seeping into every corner. "And I know you now. I couldn't place you at first, but now I recognize you."

Alex pulled at his coat, feeling unsettled and even more chilled than before. It was so *cold* down in the cellar; he could feel it slipping down his fingertips like frost curling over a fresh blade of grass. He stared at the cat, waiting for it to continue, but it said nothing more, instead licking a paw and sending a spray of shadowy mist flicking off the tip of one long claw.

"What are you?" Alex finally asked. "What do you want?"

"Haven't we already established that I may as well be a cat? As for what I want"—its ears swiveled—"I want nothing much. Mostly just to watch. I did want to tell you, though: do be careful. The professors..." It made a noise somewhere between a growl and a cackle. "They are not half as stupid as they might appear. And that goes double for the Head."

Alex stared.

"This is no place for one such as you," the cat continued. "So be careful, won't you? I wouldn't want you to graduate too soon."

Alex wet his lower lip. "Graduate?"

The cat let out a low hiss of dissatisfaction. "Haven't you figured it out yet?"

Alex looked up at the sound of voices and approaching footsteps above.

"I hear one of the old professors used to tend this place," came Jari's high voice. "Real green thumb."

"What happened?" asked Natalie.

"She left, like all the rest," said Jari. "Got replaced. Here we are! And down we go."

When Alex glanced back, the cat was gone.

CHAPTER 16

ONCE JARI LEFT THEM TO HEAD BACK TO THE manor, telling them with a wink that he would return in an hour, Alex and Natalie found themselves alone in the small, cold cellar. Hopefully alone.

Natalie looked tense and excited, her eyes shining. "Now we will escape, yes?"

"We're going to try," Alex replied. "I was thinking we should start simple, with the gates. That's why I wanted to come out here. Well, that, and so we could talk with more privacy."

She nodded, her hair gleaming warmly in the torch-light. "It's a good start."

They climbed back up the wooden ladder and headed across the devastated garden, picking their way around heaps of rubble and long-dead trees.

"It's so creepy here," Natalie said as they walked, holding her arms around herself. "It's even worse than inside."

"I don't know," Alex replied as he held back a leafless branch so she could pass. "At least the gardens aren't trying to hide what they are. Inside, it's pretending to be a school, but it's not really, is it?"

"What do you mean?"

"Well, the teachers here aren't really teaching much, are they? They only ever cover focus and control." He paused, hesitant to scare her with all he had heard tonight. She probably didn't need to know about the dark crater in the garden, or Aamir's deep-seated fear, or the cat-creature. "And nobody seems to know what it means to graduate, but it doesn't sound good," he finished.

"You're right. And it does not feel very much like a school. The students are strange and quiet, and it's hard to make friends. Maybe everyone is scared."

"I wouldn't be surprised." He remembered something he'd been meaning to talk to her about. "Hey, do you remember me asking you about a gray man in rags?"

"In Professor Derhin's classroom?"

"I mean before that. In the nurse's office at Middledale High."

"No...I don't remember very much from that time,"

she said, sounding rueful.

"Well, I'm thinking that must be 'Finder'. He finds magical people and enchants them to come here. That's another creepy thing about this so-called school."

"But he's supposed to be invisible, isn't he?"

Alex paused, and she nearly bumped into him. "Is he?"

"That's what the girls in my dorm said. He's supposed to be invisible, and nobody has ever seen him."

They started walking again, Alex mulling this over. *What did this mean?*

"Alex," Natalie said, stopping suddenly on a chunk of cracked pavement. "If we find a way to escape, if we succeed…We can't just leave the other students here, can we? Haven't they all been taken from their homes too?"

He sighed. He hadn't yet asked Aamir or Jari for details about their personal history, though she was probably right. But a mass escape? How would they pull that off?

"Let's just focus on how to escape at all first," he said as they approached the gates.

The great gates of the manor were much as Alex remembered them. Rusting bars of iron as thick as his arm, covered in so much ivy that he couldn't even see the world beyond through the slits. On either side, tall brick walls rose high above the garden, topped with treacherous curves of barbed metal.

He strode over and reached through the ivy, seizing one of the bars with both hands. It was strong, immovable, and freezing cold. Thinking to climb up it, he steadied his grip, but the cold intensified, shooting down his arms, sinking into his bones. He grunted and let go, leaping backwards and rubbing his arms vigorously. The cold lingered, and he shuddered.

"Let me try," said Natalie, stepping forward through the ivy.

"No, don't!" said Alex quickly. "It's so cold it hurts."

"I will just try," she insisted, brushing past him.

After testing both gates' strength for herself, not even flinching from the cold, Natalie stepped back again, closing her eyes in concentration. Just as it had in class, her golden aura came to life, flicking lightly all over her skin. She frowned and extended her arms, pushing the magic away from her, toward the gates. It didn't quite reach, seeming to sputter and rain down upon the ivy, where it disappeared.

She tried again, this time with her hand directly on the metal. Her hand looked wreathed in golden flame, but the flame died quickly, dropping down to the ivy once more. It was the same on the third try, and on the fourth she could not muster an aura of the same strength.

"I don't see how we're going to do this," Alex murmured. Aamir's words rang in his ears, and he racked his brain for a solution. Maybe he could construct something they could climb, or something that would propel them… The ladder in the cellar was much too short, but maybe he could use it somehow. Building something would probably attract a lot of attention, though. How could he go about it in secret? And what kind of defensive spells might be at the top?

But then he looked to Natalie, and he forgot his plans and the freezing cold permeating his body.

Natalie had slumped dejectedly to the ground and buried her face in her hands. Alex sat beside her, putting an arm gently around her shoulders. She leaned slightly into him, crying softly and pulling her knees up.

"Hey," he said gently after a minute. "Don't lose hope. We're going to find a way out of this mess. I promise." He wasn't sure how he'd fulfill that promise, but he could never give in.

She stopped crying after a moment, gathering herself quickly and wiping at her eyes. "My family must be so worried about me," she said with a quiet sniff, sitting up a little. "My sister Elena…she is just starting middle school. We were going to talk every day."

Alex thought again of his mother and felt pain in his chest.

"You'll get back to them," he said firmly, as much to reassure himself as to comfort her. He managed to smile. "I've got no choice in the matter—I promised your little sister I'd look after you."

She sighed. "Yes, you did."

A few more moments of silence passed between them,

and then she tensed and set her jaw, looking again at the gates. "I have a plan," she announced, rising to her feet. "We will stay here, just until I get strong enough. I'll practice all the time. And then we'll come back here, and I'll use magic to blow the gates away, and we'll tell all the students and get everyone out." She looked at him, her eyes glinting. "You can help me practice, and learn the way out here."

He didn't say anything for a minute, trying to think of another approach. It couldn't be that simple. Countless students must have tried that. If Natalie were the one leading the escape, she would be the one facing punishment, or possibly worse.

"It is a good plan," she said a little defensively, watching for his response.

"Yes, it is," he replied, not wanting to deflate her. "Let's start practicing right away." There was no harm in her strengthening her magic.

And in the meantime, he had to come up with something else.

CHAPTER 17

Bᴜᴛ, ᴀ ᴡᴇᴇᴋ ʟᴀᴛᴇʀ, Aʟᴇx ʜᴀᴅ ɴᴏᴛ ᴛʜᴏᴜɢʜᴛ ᴏғ ᴀ better plan any more than he had mastered even the simplest of magical exercises. He had at least become more familiar with the hallways, but was feeling increasingly trapped, and growing increasingly closer to despair. When Alex had first arrived, Aamir had said he had a few weeks before he would *seriously* be expected to start performing magic, but the days were slipping by at a worrying speed.

Natalie, for one, was progressing beautifully, and believed that in just a little more time she would be ready to try the gates again. He felt he had no choice but to continue pursuing their current plan, as worried as it made him. After managing several more solo trips to the gates, he was convinced they were impenetrable. He couldn't even touch them for more than twelve seconds, and he couldn't imagine they were unguarded by more dangerous magical means.

At Natalie's suggestion, Alex had started making a sincere effort to befriend Jari and Aamir. She pointed out that they probably knew lots of things he didn't, and even suggested they might want to help.

"Don't you think everyone here must want to escape as much as we do?" she had asked earnestly.

"They might be too afraid," he had countered, thinking of Aamir. "They might decide to rat us out to ensure their own safety."

"Just be careful, then," she had insisted.

Now, he found himself following Jari and Aamir into the mechanics' lab. The two of them were working on a project, the scope of which was mysterious but intriguing to Alex. He sat on a stool beside their workbench, watching the two boys bickering as they stared down at a minute piece of machinery through magnifying glasses strapped to their heads, each holding a delicate pair of instruments in their hands. The room was full of little clicks and whirrs, the sounds of clockwork all around him.

Indeed, the walls of the large, yet crowded room were hung with clocks of every shape and size. What was more, they all seemed intent on telling a different kind of time. One ran between "start" and "finish," and seemed to be stuck on the latter. Another had been carefully calibrated to chime five minutes before class would begin. And another, rather ominously, appeared to be counting down, with only a few hundred hours left before it was out of time.

"So," Alex said, interjecting himself into his roommates' argument, "if technology doesn't work here, how does all this function?" Alex had been carrying his cell phone when he left Middledale High to follow Natalie, but it must have slipped from his pocket during his struggle with her on Spellshadow Lane because he no longer had it. Natalie hadn't been carrying a cell phone at all and neither wore watches, so he hadn't been able to test the no-technology theory the boys had informed him about a few days ago.

Jari swiveled, and Aamir took the opportunity to begin poking and prodding at the piece of machinery that lay on the table.

"We mostly use clockwork," the blond boy said, his expression sage-like. "Electrical engineering just doesn't work, but we can use a little magic and good old-fashioned physics to keep basic things like this going. Not to mention, once you mix magic and clockwork, there's really all manner of things you can do."

Alex watched as Aamir reached down, a little bloom of

golden fire slipping from his fingertips and into their machine, which shuddered, then lay still.

"Told you it wouldn't work," Jari said without looking.

Aamir let out a grunt of irritation.

Alex looked down at the gears. They fit together so elegantly, so precisely, that he found himself drawn to them. Here was something he could grasp easily.

"What does this do?" he asked, looking down at the project.

"Well," Jari said, "it's *supposed* to get up and walk around a little, only Aamir here doesn't know how to make a proper set of hydraulics."

"Oh, and you do?" Aamir retorted.

Jari leaned down, looking the device over.

"Pull your magic out," he said.

Aamir sighed, then reached out, retrieving the little bloom of golden fire.

Alex watched with interest. "Couldn't you have done that?" he asked Jari.

Jari grimaced. "It's damnably hard to get someone else's magic to do what you want—all the books on how to do it have been hidden away. And dispelling it altogether is…well, impossible, for us."

He adjusted the magnifying glass over his eye, tilting forward until the glass lens was almost touching the machinery. He made a couple of minute adjustments with the tool in his hand, then looked over at Alex.

"Care to put the finishing touches in?"

Alex ran a hand through his hair. "Well, I would, but I still can't do any magic."

Jari laughed. "No need for magic. Here."

He pulled a magnifying glass from nearby and handed it to Alex, who strapped it over his eye. At once, the machine below him lurched into focus, each tiny gear sparkling and plain to see.

"See where that cog connects to that other one?" Jari said, pointing the two places out.

Alex nodded.

"Now watch this."

A lick of gold wisped its way out, settling into the gears. At once, they began to turn, ever so slowly, as if in response to the power. Alex stared at it with fierce intensity. The machine was almost ready to move, but there was something missing. A link between the two cogs that Jari had pointed out.

The boy handed Alex a small pair of tweezers, squeezing the end. He looked at the tips of the tweezers through his lens and saw they were pinching the missing piece.

Slowly, painstakingly, Alex inserted the gear, then fastened it in place. When he was done, his hand was stiff from having been held so still throughout the process, and his neck was aching, but he felt satisfied that he had done a good job. Jari made no comment throughout, only nodding, and Aamir stared down at the machine in concentration without interfering.

When Alex was done, Jari reached out, adjusting the magical flow within the machine. The gears started to turn. With a click and a whir, a little puff of steam boiled up from some hidden, internal organ. The machine's little legs began to kick and flick the air like a beetle turned on its back, and Alex instinctively reached out, righting it. Its legs hit the tabletop, and it skittered off along the wood workspace to collide with another boy's project.

A volley of curses, insults, and threats followed. Alex ducked away, moving to where the beetle had fallen and picking it up. Its legs continued to move, but they seemed weaker, less coordinated somehow. Little trails of steam rippled up through the gaps in its clockwork hide.

A shadow fell over the machine, and Alex looked up to see Aamir standing over him, his dark eyes sparkling with amusement.

"You have worked on something like this before?"

"Sort of," said Alex. "When I was a kid I went to a robotics workshop. I've never done anything exactly like this, but it's just basic engineering, isn't it?"

Jari bounced up beside Aamir with a broad smile. "We'll have to come more often!" he said. "We always mess up the engineering part. Magic is way easier."

Aamir glared. Jari returned the look, then corrected himself.

"I guess Aamir doesn't *always* mess up the engineering."

Aamir let out an offended huff of breath, and Alex looked over to see him leaning toward Jari with a scowl darkening his features. The two boys were an odd duo, to be sure. Alex watched as they turned in unison to a diagram on the table, each making sharp gestures as they shot their opinions at one another.

In his attempt to become more friendly with them, he'd asked about their backgrounds. Aamir was taken from New Delhi, India, while Jari had Greek roots, though he'd been living in America when he'd been "found". Both had been strangely guarded when Alex had asked about their families. They'd tensed up, discomfort tracing their eyes, and returned similar answers—they'd prefer to not talk about it. Their responses had left Alex's stomach feeling like a hollow pit: why had they been so reticent? After considering it, he came to the conclusion that it must simply hurt too much. Both were convinced they'd never escape this place. Thinking or talking about their families was just a recipe for pain. It scared Alex to realize he had already found himself constantly trying to push thoughts of his mother aside in an attempt to keep himself together—he was already utilizing Aamir and Jari's method to cope with the separation.

But he could not end up like them. *He could not.*

"What do you think?"

Alex blinked, looking up just in time to see Jari and Aamir staring at him, both of their faces similarly demanding.

"Think about what?" he asked, pulling his mind back to the present.

"The design," Aamir said, stabbing a finger at the little metal bug in Alex's hand. "I think the methodology employed had some serious flaws."

"At least it didn't just give up and die," Jari said.

"It lived *too much*."

At this last note, Alex noticed that the student down the table, who had been fastidiously ignoring them, nodded sharply. Alex shrugged.

"I think it's better to move than get stuck in one place. At least something happened. Here, let me see…"

Jari beamed at him, and Aamir sighed, running his hands through his hair. For a moment, his eyes seemed to glaze, looking at something else, somewhere else.

"I suppose," he muttered.

There was a clattering from the walls, and the clocks began to chime, a cacophony of deep, booming notes mixed with high, tinny clinks.

"Curfew?" Alex asked, holding his ears.

Aamir continued to stare into space, so Jari stepped in to answer the question. "Yes," he said. "We've got to get back to our rooms."

"What if we don't?" Alex asked, thinking of his after-dinner strolls in the garden.

Aamir shook his head, snapping out of his apparent trance. "You want to be back to your room before curfew," he said simply.

"Hm," said Alex. Another non-answer from Aamir.

As the trio made their way toward the door, Aamir suddenly stopped and threw out a hand. "Wait, wait," he said, turning to Alex. "You don't still have the beetle, do you?"

Alex nodded, holding out his hand to reveal the little clockwork creature, its legs now completely still.

Jari winced. "Ah, good point," he said. "Alex, you can't take those with you outside of the lab. They're considered contraband."

Alex proffered the item to Jari, who took it to the back of the room and put it in a little box labeled *Petra*. Then he came back to Alex and clapped him on the shoulder.

"Off we go, then!"

When they reached the room, Jari skipped across it in one bounding step to flop magnificently upon his mattress, bouncing once before landing on his back. Aamir watched him with a disapproving sigh, then looked at Alex as if to say, "Well, no helping that."

"Here," he said, reaching into a pocket and rummaging around. He pulled something out, and pressed it into Alex's palm.

It was cold and firm, with a pleasing weight. Alex looked down to see a screwdriver, complete with a set of bits. He looked up at Aamir, surprised. Aamir pressed a finger to his lips and gave him a knowing look.

"You looked...happier. More at ease, near the machines," he said. "I know how hard that can be when you first get here. Hell, it's still hard now. So take that. It's minor—I doubt you'll get in much trouble for getting caught with it."

Alex turned the screwdriver over in his hand, admiring it. This could be a very useful tool at some point. And Aamir was right, too—he had momentarily forgotten his constant tension in the lab, and focusing on something besides escape had been almost meditative for him.

"If you don't want it," Aamir said, "I can always take it back and—"

"No," Alex said quickly. "Thank you. I appreciate this."

A rare smile cracked Aamir's lips. He gave a quick thumbs-up to Jari, who was sitting on his bed with an attentive expression.

Alex flopped backward. Well, Natalie had been right. He had learned a couple of new things about the manor, and it felt good to be on friendlier terms with his roommates. They certainly seemed excited about it.

But he still wasn't sure he wanted to trust them with his secrets.

As he waited for Derhin's class to begin the next day, Alex prepared himself for yet another awkward session where he would stand out as exceptionally incompetent. It was a disconcerting feeling, given that all his life he'd always been one of the, if not *the*, top student in his class.

"I can't believe you still aren't doing well," said Jari later in Derhin's class, shaking his head. "You and Natalie seem closer than ever. You're always in the library together, or practicing at the tables. You shouldn't still be having so much trouble!"

Aamir looked pensive, but said nothing.

Professor Derhin cleared his throat, a noise that was somewhere between a smoker's rasp and the cry a mouse might make if stepped on by a steel-toed boot.

"Now that the class is actually here," he said, eyeing some latecomers, "I think we can begin. However, first off—Webber, I'd like you to come to the front of the room."

Alex almost didn't register what he was hearing. He looked up at Professor Derhin with an uncertain expression, and the man waved with uncharacteristic enthusiasm. "Come on," he said. "I've decided that today is the day we break that little block of yours."

Alex felt his blood run cold.

He was supposed to have more time. He'd had an idea that if worse came to worst, and they were still at Spellshadow by the time his "few weeks" grace period was over, he'd ask Natalie to fake his magic. But he hadn't

139

discussed it with her yet because he was supposed to have at least one week more to go. He shot a look over his shoulder and saw Natalie wearing an anxious frown.

Crap.

"Up, up," said Derhin, clapping his hands.

Alex rose to his feet, his eyes flicking around the classroom. Everywhere, eyes were focused on him. He became keenly aware of the cold in his bones, that cloying, ebbing feeling of emptiness. He had no magic.

"Sit on my desk," Derhin instructed.

Alex scrambled up onto the polished wood surface and sat cross-legged. He straightened his spine and raised his hands near his heart. He knew the procedure, at least.

"Excellent," said Derhin. He circled Alex, looking him up and down with an academic air. "Yes, this is a good starting pose, but you need to remember to breathe. The breath is crucial to this focusing technique."

Alex pulled in a breath, slowly, through his nose, just like he'd learned.

"All right," Derhin muttered, as if trying to figure out how to tackle a complicated math problem. "Go through the stance for us. Give it your best."

In dead silence, Alex raised one hand, opening his palm toward the sky as he brought his other hand over his heart. He closed his eyes and tried to visualize the flow of energies in his body as they traced the lines of his breath, but there was nothing but cold.

"Link the heart and mind," Derhin said, softly. "Pull them together, and make them one. The breath is your heartbeat, and the heart draws air. Focus your energy like a great funnel, blossoming from its point at your gut and flowing free at your fingertips."

Alex tried; he really did, but he felt nothing. Derhin poked and prodded at him, trying to adjust his stance, his words still coming in dull mutters.

"It really should work," he was saying. "Webber, try twisting your hand—no, the other one—I've heard that helps. Maybe…no."

Alex felt panic rising in his throat. This was it. This was the moment he proved that he wasn't supposed to be here. They would place his connection to Natalie, figure out that he had followed her, and then…who knew.

He focused as hard as he could, squeezing his eyes shut…

"Aha!"

Alex opened his eyes to see Derhin standing in front of him, but rather than looking disappointed, his face was a mask of triumph. He stepped aside, gesturing toward Alex.

"See? All it takes it a little practice," he was saying, but Alex couldn't hear him.

All around his body, little golden flames licked across his skin. He did his best not to break his stance as he stared at the strands of light that spiraled around his wrists and fingers, sending crackles of energy through him. He shot a look at Natalie.

She sat, looking pleased, with her legs crossed and one finger held idly out. Around it was tangled a little wisp of golden flame. She gave her hand a twitch, and Alex felt a little bite of cold at the back of his neck.

Oh…she's good.

The three boys went back to the dorm room after class. When Aamir finished congratulating Alex and Jari finished gloating, Alex excused himself to go meet Natalie in the library. Jari made catcalls at him until the door to their room was shut behind him, and even then they followed him as ghostly yowls of provocation. He shook his head, chuckling.

Now that Alex had had more time to practice finding his way around and the shifting hallways had become less mysterious than they'd seemed at first, he found it easy to predict their movements, though it still took quite a long time to get anywhere. On his way to the library, he continued his search for workable shortcuts, determined to master *something* about this place.

He opened a door that he thought might cut through

another hallway, and nearly took a spinning cog to the face. He ducked, and the thing ricocheted off the window behind him, hitting the floor with a dull *plink*.

"Sorry!" someone yelled from inside, followed almost instantly by, "Shut the door, idiot!"

Alex did so and went on his way, going down one nondescript hallway, then another, until he sensed he was near the library.

"Signs!" he heard a frustrated Natalie exclaim from somewhere behind him. "Why are there no signs here? It would be so simple!" She followed this with a string of what he assumed to be French curse words, though he only recognized a couple.

He turned back, grinning, and when she caught up, he was leaning casually against the wall.

"You lost?"

"Do not tease me right now, Alex," Natalie snapped, her brown eyes bright with irritation. "I have had it up to here with this place! Why do they not simply put up signs?"

"Like this one?" he smirked, gesturing to a sign that read "Library" with an arrow pointing the right direction.

She huffed in exasperation, then looked suddenly triumphant. He glanced at the sign again, watching as the arrow slowly turned to point the opposite direction.

"You were saying?" she asked, looking smug.

"Right," he said, shouldering off the wall and leading

the way. "Well, I think they make it confusing on purpose, anyway. They want students feeling lost and trapped in here." They rounded the corner. "Hey, thanks for saving me in class, by the way. That was some really impressive stuff."

Natalie smiled at him, but her face quickly fell.

"It was not so hard. And not so impressive, either. I still cannot give form to my magic. I tried to make a lovely bouquet, but…" She sighed. "All I could manage was golden petals."

"Don't be so hard on yourself. It's something, and you've improved really fast."

"Mirian—she is across the hallway from me—she says I need to read more. She tells me crafting things is the essence of magic."

"Okay, we can work on that. I'm sure I've seen books on that in the library."

Natalie turned, staring out a nearby window where a blizzard had just begun, sending splashes of icy snow over the glass. In the distance, Alex could just make out jagged, stony mountain peaks beneath gray clouds.

He thought he could guess what she was thinking.

"We'll get home," he said, putting a hand on her shoulder. "You're more than capable. Let's go find some books."

"Yes," she replied, sounding distracted. "We might as well."

At the base of the great iron staircase that wove around

the library's central pillar was a little sign, listing a variety of subjects. Alex glanced at it to remind himself where the Spellshadow Manor history books were located. He hadn't found anything useful there yet, but he held out hope.

"If you're going to keep covering for me in class," he said, his voice muffled by the quietening charm, "we might need to find some new techniques to practice. You'll have to do twice as many projects as a normal student. Think you're up for it?"

"I suppose so," she said listlessly.

"Okay...what type of spell do you feel like practicing today?"

"I do not care very much. Whatever you think is best." She trailed her finger along the plaque, looking absently at the categories. "No, wait—what about destruction?" Her eyes gleamed dangerously. "Yes," she said with more certainty. "I will be back."

Alex was dubious about the safety of studying destruction, but figured it might come in handy, perhaps as defensive magic.

Natalie pushed off lightly from the handrail, levitating into the air with her arms and legs held close to her body. On the ground, Alex watched as she twirled, rising and falling with a dancer's ease before starting to look for the section on destruction. Apparently not all new students could master the ability to fly easily, which was why they still had ladders climbing the three columns. He couldn't help but feel jealous—how awesome would it be to fly? He hoped it would cheer her up somewhat—she loved floating to retrieve books.

By the time they left the library, laden with books, Natalie was indeed flushed and excited again. She had quickly found a book called *Pyromancy and You*, and had spent the rest of their time happily floating up and down to find all the books Alex listed. It was her favorite part of studying, and Alex was pleased she seemed back to normal. Though he had his doubts about her escape plan, it was necessary to keep her hopes high. Natalie was prone to bouts of despair, and he didn't want her to give up, to succumb to the numbing energy of Spellshadow. He just needed more time to come up with something, and the key might be figuring out what else was going on at this so-called school.

The tables in the study hall where they headed next were a small sea of mostly abandoned rounds that sat before the great window overlooking the gates. Beyond them, Alex could just make out the great, snake-like building that rose up over the walls, backlit by the sparkling lights of a faraway city. As they settled down, Alex unloading his armful of books onto the table, Natalie seemed unable to take her eyes off the horizon.

"Is that your home?" she asked eventually.

Alex looked over. "Maybe," he admitted. "Hard to tell

at this distance, isn't it?"

Natalie bit her lip, her fingers running over the embossed letters on the cover of *Pyromancy and You*. "It looks so close. Why can't we just…?" She trailed off.

"I don't know," said Alex. "There's something going on here." He tapped the pile of books in front of them. "That's why we have these."

Natalie rallied, flipping open her book. "Yes," she murmured.

It took maybe ten minutes for her enthusiasm to flicker, sputter, then go out like a candle in a hurricane. She sprawled, her arms splayed out on the table, her hair forming a dark halo around her head.

"It is impossible," she moaned. "I cannot read any more *English*."

Alex looked up from where he had been reading about the mental process of making inner fire into proper fire. "Let's move on to practical magic, then. Sound good?"

"Very well," she sighed, raising her face to look at him.

"All right, then," said Alex. He looked over the page he'd been reading, then stuck a bookmark in it and turned to Natalie, who sat up a little straighter.

"Conjure some magic, please," he said.

She nodded, cupping her hands in front of her. A little whirl gathered there, and she released a ball of light into the space between them.

"Now what?"

He looked down. "You need to fix the idea of heat in your mind. Of burning. Of everything that is fire. Then, you need to fill your magic with that."

Natalie tilted her head, staring at the ball. Nothing happened.

"It won't work," she said.

"Let's try something else," he replied, picking up another book. Reading about Spellshadow's history would have to wait.

They went through the next half hour with Alex gathering tip after tip from the books arrayed before them. Natalie, in turn, practiced her control while she waited for further instruction. Before long, she had three little balls going at once, her brow wrinkled in concentration.

Alex paused in his research, looking up at the three spheres.

"Nice!" he said. "You're multitasking really well."

She smiled faintly, her eyes fixed on her magic. "It is strange," she said. "In class, it felt so easy, but just making three of these is difficult now."

Alex nodded, tapping one of his books. "That's called having range, but not focus."

Natalie nodded, a little disappointed.

"Then we will practice focus next. Anything else?"

Alex referenced yet another book. Making fire was supposedly the simplest technique that destruction magic had to offer, but something was holding Natalie back.

"But I don't understand," she muttered. "I had four balls in my room earlier, and it wasn't nearly this hard." She looked at him. "Perhaps it is because I feel monitored."

"Just pretend I'm not here," he said absently, scanning the book in front of him. "Now, new tip. This one says you should be trying to make the fire come from within the magic. Picture your power like an egg, then hatch it with your mind."

Natalie raised her eyebrows, then looked at the rightmost ball of her trio. She frowned, then made a sharp little motion with her finger.

The ball cracked up the center, and Alex stared in awe as little flashes of red and orange crackled along the line. Then, in a puff of crimson, the ball ignited, burst, and vanished. He sat back in his chair, his face feeling hot from the detonation. Natalie only stared at the place where smoke was now rising from thin air. Her other two spheres winked out of existence.

"That..." she said, "was so cool!"

Alex smiled. "Let's see if you can make it stay next time."

Natalie pursed her lips, held out her hand, and tried again. The flickering orange light bounced off the great window of the library, reflecting up the columns and into the rafters high above. The distant city lights sparkled, unchanged.

CHAPTER 18

THE REGULAR TEDIUM OF CLASS WAS INTERRUPTED the next afternoon when Professor Derhin strode into the classroom with a slightly vexed expression on his face. He looked around at his silent, attentive class and actually gave a small huff of annoyance.

"I've been informed," he said, "that today will be spent reviewing student policy. Apparently, we need to touch base on school rules for the newcomers. So. Let's get that out of the way, and then we can do some actual learning, eh?"

In spite of his protests, Derhin's attempts to 'get that out of the way' seemed anything but hasty. He started with the smallest, most minute rules and worked his way forward, with a sort of enraptured glee, in what Alex quickly realized was alphabetical order. Aamir's head sunk lower and lower until his brow was pressed against his desk.

"And that covers proper use of lighting during curfew hours," Derhin said, rolling his knuckles along his desk. "Moving right along, you may have noticed that there are certain colored lines throughout the school. Blue and gold. Given that we haven't had any trouble from the new students, I would imagine you were properly warned, but do *not*, under any circumstances, cross either. The blue marks where student territory ends and teacher territory begins. The gold lines, on the other hand, are only to be crossed by the administrative staff, which is to say the two heads of the academy or Siren Mave."

Two heads? Alex's eyebrows rose, but he refrained from raising his hand. Asking Derhin a question would likely get him a thirty-minute answer that would cause the lecture to bleed over into their other classes. Instead, Alex leaned forward and tapped Jari on the shoulder. The boy turned, looking bored, and it occurred to Alex that this wouldn't be the first time that he had heard this lecture.

"What's up?" Jari whispered.

Alex gestured at where Derhin's nasal drone was flooding the front of the room. "*Two* heads of the academy?" he said. "I thought there was only the one."

"Yeah," said Jari. "You might know him as the invisible

force that compelled you to come here."

"Finder?"

"Yeah, that's him."

In all the time he had been at Spellshadow, Alex hadn't seen so much as a hint of the man, though he was sometimes mentioned. Whereas the Head's influence was visible at every turn, Finder seemed a reclusive sort. It was strange to Alex to hear them mentioned on equal footing.

He weighed his options, finally deciding that any information he could gather might be worth the risk. "He wasn't invisible to me."

Jari froze, his mouth half open. For the first time since Alex had met him, the boy seemed truly at a loss for words. "You…Excuse me?"

"I could see him," Alex repeated, wondering whether he had just made a grave mistake.

Aamir glanced over at them. "What's going on?"

"Alex *saw* Finder."

The two exchanged a look.

"Let's talk after class," said Aamir.

When they met in the dining hall after class, Aamir's interrogation was thorough.

Jari, while also interested, seemed perfectly content to let Aamir do the grilling, leaning back in his chair with a fascinated expression. Natalie had also opted to join them.

"He sounds less impressive than I had pictured him," Aamir admitted, when Alex had finished describing Finder's rotting clothes.

Alex frowned. It was hard to convey Finder's unnerving quality with words, he was finding. He was both eerie and powerful, more like an omen than a man, an apparition that brought with him a sense of ending, of finality.

"Did *you* see him?" Aamir asked, swiveling toward Natalie.

She shook her head. "Alex mentioned him to me," she said, "but I didn't see him…I don't know if I heard him either. I was in a weird way. I didn't really understand what he was saying—or don't remember it now."

"Don't worry," said Jari with a bright smile. "Nobody can see Finder. It's part of his magic." He stared pointedly at Alex here.

Alex made a face, then turned to Aamir. "All right. My turn to ask some questions."

Aamir nodded.

"Finder. Who is he, and how does he…'find'?"

Jari leaned forward, answering before Aamir could. "He's, like, this old master of the school," he said. "Dedicated his whole life to scrying and detection magic. They say if there's a drop of magical blood in someone's veins, he can find it. That's why he's called Finder, see? Because nobody knows his real name; they just know what he does."

Alex nodded slowly. "Doesn't he have a more active role here? Beyond finding new students?"

Aamir shook his head. "No. At least, not that I know of."

"He wanders the hallways at night sometimes," Jari said.

"No, he does not."

"Does too!"

As the two began to argue, Alex rolled his eyes at Natalie, to see her staring down at her bowl.

"*Anyway,*" Aamir broke off, all but palming Jari in the face to shut him up, "Finder has always been called one of the school's Heads. Beyond that, nobody knows much."

"But," Jari interjected, "if you see him at night? Run. I've heard some nasty stories."

Alex glanced at Natalie again. She was still looking at her bowl. She gave the contents an idle stir with her spoon, looking pensive. When she realized that Alex was watching her, she looked up.

"Alex," she said softly, "do you feel like getting some fresh air? I am feeling restless in here."

Jari broke away from his second argument with Aamir at once, gazing delightedly between the two of them.

CHAPTER 19

"SO YOU'RE READY TO TRY THE GATE AGAIN?" ALEX asked.

The crisp air turned his words to mist in front of him. Natalie was wearing a thin black T-shirt and jeans, but he didn't see so much as a bump of cold on her arms. He wondered if she was using magic to heat herself.

"Yes," she said. "But I don't think it will work."

He started. "You don't?"

"Of course not. I am not stupid. I thought it might when we first got here, but that was before I learned more about magic." She looked at him skeptically. "*You* do not think it will work, do you?"

"Well, no," he admitted. "The gate's probably guarded by loads of charms. But I guess I didn't want to disappoint you. You seemed happier, more hopeful, when we were planning this."

Natalie scoffed and rolled her eyes theatrically. "I am not some precious flower, Alex. You do not need to protect me from disappointment. I thought we were on the same page." She glared at him, then continued slowly, deliberately. "Anyway, it is important to know what we are up against. And to know that, we must try magic. So I have practiced, and you have helped, and now we test the Spellshadow defenses."

She strode briskly forward and grabbed one of the metal rungs of the gate.

"I have a family, you stupid gate," she growled. She pushed, a light sheen of sweat appearing upon her arms as she heaved at the metal bars. Alex watched in awe as golden fire flared up around her, then surged toward her hands, but before it could strike the bars, it diverted, flowing straight into the gray ivy. For a moment, the plant trembled, the leaves growing a sickly green. Then it fell still, limp and colorless once more.

"Did you...?" Alex said.

Natalie only stared, panting, her eyes flashing dangerously.

"The ivy *ate* my magic," she said indignantly. "I could feel it. It was like..." She shuddered, unconsciously backing away from the gate.

"I'm guessing your magic isn't going to work," Alex said.

Natalie shook her head. "I did not think so." She looked at the walls. "Could we climb?"

Alex stared at the bricks, perfectly fitted and at least ten times his height. "Not a chance," he said. "And even if we could, what are the odds there aren't spells at the top of the wall?"

Natalie sighed. "Low."

She strode over to the wall, pulling one long strand of gray ivy away from the stones. She closed her eyes. A whip-like line of magic came into existence over her head, and she frowned deeply. All at once, the golden line burst into a great saber of flame, which carved down at the thin strand of plant. Alex yelped, skipping back a step, but once again, nothing happened. The fire struck the ivy, writhed for a moment, then sank into the plant. The ivy glowed red for an instant, then green, then went limp. Natalie dropped the strand of ivy back against the wall.

Alex stared at her.

"I take it you spent some more time practicing yesterday?"

Natalie nodded. "I am starting to get the hang of it," she said. "Although, the other girls tell me the mark of good magic is keeping your essence from appearing. I am not yet that good."

"Still," Alex said, his tone appreciative. "You improved really fast."

Natalie rubbed her temples. "It is not enough," she said. "I wonder what it would take to break this."

"I read something about an old practice called anti-magic," replied Alex, recalling a book that had mentioned it in passing. "But that was only usable by a scarce bloodline called 'Spellbreakers', and they went extinct."

Natalie tossed her hair and glared at the gate, seeming not to have heard him, then drew her hand back and sank a shining fist into the metal. She drew back with a cry of pain, shaking her hand as the ivy glowed.

"Hey, stop it," Alex said, stepping forward. "You're hurting yourself."

But Natalie wasn't listening. She drove her hand into the gate again, magic rippling out around her.

"Natalie," Alex said, putting a hand on her shoulder.

He noticed in shock that the earth around her was starting to twist, the gravel forming a swirling pattern as the dirt beneath ripped, caught up in the power Natalie was wielding. Little tendrils of pinkish light reached out from the heart of her aura, and a terrible cold washed over Alex. He reached out and grabbed her by the wrist, and it felt as though she were made of ice. He grunted, staggering back.

"I want to go home," Natalie hissed under her breath, the magic around her snapping the air into pieces. "You cannot keep me here!"

Alex knew she was speaking again to the gate. He stepped up beside her once more, keeping his voice level, trying to snap her out of this dangerous mood. She had insisted she didn't expect this attempt to succeed, but she was clearly devastated that it hadn't.

"I know. And you will." He pulled her away from the gate and put his arms around her.

The light went out. The terrible, churning magic vanished, and Natalie slumped against him, dragging a hand over her brow, shaking.

They just stood there like that for a time. Alex could feel Natalie's frustration like a tangible heat against his skin. He knew he should say something, do something to alleviate the girl's tension.

"Natalie," he began, but before he could finish, the gate let out an aching groan. Natalie's head shot up, and she slipped out of his arms, turning to where the doors had begun to open. Little tongues of magic whirled off her as she stared at a line of light spilling onto the grounds from outside.

Finder was bringing in a new student.

Without thinking, Alex grabbed Natalie by the shoulders and dragged her back. She resisted, struggling against him, her eyes fixed on the opening gate, but Alex threw them both into the thick ivy that hung down along the wall.

Natalie's magic went out as the heavy plants fell against her skin, and she spun to stare at Alex with angry confusion.

"What are you doing? We could *leave*," she spat.

"We wouldn't make it ten feet. Finder is right there!"

"But what could he do to us? The gate is *open*, Alex! We could run!"

"He could enchant you again!" Alex said, holding her a little tighter. He wasn't sure he could stand it if that happened. "And probably much worse. He's powerful, Natalie."

Natalie hesitated, then looked back up, peering through the ivy at where the gates now sat open.

Finder stood there, his hand on the shoulder of a young boy with pale skin and wide eyes. Finder eased the boy through the gate, guiding him toward the manor.

"I do not see him," Natalie said, frowning. "Is he really there?"

"Yes, he's right there," Alex said, pointing to where Finder was ushering the boy with his ragged fingers.

Natalie paled, slumping back against the wall as the gates eased shut. The ivy swung over the bars again. The sky shifted suddenly from the blue of fall to a dusky, red-gold sunset.

Natalie stared at the boy as he walked into the manor, letting out a curse in French.

Alex frowned. Finder hadn't entered the manor alongside the boy, but had stridden off to one side, cutting through the grounds with long, purposeful footsteps. His ripped robes trailed behind him like smoke behind a burning branch.

Natalie must have noticed Alex's eyes tracing his path along the edge of the building.

"Finder did not enter, did he?" she asked, frowning at him.

Alex shook his head, his eyes narrowed, then came to a quick decision.

"Let's follow him," he said, jumping softly to his feet. "We'll have to be very quiet, but this is a rare opportunity for information."

Natalie looked reluctant, but stood too and reached for his hand, her irritation evaporated.

"Are you sure this is a good idea?" she whispered as they jogged as quietly as they could.

"Well, no," he replied, "it might be a terrible idea. But I'm going after him. I'm sick of biding my time, hiding in this place. We have to take some risks. You can go back to the manor if you want; it could get dangerous."

"No," she said firmly. "I will go with you. I am not a precious flower, remember?"

"Yeah, I remember," Alex muttered, his eyes on Finder's retreating form. He was heading around toward the back of the building.

They set off across the grass, Natalie's dark hair swinging behind her in a streak as she danced silently over the scattered tendrils of ivy that reached for her legs. Alex kept hold of her hand.

The grounds of Spellshadow Manor were as eerie and derelict an environment as ever. As they passed through them, Alex thought he could see ghosts of places past. A great lawn, lined with magnificent figures of marbles with onyx eyes. A gazebo made of white iron, all intricate patterns and delicate workmanship. A stand of trees in neat rows, presumably an orchard of some sort.

But those places were gone now. The statues lay in rubble, the lawns coated with ivy and brambles. The gazebo was a mess of tangled metal, and the trees had grown dark and sinister looking, shrouded in a funeral veil of gray ivy that simply climbed over their branches in smothering loads.

Rounding the manor, Alex drew up short. There, tucked against one of the back walls of the manor building, was a small stand of stones, lined in a neat row upon trimmed grass. Alex just barely caught sight of Finder's robe flapping behind him as he vanished into a cave-like passage that led down between them.

Natalie looked at Alex, and he jerked his head toward the opening. She nodded, creeping up to examine the row of stones.

"Graves," she whispered as Alex drew closer. "Old ones."

They weren't just old, Alex soon found. They were

ancient. The dates and names had been worn from their surfaces by time, until nothing but smooth stone remained.

They moved on.

The passage Finder had entered was a strange thing. There was no door, just a deep hole of darkness that led to a staircase which plunged down into the earth. Natalie stepped forward, and with a flick of her hand she conjured a small flame at her fingertip, casting a pale pool of light around them. She made to move farther in, glancing nervously back at him.

"Natalie!" Alex caught her arm just in time, gesturing to the thin golden line that crossed the hallway and pulling her away from it. "Aamir warned us about those lines. The blue ones we could probably risk, but the gold lines I'm not so sure about."

"What will happen if we cross it?"

"I'm guessing something horrible."

She fell silent, looking at the golden line with him. Alex could already feel the line's hostile presence, beating cold as ice against his skin. He looked over at Natalie, who was edging away from the line with a cautious expression on her face. Well, they had come this far. And they might finally be close to some real answers.

He made his decision.

"I'll go first," he said. "But if something bad happens, you run, okay? Run back to the manor right away."

She was shaking her head. "No, Alex—"

"It doesn't make sense for both of us to get in trouble!" he insisted, and finally she relented.

He took a deep breath and moved forward. He hesitated just shy of the border, his heart racing, the chill air beating against his skin. He bit his lip, drew in a breath, then threw himself forward.

It hit him as though he had swallowed a gallon of ice water, and now he could feel it swashing about in his gut. He doubled over, his breath coming free in a great cloud of frost. Natalie leapt forward, her feet kicking up golden dust from where the line was writhing and twisting, its ends broken on the ground, as Alex continued to heave up frost and snow, his eyes bulging as he clutched his sides.

"Alex! Are you okay?" Natalie asked, rushing to his side.

"Cold," gasped Alex, his teeth chattering as ice wrapped around them.

She held him a moment, rubbing his arms up and down. The cold wasn't getting worse, but he could feel it in his bones, could see his fingertips paling, then darkening with frostbite. Natalie clearly saw it as well; she reached out, and warmth poured from her hands as little bubbles of fire gathered in her palms, warming Alex's skin.

"Honestly, I thought it would be something worse." She poked at the broken line with her toe. "You are feeling better?"

"I need a minute," he grated out.

Natalie bit her lip anxiously. "I think we should keep moving," she said. "We should not stay here long."

It took a few minutes before Alex was ready. Natalie insisted on draping his arm over her shoulder like a wounded soldier as they limped down the stairs into the dark.

There was no light save for Natalie's little flame. The air around them grew moist with the smells of dirt and decay, and as Alex watched, the walls changed from the manor's coarse bricks to a smooth, black marble.

He knew what the place was before they saw the first tomb. It lurched out of the dark, a great statue of a man in a crisp suit, one hand outstretched and covered in delicate veins of ice, carved to look like lightning. They stared at him, and the plaque beneath him.

Gifford White, the Stormcaller. Lord of Spellshadow Manor.

Set in front of him, on a little white sheet, was a skull. Natalie gasped at the sight, covering her mouth with her hand.

They kept moving. There were other figures, other names. Women with rubies for eyes, and men with ever-flowing fountains of water pouring from their hands. Beneath each, a skull lay upon the white sheet.

The hall of dead lords and ladies was long, and it took some time before they reached its end. With each step, Alex grew more concerned that Finder would be there to step from the shadows, pale hands reaching out and condemnation on his lips, but there was no sound or movement as they approached the final statue.

"Is he here?" Natalie asked warily. "Finder?"

Alex turned to the final statue, and hesitated.

The man the last statue depicted was tall, his shoulders broad and muscular, his cloak a crisp cut. His eyes had been wrought from gold and steel, irises gleaming from beneath a low-hanging hood.

Malachi Grey, the plaque beneath him proclaimed. *The Finder. Lord of Spellshadow Manor.*

Beneath the statue was a skull. It frothed with a cold so intense that Alex could feel it against his skin. Between the two gaping eye holes, a third hole had been carved into the bone. It seemed to stare at Alex as he looked, his mouth dry, his hands clenched.

Finder was *dead.* How was that possible?

"Time to go," Alex stammered.

Without waiting for Natalie's response, he grabbed her by the wrist and hurried from the little crypt. As he went, he thought he could still feel the skull's regard, the three empty sockets watching them go.

CHAPTER 20

"**N**ECROMANCY?" PROFESSOR LINTZ SAID, HIS heavy brows lifting. "My boy, that was outlawed a long time ago."

Alex was seated in the professor's office in the student wing. It was a lavish room, adorned with several gold-framed portraits, which appeared to depict Lintz himself, and a display case containing a rather impressive collection of scepters.

"No, no, no," Lintz continued. "It's a forbidden magic. Anima's nasty cousin, you know?"

"How's that, sir?" Alex asked interestedly.

"It deals in magic that shouldn't be touched," Lintz

said, his eyes darting toward the closed door and then back to Alex.

The man was nervous about something. Ever since Alex had come in, Lintz had been on edge, scanning the room as if he suspected something was lurking there. For a moment, Alex wondered whether Finder was invisible to the instructors as well. He knew he would be jumpy if Finder made a habit of popping up out of nowhere.

"Look," said Lintz, leaning back in his chair and rummaging under his desk to bring out a green bottle of murky liquid. "There are two kinds of magic, okay?"

Alex watched as Lintz poured himself a generous glass of the contents of the bottle, then immediately downed half of it. A thick, tangy scent filled the room, mingling with the smells of leather and cologne.

"I'm not sure I do, sir."

Lintz finished his glass and poured another, his cheeks turning faintly pink.

"Magic is always gold, right?" he said. "When you summon it in your aura?"

Alex nodded slowly. When he thought of magic, he pictured a gold light.

"Incorrect," Lintz said, smirking as he tapped one heavy finger on the tabletop. "Normal magic uses your vim, boy. Your fighting spirit! It's a healthy, natural art. But there is another force: life magic." His hands folded together on the table in front of him.

"Sir?"

"There are two wells of power in a person," Lintz said. "One comes from your essence, and we call this magic. Life magic, on the other hand, comes from your soul itself. To tap into it, even once, can cause irreparable damage to a person's very existence—but it will give a wielder unimaginable power."

Alex paused as he took in the information. "What does this have to do with necromancy, sir?"

Professor Lintz's cheeks grew pinker still, his eyes darting away as he took another sip from his glass. "I shouldn't say," he muttered.

"Very well, sir. I'm sure I can find it out for myself," Alex countered.

Lintz waved his hands, his eyes widening. "No, no, there's no need for that. I'll explain, just…promise me that you'll leave this dangerous business behind you once I have?"

Alex nodded emphatically.

"I am only curious, sir."

"Necromancy is wrong on two levels," Lintz said, his voice dropping to a whisper. "The first is that it taps into a school of magic which is devoted to ripping the magical essence out of another person. The second is that it involves the removal of a person's life magic." He shook his head. "The outside world, it has these notions that necromancy is something you do to a corpse, but it's not like that. You kill your target, and then their ghost—the remnant of their life magic—becomes your thrall, your slave, bound to your will."

Alex took that in. He thought again of the little plinth in the catacombs, where only the Head was allowed, and the unnatural extra eye carved into the skull that lay upon it. He swallowed.

Lintz, seemingly of the opinion that Alex was disturbed by the magic itself, nodded. "Grotesque, is it not?" he said.

Alex tried to organize his racing thoughts. "So when you say necromancy is the cousin of anima," he said, "do you mean that you steal a person's life magic, then use that essence to form a homunculus?"

Lintz blinked. "You…are marvelously well-informed," he said, eyes narrowing.

Too far, a little voice in Alex's mind cautioned. "Just something I overhead," he said quickly. He glanced at the clock on the wall, then pretended to be surprised.

"Is it already three?" he said. "I told someone I would meet them."

Lintz's eyes remained narrowed, but he only took another sip of his drink before folding his hands over his large belly. "Be on your way, then. And leave this necromancy nonsense alone."

"Yes, sir. Of course."

Alex rose from his seat, but hadn't gone two steps

before Lintz called after him.

"Webber."

Alex turned back, a politely inquisitive expression on his face.

"Sir?"

For a moment, Lintz seemed unsure of himself. He chewed at his lip, one eyebrow twitching. Then he spoke.

"Do not speak to Professor Derhin of this."

Alex blinked. He had been meaning to talk to Derhin the next day. "Why not, sir?"

Again, it took a moment for Lintz to reply. "It's not that he's a bad man," he said carefully. "He's a good man. Great, even. I am happy to call him a friend, it's just…" He trailed off, his words jumbling together.

The sky outside flickered, and then turned suddenly gray. Rain began to slash the window, filling the air with a hard pattering sound.

"He has had to do things to get where he is," Lintz said, and there was a strange look on his face. Alex noticed the way his lips tightened, the way the veins on his neck seemed to bulge. Before he could speak, Lintz continued. "Things that, frankly, I wish he hadn't done. He did them for me, some of the time, but all the same, I…well. Take me at my word and do not speak to him of this. Nothing good will come of it."

Alex licked his lips, nodded once, then turned away and stepped out into the hallway beyond. Students walked along it, some laughing with their friends, some with their noses in books. Alex recognized the strange expression on Lintz's face. It had been similar to Aamir's.

Fear.

Alex was sitting in the library, watching the rain sweeping the grounds, when Natalie finally found him. She sat down opposite him, and it wasn't until he looked up that he noticed the sleek gleam of her hair, her darkly lined eyelids, and the vivacious shine of her cheeks.

"What...?" he began, staring at her. She looked like she was made of plastic, or porcelain. More like a doll than a person. It was unsettling. "What happened to you?"

She burst into angry tears, covering her face.

"Esmerelda tried to teach me beauty magic," she wailed. "Don't look at me! It is not my face!"

"But why on earth would she do that?" he asked, bewildered.

"I asked her about necromancy. But she thought I was trying to learn something daunting, to impress a boy. And then she did this to me!"

Alex frowned. "That seems like a strange thing to do, change your face so much. Makeup is one thing, but this…I mean, I thought you looked pretty before."

She glanced at him through her fingers, then lowered her hands.

"Really?" she asked, the natural sparkle in her eye visible through the glamor.

"Yeah," he said, feeling suddenly embarrassed but glad at least that she'd stopped crying. "This looks weird to me. I hope it wears off soon."

"Well," she sniffed, "I hope so too." But she looked a little happier.

"Did she say anything about necromancy?" Alex asked, hoping it had at least been a productive visit.

Natalie let out a long sigh, drooping and leaning her chin on her hand. "No. It was a dead end."

The two of them had spent the entire previous day scouring the library for anything on the subject. There wasn't so much as a book referencing the topic, however. Ultimately, it had been Jari who'd confirmed that the magic did exist, but that the methods had simply been locked away from students.

"It's a mystery," he'd said with his usual theatrical tones. "Nobody knows why!"

Alex, of course, had some idea why. It had to do with a long-dead lord of the manor continuing to walk around.

Alex heard the sound of footsteps approaching them, and swiveled. He was surprised to find Jari looking down on them with a frown on his face. He strode up to the table, and Natalie rolled her head to look at him.

"Sorry to interrupt, uh, whatever this is," Jari said, "but can I borrow Alex for a bit?"

Natalie could probably use some more cheering up, but Alex rose anyway. There was something *off* about Jari. The boy's usual vigor had vanished, leaving him strangely listless. Also, outside of class, it was somewhat rare to see him without Aamir.

"We'll have to finish our talk later," Alex told Natalie apologetically, and she nodded, her eyes flicking to Jari. He was staring outside at the rain, his eyes shrouded. Alex had to take him by the sleeve and give him a shake to get his attention.

"Huh?"

"Jari. What's wrong?"

Jari smiled. "Just something I wanted you to take a look at. Come along!"

He made his customary grab for Alex's hand, and Alex followed him out of the library. A glance back told him that Natalie was attempting to remove the "beauty charm" herself, looking focused. She would be fine.

They had been walking for a few minutes when Alex realized they weren't heading back to the dorms.

"Where are we going?" he asked. "Where's Aamir?"

Jari sighed, shooting a look over at Alex. "I need to ask you something," he said. "And you aren't in trouble. I just need you to be honest with me."

Alex nodded slowly. "Okay, shoot."

"Did you talk to Aamir about graduation?"

The question hung in the air for a time.

"I suppose," Alex said. "But it was a while ago—and just in passing."

Silence.

"I thought that might have triggered it," Jari said.

Alex found himself almost jogging to keep up with Jari, who may have been small, but didn't lack for speed.

He waved a hand in the air, his fingers twisting like talons. "Aamir," he said, "he's...well, he gets stressed out about graduation. You may have not noticed, but *I've* noticed that, gradually, he's been throwing himself into his studies more and more of late. It's gotten to the point where he's getting...really strange notions."

Alex blinked. "Isn't that just Aamir?" he asked. "He always seems intense."

"To an extent," Jari admitted. "But this—well, I'll just let you see."

Jari led Alex through a door out onto the grounds, through the same exit that led to the older gardens and the cellar. Before Alex could even cover his head against the rain, a shimmering barrier of light burst into life around them, and without so much as breaking stride, Jari made his way across the muddy lawn.

Alex's boots squelched as they walked, and he looked up in wonder at where the rain was ricocheting away from them. He was about to say something appreciative when a drop of rain punched through, spattering on his cheek. He looked over at Jari, but the boy didn't seem to notice that his spell was anything but flawless. His eyes were downcast, his hands balled into fists.

They reached the cellar, and Jari motioned for Alex to stand back as he leaned down. As he shoved the layer of ivy back from the door, his magic winked out, and Alex found himself abruptly drenched in rain. Jari threw open the hatch, seeming not to notice, and Alex was about to step forward when a roar of energy split the air. He staggered back a step, feet slipping in the mud, and Jari pointed two fingers down into the cellar. A burst of light flashed from his fingertips, and for a moment a bright, clear glow emitted from the hole.

"Okay," Jari said. "Go on in."

Alex looked at him, dubious. "Aren't you coming?"

Jari sniffed. "It's your turn. He's not being sensible."

Alex supposed he would just have to see for himself whatever was going on with Aamir.

CHAPTER 21

H E FOUND THE LADDER WARM AND DRY, IN SPITE
of the rain. As he descended, the cold was
replaced by a searing heat, causing sweat to
prickle out over his back and arms. The air in front of him
rippled, and he was starting to feel a little lightheaded by
the time he dropped down into the cellar.

Aamir stood on the other side of the room. He had
stripped off his shirt, and his lean frame glistened with
sweat. He turned toward Alex, showers of sparks rolling
off his body to cascade over the ground, then paused and
blinked when he saw Alex standing there. With a flick of
his wrists, he shot through the air, landing in front of Alex

with a dull impact that made the ground roll under Alex's feet. Overhead, Jari shut the door.

"Jari is making you check in on me?" Aamir asked.

He was radiant. Wisps of magic flickered around him, gathering in pools on his coffee-colored skin. Staring at him, Alex realized that this was what magic could be. Maybe should be. Not the strange, monotonous routines of the classes, but this raw, burning power.

"Yeah," he said. "So what's going on?"

Aamir let out a snort and did not answer. The energy around him faded, and he reached out a hand, his shirt flinging itself from a dark corner of the room and landing on his outstretched palm.

"Jari worries too much," Aamir said. "I'm just practicing."

"I can see that," Alex said, sweat still running down the back of his neck from the heat. "I think he's worried that you're overdoing it."

Aamir's eyes went flinty. With a complex twist of his fingers, he drew a chair of earth up from the ground, and then a second behind Alex. He motioned for Alex to sit as he slumped down.

"I am graduating in a few months," Aamir said, his voice hollow. "Just a few months, and then…well, who knows? We spoke of it before; what do you think happens?"

Alex licked his lips. He looked around at the dusty,

abandoned cellar, sighing and leaning back in his earthen chair.

"To be fair, we don't know—"

"Alex."

Alex looked up, his face grim.

"You disappear like the rest," he said finally.

Aamir nodded. "At least you admit it," he grumbled. "Jari, he seems to want to carry on like nothing is wrong. Like I will be able to invite him over for coffee at my New Delhi apartment and we can chat about his studies. But that is not how this works." Aamir stared at Alex, and his stern mask broke to reveal the pleading face of a boy not much Alex's senior.

"I am afraid," Aamir said, his voice cracking. "I do not know what happens, but I do know it will be bad."

Before Alex could say something reassuring, Aamir was talking again. "I have a plan."

Alex sat forward, interested. "Tell me."

Aamir drew in a deep breath, as if trying to decide whether or not to let it out. Then he spoke. "I'm going to challenge one of the teachers for their position."

The room grew very still. Overhead, Alex could hear the storm still pattering away against the hatch.

"Challenge…?" he repeated.

"A teacher, yes," Aamir said. "Jari thinks I have lost my mind, but there is precedent. The only permanent staff here are the Head and Finder. All others come and go. The woman who tended the gardens, the men in the pictures on the walls, they are all gone. Students who surpassed them took their places."

Alex shook his head slowly. "But that's not a solution. You'll still be stuck here. I mean, the teachers don't leave, do they?"

Aamir shrugged. "It'll buy me time. That's what matters," he said, looking tired.

"Who do you plan to challenge? How does it work?"

"Derhin, probably," Aamir said after a moment of thought. "As for the how, I don't know. I'm preparing for everything I can."

Professor Lintz's terrified face crept into Alex's mind.

"I wouldn't recommend Derhin," Alex said quickly.

Aamir raised an eyebrow. "Why not?"

"I spoke to Lintz recently, and he seemed afraid of him. I think there's more to Derhin than it seems."

Aamir tipped his head in contemplation. "I will think about it," he said. "But I still think he is the best choice."

The two boys sat in silence for a long time.

"Jari seems very worried about you," Alex said at last.

"He is an idiot," Aamir muttered. Alex was silent, sensing that Aamir wasn't finished. "He just doesn't get it. He thinks things will work out, and they just…won't. I can't just sit around and wait for my fate to find me. I need to *do* something, you know?"

Alex thought of Natalie, led away by Finder. The black

cat made of shadows. The Head, surrounded by impossible amounts of inky power. His own foot, crossing over that thin, forbidden golden line.

"I know," he said, looking Aamir in the eye.

The weather changed with its customary abruptness, the rain fading away and leaving only the sound of the two boys breathing. They stared at each other for a time, then Aamir rose, throwing his shirt aside. Golden lines of power wrapped around him, and as Alex watched, he began to draw snow and ice out of the air. He swirled his hands, the storm gathering around him with little crackles of blue light.

"Tell Jari he is wasting his time," Aamir said. "My mind is made up. There is no other option."

Alex knew that feeling, and could not bring himself to dissuade his roommate. Perhaps it was a bad idea, and perhaps it would lead to Aamir's failure, even his death. But if it were Alex, if he could, he would likely do the same.

Alex watched Aamir as power gathered around him. Then he turned, and clambered up the ladder and out onto the grounds.

The rain had been replaced by a gentle, wintry breeze, suffused with the smell of pine resin and salt. Alex drew in a deep breath as he looked around at the ruined gardens. Jari, it seemed, had left. With a heavy, worried sigh, Alex headed toward the nearest door into the manor.

He'd gone about twenty paces and was crossing under

the crooked corpse of a half-fallen tree when he had the sudden feeling that he was being watched. He stopped, glancing around, but around him there was only the wind blowing, cool and sharp.

"Hello," a voice purred from above him.

Alex jumped back, staring up at the tree's tangle of leafless limbs. A shadow detached itself from the thicket, one claw dragging a thin black line over the rough bark.

"You again," Alex said, narrowing his eyes and stuffing his hands into his pockets. "I'm in no mood for riddles today."

The cat let out a cackle. "Feisty!" it exclaimed.

"Tell me your name," said Alex, sticking his chin out. "Or I'm walking away."

The cat's tail dangled off the branch.

"Elias," it said. "Nice to meet you, Alex Webber."

Alex stared at the creature, not even surprised it knew his full name. He wasn't as disturbed by it as he had been the first time, but he was smart enough to keep his guard up around it.

"And what are you?"

"What indeed," said the cat. "That, kid, is an excellent question. I wish I knew."

Alex regarded it, gathering his thoughts, determined not to let the little creature get the best of him this time.

"Homunculus," he announced.

The cat was silent for a moment, then tilted its head.

"Perhaps…"

"Who made you?"

A grin of inky teeth. "Elias made me, and I am Elias."

Alex opened his mouth, a question on his lips, but Elias chose that moment to slide off his branch. As he did so, he seemed to liquefy, spilling down in a cascade that settled into the form of a long-haired young man of Alex's height, made entirely out of shadow.

Elias looked Alex up and down, folding his arms.

"I'm not your enemy," he said.

"Then what are you?"

Elias laughed, clapping his hands together. "A benefactor, of course," he said. "This time I've come strictly to help."

Alex stared blankly at him, and Elias's dark face contorted, looking hurt. "Come now," he said, "don't give me that. I wanted to tell you something, really!"

Alex was silent for a time, thinking carefully before responding. "And that is?"

Elias smiled, and the expression was somehow even more disconcerting on his human face than it had been as a cat. His lips lifted a little too far, splitting his cheeks almost up to his eyebrows in glee.

"Finder is dead," he said.

"I know," Alex said with a huff.

Elias nodded. "I know you know. You've been looking for information about necromancy." He turned away, examining his fingers. "I may know where you could find a book," he said.

Alex tried to still his suddenly hammering heart. "Where?"

Elias laughed. "What would you do with it?"

Alex observed the shadow coolly. He didn't trust this creature a bit, and didn't want to give away the plan he had been formulating since the day before. But he thought of Aamir, throwing himself at the cellar walls, desperate to escape his fate. He thought of Natalie's desperation the previous day. He thought of his mother, alone and devastated. Their lives might depend on this book.

"Why do you want to know?" he asked, folding his arms.

"Call it curiosity," replied the young man, also folding his arms.

We have to take some risks, Alex thought, looking Elias up and down. *And he will just find it out anyway.*

"We would destroy Finder," he said finally.

Elias let out a low whistle. "That," he said, "is an incredible plan. Really well thought out."

"Well—"

"The book you're searching for," Elias interjected, "is in the Head's office."

Alex was silent for a long time. That was probably the least accessible place for a book they so desperately needed.

"But how do I get to it?" he asked at last.

Elias reached up, and his arm extended grotesquely to grip the branch of the tree before hoisting the rest of him skyward. The shadows swirled, then coalesced into the form of the cat once more.

"You've got your own little talents," he said. "Naughty interloper that you are. Why don't you use them?"

Alex had already opened his mouth when the cat lay down and melted into the tree. He knew before any words came out that Elias had disappeared once again, lost in the manor. What was Elias in his previous life? And why was he following him around, spying on him, giving semi-helpful advice?

Wondering how he would even begin to research something like that, never mind sneak into the Head's office, Alex looked at the world around him. Ruins as far as the eye could see. Dreams that had stopped. A manor, ruled by a man who appeared to keep its rightful lord as an undead slave.

Alex made his way back inside, his hands brushing the Ouroboros handles. He walked slowly toward his room, thinking.

But if he thought his adventures were done for the day, he was wrong.

CHAPTER 22

A scream pierced the air just as Alex was turning past the door to the library. Suddenly alert, he stared down the vacant hallway in the direction the noise had come from.

The scream came again, jolting Alex forward. Before he knew what he was doing, before he could think, he was pelting off down the hallway, skidding around the corner to find a horrible scene.

A girl pressed herself against the wall, recoiling from where a boy lay, crumpled on the floor. Alex recognized him as Blaine Stalwart, a boy Aamir admired for his magical skill. His arms and legs were stiff, his face hidden in shadows.

At his feet ran a small, golden line.

"Oh my," came a leisurely voice from behind them. "Somebody's been bad."

Alex spun to see Professor Derhin approaching with long, uncharacteristically graceful strides. He strode up to where Stalwart lay, then shifted a viperous gaze onto the girl.

"H-h-he said it wouldn't be as bad as people made out," she stammered. "That it'd sound an alarm. Some foolish nonsense."

"*Just* sound an alarm?" Derhin said. "This isn't a blue line, is it? It did sound an alarm, but messing with a golden line is exactly as bad as people make out. That's why I'm here. To collect."

He looked down at the body on the floor.

"Is he…?" the girl said.

"He broke the rules and got caught," said Derhin pointedly. "He'll be transferred to Stillwater House."

Alex stared at Blaine. The boy wasn't moving. He didn't even seem to be breathing. Little curls of magical power spun over his skin, and Alex wrapped his coat tighter around himself. It was cold in the hallway. So cold.

Derhin turned, fixing Alex with a stare.

"Did you have anything to do with this, Webber?" he asked.

Alex shook his head.

"Heard the scream. Came running."

Derhin nodded in satisfaction. "Very good. You may leave."

Alex hesitated, staring at the body, and the terrified girl who seemed to be trying to disappear into the cracks in the stone. The eerie light streaming in through the distant window rippled and swirled over Derhin's pale features.

"Now, Webber," he said softly.

Alex turned and hurried away, too late to help, feeling the professor's eyes following him as he went.

His thoughts went to the golden line he had somehow broken.

CHAPTER 23

TRUE TO DERHIN'S WORD, BLAINE STALWART vanished from classes. The girl who had accompanied him, Claire Goldfield, did come back to class, her eyes low and distant, after missing several days. When her peers asked after Blaine, she said nothing, just grew pale and shook her head fervently.

Alex had been expecting a bigger deal to be made about the whole affair, but the other students had dropped the issue almost immediately. Aamir, for example, seemed more irate than afraid.

"Honestly," he said one morning over breakfast, lowering his voice and glancing over at where Siren Mave was sitting like an imp behind the breakfast buffet, "he should have known better. Even the newest students know that crossing one of those golden lines is as good as a death sentence."

Alex frowned at his toast, feeling Natalie's curious gaze on him. He knew she must also be wondering how Alex hadn't been caught and punished.

"Another one gone," Aamir muttered, stabbing at his plate.

Jari entered the room, brushing his hair from his sleepy eyes and looking around to find his friends. When Aamir spotted him, he rose to his feet, excusing himself and slipping away. Jari took the newly vacated seat a moment later, staring after his friend with a tiny frown and hot eyes.

And so, life dragged on.

With Aamir mostly absent, and Jari constantly fretting over his friend, Alex and Natalie were left with a great deal of time to themselves over the coming weeks. Natalie continued to cover for Alex during class, and they sailed through their first practical exam with ease. Natalie showed off her pyromancy, which earned her an approving clap from Lintz and a disappointed sigh from Esmerelda, who had probably been hoping that she would find a more "womanly" way to apply her talents.

Alex, for his part, had decided to "learn" a modest

spell from the illusion school of magic. It had been a bit tricky, and had required a lot of reading, but, with his assistance, Natalie had gone along with it happily enough. Alex had gone to the front of the class, made the gestures, and Natalie had wreathed him in shimmering light until he was surrounded by the appearance of rain, streaking the air around him. Derhin had even bestowed mild approval.

"That's certainly an improvement, Webber," he had said as Alex lowered his hands. "I'm glad to see you settling in at last."

Alex had shot a look at Natalie, and she had smiled before making a motion with her hand under her desk. The rain had disappeared.

Aamir's examination had followed Alex's, and the older boy had caused a full tree to burst from the classroom floor in a shower of splinters and leaves. Derhin had been knocked to the floor, where he had adjusted his glasses and sighed drearily.

After some thought, Alex and Natalie planned their break-in to the Head's quarters for New Year's Eve. Alex had related his previous encounters with Elias and explained that he could very well have lied, but Natalie still insisted on coming along. She had heard from a girl in her dorm that the Head always gave a speech on New Year's Eve, so it seemed like the perfect opportunity. The students, teachers, and the Head would be distracted. They would still need to contend with Finder, but Alex had the advantage of stealth where the old master of Spellshadow was concerned.

"The main thing is you can cross the golden lines," Natalie said, even as worry touched her voice.

"Yes," he said emphatically, then hastily dropped the subject. He was troubled and curious about why he was so mildly affected by the lines, and had wanted to explore forbidden areas of the Head's domain immediately. But Natalie had pleaded with him not to unless it was absolutely necessary, and he had reluctantly promised her he wouldn't.

As Christmas approached, Professor Esmerelda hung mistletoe and garlands above the doors, and the students dove into the rituals of the season. The windows showed them more and more snow, falling softly apparently just outside, but just out of reach.

Jari, whether in an attempt to lure Aamir from his studies or just out of pure festive spirit, decorated their little room with a collection of trees and constant, warm snow that tasted faintly of chocolate. Aamir, in response, stopped studying in his bed, telling Alex that he couldn't concentrate under these conditions.

"He can't dodge me at Christmas," said Jari, his brow scrunched up. "That one I'll get."

On Christmas Eve, Alex and Natalie found themselves sitting in the library yet again, but for once, neither of them could focus. The two of them stared at the ice crystals that were blossoming from the frame of the huge window, spreading in glittering strands across the view beyond.

Distantly, Alex could see lights again. He stared at them, wondering, as he always did, if that was their home. He pictured the Christmas tree he usually set up, twinkling with colored lights in their darkened living room, and thought with a pang that his mother wouldn't have it up this year without him.

What was she doing now? How was she managing everything? How was her health? Did she think he was dead?

His gaze became hazy as tears formed in his eyes. He blinked them away just as Natalie sighed, looking down at the book she had propped open in front of her and then shutting it.

"I cannot focus," she muttered.

"Neither can I," Alex replied quietly, attempting to rein in his emotions. "What do you say we take a little time off for Christmas?"

Natalie shrugged, looking down at her hands. A little trail of fire wove between her fingers. "I guess," she said. "It just doesn't feel like we have time for anything."

Alex looked between her and the quiet lights outside, then rose to his feet. Perhaps a celebration would feel odd under the circumstances, but it might be just what she needed. They had been lost in their plotting too long now, and Natalie was growing increasingly gloomy.

"Come on," he said. "Let's go for a walk. We'll get Jari and Aamir."

They found Jari sitting in his room, staring up at where he had conjured a collection of bubbles in the air above him. As Alex and Natalie entered, they popped, and the boy looked over sulkily.

"You two need the room or something?" he said.

Alex chuckled. "Funny, Jari. We actually came to get you."

Jari perked up at that, swinging his feet off the bed to look hopefully over at them.

"Get me? For what?"

Alex gave his best smile. "It's Christmas Eve, Jari," he said. "Let's get Aamir and do something other than what we always do."

Jari didn't need to be told twice.

Aamir was in the study, tucked away into a corner of the room, far from where the other students were gathering around the fireplace and sharing mugs of cocoa bobbing with little marshmallows. He looked up as the group approached him, scowling.

"What is this?" he said. "An intervention?"

"No, it's Christmas Eve!" Jari proclaimed, darting forward.

A look of puzzlement crossed over Aamir's features, followed by a sheepish smile. "Is it?"

"It is," said Natalie gently. "Come on, we are going for a walk in the snow, and you must come with us. It will be fun."

The four of them made their way out onto the grounds, where a chill wind had gathered. The grass crunched under their feet as they walked, Jari darting out ahead and spinning around in the drifts of white. Aamir smiled.

The cold didn't seem to bother Natalie, who was in short sleeves again. She exhaled through her nose, and twin jets of steam speared out into the air, swirling up as though she were some sort of dragon. She laughed at the sight, looking over to Alex.

"You really aren't cold?" Alex said, sidling up to her as he shoved his hands into a pair of gloves. He was wearing not one, but two coats today, and he could still feel the chill whirling in his gut.

"No," Natalie said. "Perhaps that is one advantage of being magical."

They set out across the grounds, coming to a large, frozen lawn before Jari turned.

"Aamir!" he called.

Aamir looked over from where he had been watching the snow falling.

"Do that thing with the tree."

"Thing with the tree?"

"You know what I mean!"

Aamir smiled wanly, then ushered Jari away from the center of the lawn. Alex watched with interest as golden light began to swirl and rise around Aamir, his hands spreading, his brow suddenly glistening with sweat.

A rumble spread through the ground, and then, all at once, a great tree burst from the ground, even larger than the one in class. Bits of dirt and stone spewed out in all directions as branches unfurled from the trunk, and within an instant Alex was admiring a massive evergreen.

Jari dusted off his coat, shooting a disparaging look at Aamir. "Couldn't you do that *without* making a mess?"

Aamir glowered at him. "It is much more difficult to use anima magic if you don't mirror the natural process," he said. "You know that."

Jari leapt into the argument with enthusiasm, and Alex and Natalie walked a little way away, giving the two friends some space while they stared up at the huge tree.

Natalie didn't speak, but spread her hands, her brow furrowing. One at a time, little lights began to pop into existence around the trunk, glowing red and green and blue, shimmering out from amid the tree's needles.

Alex smiled appreciatively. "When did you learn to do that?"

Natalie laughed. "I'm making it up as I go," she admitted. "It is good they didn't burn down the tree. I sort of…It is hard to explain. I combined the illusion from your project with the fire from mine."

The wind rustled the leaves of the tree. Aamir and Jari had turned as Natalie had begun to decorate the tree, watching happily as the lights appeared, and now they began to work as well. Jari crafted a golden star out of thin air and sent it up to alight gently atop the tree, while Aamir worked the air with his hands, throwing down garlands of shining light around the tree that wrapped it in a corkscrew of power. Before long, it lit the grounds around it like a miniature sun.

"It's beautiful," Alex said, looking at her.

"It is, yes," Natalie agreed, staring up at the gleaming tree, but her voice lacked emotion. "It's also...lifeless. Pretty things are easy, common. They are everywhere in the manor. It is full of wonders, and magic, but somehow...there is nothing there. It is empty, this prettiness." She stared at her feet.

Aamir finished his garland and walked over, offering Natalie an encouraging smile. "This is your first Christmas away from home, isn't it?"

Natalie nodded, a tear coursing down her cheek.

Aamir patted her on the shoulder. "Don't worry," he said softly. "It gets better. It just takes time."

Jari stepped up beside them, little lights trailing him through the air. "He's not kidding," he said. "It gets better."

Alex glanced over at where the small boy had stuffed his hands into his pockets. Little flecks of snow littered his golden hair, and his cheeks were tinted with pink.

Then, unexpectedly, Jari said, "You never stop missing family, though." His eyes averted to the ground, and his lips formed a melancholy smile. "My dad was a real goof," he continued, and Alex got the feeling from his distant expression that he was talking more to remind himself than inform them. "Always liked to pull stupid pranks on me and my brother. And Mom was an artist, always quizzing us on color and form."

As if Jari's openness had triggered something in Aamir, the older boy also began to reminisce. "My grandfather used to paint. He wasn't very good, though my grandmother always encouraged him. He liked to say it was more about the act of appreciating beauty than creating anything worthwhile."

"My mother is a firefighter," Natalie cut in. Everyone glanced over at her in surprise—Alex included. Natalie grinned, her face lighting up with pride. "She is the only woman at her station and kicks my dad's butt in the gym. She loved to take me running when I was younger."

Three heads turned expectantly toward Alex, and although he was afraid he might choke up again, if Aamir and Jari could say something about their family at Christmas, so could he.

"My mom was an elementary and middle school teacher," Alex said. "She stays at home now, though, mostly. She's not well, but...I'm hoping she'll get better."

A long silence followed, and was broken only by

Natalie giving a loud sneeze. She rubbed at her nose, her cheeks pink, her still-bare arms covered in bumps.

"Better cover up," Alex said, thinking that he might finally be witnessing Natalie experiencing coldness. He took off one of his coats and offered it to her. "You might get a cold."

She didn't respond. She just looked up at the tree, the glittering lights reflected in her too-bright eyes.

By Christmas Day, Aamir had apparently decided he had engaged in enough frivolity, and had retreated to his corner of the study hall. And Natalie was nowhere to be found, which worried Alex. After searching for her for a while, though, he assumed she wanted her privacy, and he didn't want to be invasive or disrespectful. As a result, Alex and Jari ended up alone in the library, playing chess.

It felt wrong to have Christmas with so little fanfare, with no gifts or holiday food. The only thing marking the day as special was the absence of classes, but even that only served to make the day feel emptier. Alex saw more than one student standing around looking uncertain. He had thought to use the day for more private research, perhaps regarding anti-magic, used only by those long-dead

Spellbreakers. But he found he hadn't the heart.

And then the day was gone, just another thing swallowed up by the empty building. Everyone returned to class, and it was like nothing had happened.

CHAPTER 24

"CHEVALIER?"

Professor Derhin stared toward the back of the room, his eyes squinting at Natalie's empty chair. "Natalie Chevalier," he repeated, as if he could summon her out of thin air with his voice.

Surprising nobody, she did not appear. Professor Derhin let out a forlorn sigh.

"She's sick," another girl said.

"Sick?" Derhin said. "What with?"

The girl—Alex remembered her as Ellabell, Natalie's roommate—shrugged.

Derhin smirked, an oddly triumphant expression.

"One less for me to teach, then," he said. "We'll continue as normal—she can join us when she decides she's ready."

Alex's gut did a somersault. Without Natalie, he was as magical as the chair he sat on. While he had never been an impressive student, he had thus far managed to avoid being the abject failure he had begun as. And what did that mean? *One less for me to teach.* Derhin seemed like he might be pleased that one of his best students had fallen ill. He drummed his fingers on the desk in front of him, frowning.

"Webber, you look unsettled."

Alex looked up, and was surprised to see Professor Derhin just feet away from him. He gave Alex a knowing smile.

"Worried about the lady?" he said.

There was a titter of laughter, but Alex seized the excuse.

"Yes, sir," he said, which got a muttered wave of whispers. "Could I go check on her?"

Derhin put a hand over his heart, his eyes fluttering coquettishly. "Ah, young love." The class tittered again and Alex felt the heat rise in his cheeks. "Well, don't let me stop you. Off you go, then."

Alex rose, then hesitated.

"Will I be able to get into the girls' dormitory?" he asked, remembering Jari's warning from his first day here.

Derhin looked over at Ellabell, who shrank into her

chair. If she was trying to hide, it didn't work.

"Magri, let Webber into the girls' dorms. And if you feel the need, stay to chaperone the lovebirds," he leered.

If Ellabell was upset, she hid it well. She smiled primly. "Yes, sir."

Wondering if that hadn't been a little too easy, Alex set off toward the girls' dorms with Ellabell.

She was a small thing, with a crop of brown curls sitting over a pair of wire-framed spectacles. She walked with a brisk efficiency, her footfalls clacking on the floor.

"Thanks for letting me in," Alex said, hoping she didn't really feel the need to stay and supervise.

Ellabell shot him a look. "Just don't tell Petra where I sleep these days," she muttered. "His last salvo of affections is only just wearing off."

Alex chuckled. Aamir had told him during breakfast one morning about Jari's attempt to woo Ellabell. The girl had been harassed half to death by magic bouquets that exploded into petals over her head in class, violins bursting into song in the dining hall, and even love letters written on the face of the moon. To hear Aamir tell it, she had been driven to some rather extreme measures to get rid of Jari, trying to find information about how to perform anti-magic and eventually mastering invisibility magic.

"I'd never do that to someone," he assured her.

She gave him a crooked smile.

They traveled down a series of twists and turns, then

past doors with little brass numbers that indicated they had entered the girls' dormitory. As they walked, Ellabell's brow furrowed. She seemed to grapple with something, looking more and more uncertain until she finally spoke.

"How is she doing? I mean, how is she *really* doing?" she asked hesitantly.

Alex blinked. "What do you mean?"

"It's just," Ellabell said, lines deepening beneath her eyes, "I can tell something's wrong, but she insists she's just fine. I chalked it up to a rough adjustment at first, but now...I worry about her. That's all."

They passed a line of old paintings of teachers with stern expressions.

"I worry about her too," Alex said, hoping his secretiveness hadn't rubbed off on her too much. "I don't think she's fine. But are any of us really fine here?"

Ellabell bit her lip. "I guess not," she said, frowning.

A moment later, they stopped at a door with a brass number twenty-eight affixed to it, and she looked at Alex before knocking.

"Natalie," she called, "you've got a guest. Are you presentable?"

She opened the door a crack, and a muffled groan rolled out into the hallway.

"One minute," Alex could hear Natalie saying croakily from inside.

Ellabell nodded, then turned to set her back firmly

against the door, barring Alex's way.

"You know," she said conversationally, "I'm not sure boys are technically allowed into our rooms."

Alex rolled his eyes. "Well, I promise to behave myself."

Ellabell gave him a mocking look. "If you say so."

"All right, I am ready," came Natalie's voice again. It was nasal, cracked, and hoarse. Alex winced just hearing it.

"I'm going back to class, then," Ellabell said. "Don't get up to any mischief, and don't touch my things."

She turned, and with a whirl of her brunette curls, she melted away into the air. Alex stared at the place where she had been standing a moment before. Then he shook his head and tugged open the door to Natalie's room.

It bore a striking similarity to his own quarters, only these hadn't been bedecked with Jari's unbridled enthusiasm. There were a few modest garlands of paper snowflakes hung upon the walls, and a shimmering strand of lights hung along the back wall over the desks. As if in deliberate contrast to the simple furnishings, an acrid scent hung in the air.

Natalie had drawn her sheets up over her nose, her hands clutching the top of the blanket, so that only her eyes peeked out at him as he entered. Even by that slight glimpse, Alex could tell that Natalie's face was flushed with fever, and her hands were shaking and pale.

"Natalie, you look awful," he said, dragging a desk

chair over beside her bed and sitting down.

"I know," Natalie croaked dismally.

She lowered the blanket down to her shoulders, and now Alex saw chapped, cracked lips. Natalie sighed.

"I couldn't go to class," she said. "Ella wouldn't let me."

"I can see why. You're really sick." He looked worriedly at her, recalling what Jari had told him about magical people having a hard time getting sick.

Natalie struggled to sit up, her expression indignant. "I'm fine," she said, grimacing and putting a hand to her forehead.

Alex frowned. "You don't seem fine."

Natalie changed the subject. "Did class go okay for you?"

Alex shook his head. "Derhin let me out early to come check on you."

"That is good," said Natalie weakly.

Alex stared at her for a time, trying to figure out exactly what her symptoms were.

"How do you feel?"

"Dreadful. Like I am getting every illness I never had."

Alex licked his lips, glancing toward the door. "Are you getting any better?"

Natalie set her jaw. "I am still coming with you on New Year's Eve to get the book, if that's what you are asking," she muttered.

Their plan to raid the Head's office was only two days

away, and Natalie looked closer to a corpse than a living person. Alex watched as she shook, rolling away from him to face the wall.

"I will get better," she said, her voice full of determination.

Alex ground his teeth. "This is absurd," he said. "This is an institute of magic. There should be a nurse here, or some kind of medical expert! It should be simple to get rid of an illness, shouldn't it?"

Natalie coughed. "Wouldn't that be nice?" she said. "Ella says we don't have a nurse. Magical energy is supposed to make someone immune to this kind of thing."

Alex paused. "Then what could it be?"

Natalie rolled back toward him, her eyes full of frustrated tears. She pointed toward a metal bucket at her bedside, which seemed to be the source of the acidic smell. Alex leapt up to retrieve it, and saw that it was indeed filled with vomit.

She drew in a breath, and Alex watched as magic gathered around her. It looked...wrong, somehow. Her magic was not its normal shade of gold; it had a coppery tint that ran through it like diseased veins. As it surged around her, the little veins burned bright red before flashing angrily. The magic vanished. Natalie turned a sickly shade of green and doubled over the bucket, heaving. Alex sat next to her, holding her hair and rubbing her back.

"There," he said, setting the bucket aside. "Do you feel any better?"

Natalie lay limply against her pillows with a morose expression. "Not really." She looked over at him, blinking slowly. "What will we do?"

Alex stared at his friend, his jaw working. "I don't see that we have much of a choice," he said.

"Alex," Natalie said, her eyes frantic, "we can't just give up. We need to—"

"I'll go alone."

The words hung in the air. Natalie stared at him, her lips parted.

"But…" she started, but Alex waved a hand.

"You aren't well," he said. "You can barely stand, and you won't be ready in time. I'll go alone."

Natalie sighed, looking miserable, but then set her jaw and nodded.

After dabbing her forehead with a cool cloth and getting her fresh water, he left her room, feeling the cold in his bones and the hugeness of the manor around him as he hadn't done since he'd found her.

CHAPTER 25

NATALIE'S CONDITION DID NOT IMPROVE. WHILE she was able to get to her feet, staggering to and from class and summoning paltry displays of magic, Alex had no illusions about her ability to carry out a dangerous nighttime operation in the forbidden sections of the school. Professor Derhin almost threw her out of class when she nearly vomited after attempting a complex control exercise. Alex wished he had, as Natalie clearly needed to rest, but she was being unbelievably stubborn.

"If I cannot come with you," Natalie said, "I will at least buy you some time."

Alex eyed the girl with concern. They were in the

mechanics' lab; Alex found that tinkering with the gears and parts often helped him think. He missed his bedroom at home, with its clean lines and its solitude, and his laptop which he'd use to code all night. It was often difficult to concentrate in his dorm room—especially when Jari was excited about something, which was often. While his lack of magic meant he couldn't create anything nearly as impressive as the rest of his peers, he was happy to tinker and problem-solve.

In this instance, however, his tinkering was somewhat disrupted by the fact that Natalie had splayed herself facedown over his workspace. Her dark hair lay in lank tangles across the table. Alex was left holding the screwdriver Aamir had given him, twirling it in one hand, looking down at her.

"What are you going to do?" he asked, eyeing his friend with a worried frown.

"I do not know," Natalie said. "Throw up on someone, perhaps. Nobody can make a scene like a French girl."

Alex smiled forlornly. "Can't I convince you to go back to bed? There's some soup in it for you if you do."

Natalie's head rolled just enough to reveal a small grin. "Nope," she said.

Alex waited until it was dark, and all the other students had gone to the dining hall for dinner and the Head's subsequent speech, before sneaking off into the hallways of the manor. He had memorized the route to the Head's golden line, and now he retraced those twists and turns, his heart pounding in his ears with every step.

If he was being honest, he wished that he could have listened to the Head's speech. He hadn't even seen the man since his admittance into the manor; perhaps something in his words would alleviate some of the mystery of this place. Still, he pressed on, winding through the hallways.

With no windows to look through, Alex found himself thinking about a great many things. About Natalie, who should have been getting medical attention. About the shadow, Elias. About Finder, the ghost of Malachi Grey. About all the homes with empty rooms scattered about the world, waiting for a child who was never coming back. About the Head.

And, not for the first time, he thought about how none of it made any sense.

The line appeared before him almost without warning, leaping out from the dark like a sword swung at his feet. He stopped, hesitating just shy of it, and could feel a wave of familiar cold washing over him. He shivered, gritting his teeth. He closed his eyes, offering up a brief prayer that what he was doing wasn't just plain stupid. Maybe the line in the cemetery had been old, or faulty. Maybe the ones here had been updated, strengthened. Maybe he was being a damn fool.

But he had to know.

He stepped swiftly across the golden line.

The cold surged into him as the line snapped and whipped about at his feet, but this time he was ready for it. He gritted his teeth as twin founts of steam gushed from his nose, icy crystals pouring over his skin. He swallowed hard, gasping, watching in disbelief as a long icicle dipped slowly down off his fingertip, then broke and shattered against the floor with a dull tinkle. Though he had known what to expect, it was still a shock.

Alex didn't know how much time passed like this, but the spell eventually weakened. His limbs were shaking, but the ice had melted to cool water, which pooled around him. Breathing hard, he tried to rally himself. Whoever had created the line would probably realize soon that it had been broken. He had to keep moving before he was found.

As Alex crossed into the Head's wing of the manor, the hallways around him grew more eerie. He remembered them from that first day, but without Siren Mave's chatter, the place felt much emptier. The gray ivy grew everywhere, coating the decrepit walls. The doors were coated with moss, and the air was full of the subtle scents of ice and blood.

If he hadn't promised Natalie, he would have explored

here long ago, but as it was, he had to search every room he passed for the Head's office. Many of the doors were jammed, unmoving in their frames. Others opened onto empty rooms, or dark chambers holding four-poster beds draped in veils long since shredded by moths and decay.

He opened door after door, revealing rotting quarters, empty spaces where once life had been. He started moving faster, the images appearing only as blurs as he dashed from door to door, seeking only the one he remembered, with the stone desk and the tree-filled fireplace.

He almost didn't pause when he opened the door into a stone chamber about the size of his own bedroom, but something about the place made him hesitate. The smell of blood surged into his nostrils, and this time he let his eyes linger, sweeping the room.

It was almost empty. There was a table strewn with tools, and opposite that a grate had been built into the floor beneath a pair of manacles that hung from the ceiling, almost invisible among the hanging ivy all around them. Alex felt a shiver run through him as he approached the chains.

The ground near the grate was sticky, and Alex could guess why as he looked up at the hanging manacles. They should have been hard to see, but something about them drew the eyes. The black crust that flaked on their surface. The gleam of oil on the locking mechanism.

The smell of blood was so strong here.

Alex turned away, looking back toward the table, and for the first time he noticed a painting hanging above it. It depicted a large mouth, rows and rows of teeth layered one on top of the other, dripping with spittle, an unnaturally long tongue twisting at their center. Looking at it, Alex felt a wave of nausea roll through him.

The table itself held only a few things. A shirt, ripped at the sleeve, where a dark stain covered the fabric. A rather ordinary-looking clipboard, with a list of names and dates. The handle of a knife which seemed to have lost its blade.

Alex leaned over, picking up the list and glancing over it. There were several pages, and he flipped through them, skimming the entries. It seemed that most of the names were associated with a single date: the 7th of May. Frowning, Alex flipped to the most recent page, and saw a name there that he recognized.

Blaine Stalwart.

The boy who had been caught out of bounds.

A date, the day the boy had disappeared, was written beside his name in neat handwriting. Alex looked back at the bloody shirt, then over his shoulder at the manacles. He looked up at the painting, the mouth full of teeth seeming to smile at him.

Beside the name and date, there was another note, written in a short, frustrated hand.

Not matured enough.

Alex rose, feeling sick. He wasn't here to look at these things. He needed to get going, find the book on necromancy. For a moment, he thought about swiping the papers, or even the bladeless knife, but he thought better of it. It was best to make as small an impact as he could. He could come back for them if he needed.

He exited to the hallway, breathing hard. The torches crackled, the smell of blood mingling with the oil and smoke as he tried to get his bearings. The manor suddenly felt an awful lot like that mouth, with all of them sitting inside it, waiting for it to swallow. He looked around, then made his way deeper in.

But if he had thought to escape the image of the mouth, he quickly found that he could not. There were more paintings in a similar vein, and even the ivy itself seemed to align itself like gaping lines of teeth. The leaves brushed against him, and he could feel the way they clung to him, leaving his skin icy as they passed.

Once more he opened door after door, but now he was almost grateful when he found them empty. The smell of blood faded behind him, leaving only ice and dew and rot.

He didn't know how long he had been searching when he finally came across the Head's office. He opened the door, letting out a sigh of relief as he saw the familiar features: the stone desk, littered with papers; the bookshelves; the tree-filled fireplace; the great window overlooking a frozen lake.

Alex let himself in, his breath catching with anticipation. This was it. What he had come for. He was almost there.

He made his way over to the bookshelf.

Most of the words on the spines were in Latin. While Alex knew some basic roots, he didn't know nearly enough to understand half of what was before him. He recognized a few books of what must have been anima magic, something that read *Monstrum Dica*, a few books of what may have been more pyromancy. He was starting to wonder just how he was supposed to locate his objective when he spotted a small black book shoved into a corner of the shelf. Dust covered its spine, where faded words read:

Nobilitum Mortem.

Alex reached out, fingers ready to brush the ancient leather cover, when his eyes caught sight of a thin crimson line on the interior of the bookshelf. He cursed under his breath.

Alex would have bet anything that he was looking at another curse. He stared at it with hard eyes. His bones still felt icy after the last piece of magic he had recklessly flung himself through, but the book was right there, within his reach. They could stop Finder with it, free a trapped soul and prevent any more students from being dragged to this place. Alex clenched his fist, drew in a breath, and seized the book.

A spark of energy started in his toes and crackled up

him, sending him twitching to the ground. He only just managed to close his fingers around the book and yank it free before agony rolled through his being, his vision washed away by a blur of multicolored sparks and pain. He must have cried out as ice erupted within him with the sensation of being impaled upon countless spears. His body convulsed, and he felt bile frothing up into his mouth, his eyes wide, mouth gaping like a fish out of water, hands clinging desperately to the book in his hands.

He was only dimly aware of it when the door opened and a dark figure stepped inside. He heard the shuffling of rags, smelled the scent of grave dirt.

Through his pain, he heard a voice.

"There was a puddle of water by the entrance," it said softly. "A puddle of water. How strange is that?"

Finder.

No, not now...

There was the soft tread of boots as the man in rags crossed the room to the window. Alex bit back a groan as his spine convulsed, arching in pain.

"That spell does not make water," Finder continued. "And yet there was water. There was ice."

He turned, sweeping the room, but once again seemed thankfully unable to see Alex. His robes hung in tattered streams at his sides, dragging over the ground in his wake. In the midst of the pain, with his whole body tense and burning, Alex couldn't help but think how very real the man looked. He didn't look like any ghost he had ever heard of—Finder looked solid, present, as he dragged one finger along the windowsill, sending a cascade of dust spinning through the air.

Alex tried to keep himself from crying out as another crackle of energy ran through him.

"I bet you've been so very cold," Finder said. To Alex's surprise, the man crouched, sitting against the wall and looking toward where the stone desk stood at the end of the room. Could he sense Alex? "Your kind are supposed to feel magic's touch so keenly."

Alex's back slumped to the ground, the magic finally seeming to relent, and he drew heavy, quiet breaths as he watched the ghost. Finder's hood was drawn low over his face, and he sat in a position which Alex would almost have described as dejected.

"So cold that it enters your blood," Finder said. "So cold it crackles through your bones."

Alex shoved himself to his knees, shaking. The biting, icy touch of the manor had infested him, drawing pale lines across his bumpy skin. He clenched his jaw to keep his teeth from chattering, looking at where a little curl of blue magic was looping down his arm, the occasional spark of power straying to nestle, burning cold against his skin.

Finder rose.

"If I had found someone here," he said, voice careful, "I would have taken them to him. However, I see nobody.

And so I take my leave."

Alex watched as Finder reached out, his fingers seeming to slip into the handle of the door for a moment before they found a hold and gripped it. He paused.

"I used to kill your kind," he said. "Long ago. They hunted me to this manor, and I slaughtered them. Threw the bodies in the lake, and let the fish gnaw on their bones. But then he came."

Alex clutched the book of necromancy to his chest, shuffling away from where Finder still stood in the open doorway.

"He told me I had a duty," Finder continued. "That I had hidden for too long, and he was right. I had to help. I watched the last dragon die. Did you know that, Spellbreaker?"

A bitter note crept into the old ghost's voice, and he let out a long sigh. Wisps of ghostly magic curled in the air around him, pale mist pooling about his feet.

"I watched," he said. "And I did nothing. Now I wonder if I have done too much." He shook his head, throwing the door aside with a sudden, savage motion that made it bounce off the wall with a sharp bang. "I wonder if you can do any better, magic-killer."

He vanished, and Alex was left standing alone. He swallowed, shivering. He was so cold. He looked out the window and saw the great frozen lake as if for the first time.

Threw their bodies in the lake.

Spellbreaker.

Magic-killer.

Feeling sick, Alex made his way quickly out of the office, running through the overgrown, decaying hallways toward safety as fast as he could.

CHAPTER 26

WHEN HE KNOCKED AT THE DOOR OF ROOM twenty-eight, Alex was greeted by a bleary-eyed Ellabell. She rubbed at her face, trying vainly to paw her hair into some semblance of order.

"Alex?" she said, squinting at him and fumbling with a pair of glasses.

He faltered. He had forgotten, in all the excitement, that it was the middle of the night. He gave an awkward wave.

"Yep, it's Alex," he said. "Sorry to wake you."

Ellabell tried to draw herself up straighter, her eyes narrowing.

"How did you get here?"

"I found a girl by the entrance," Alex replied. In truth, he'd figured out his way back here alone, and if there was magic in place to stop boys from entering, it hadn't deterred him.

"What do you want?"

"Just looking for Natalie," he said quickly. "Have something I want to show her."

Ellabell stared at him blankly. "And you two claim you aren't dating?" she said after a long moment.

"Ella," he intoned, drawing out her name through a smile.

"Alex," she countered, unmoved.

The two glowered at each other for a moment, then Ellabell rolled her eyes, yawning. "Natalie is sleeping, and she damn well needs it after the scene she caused."

"Scene?"

Ellabell quirked an eyebrow in surprise. "Yeah, at the Head's speech. She threw up all over Petra and caused a huge commotion. I had to haul her back here myself. Weren't you there?"

"Had something to do."

Ellabell grunted. "Well, you can talk to her in the morning."

Alex frowned. "Can't I—"

"No," said Ellabell. "You cannot. You can see her in the morning. Them's the rules. Now go, get out of here. I'm tired."

She shooed him away with a couple sleepy waves of her arms, then shut the door in his face. Alex huffed, feeling the weight of the stolen book heavy under his jacket, and made his way back down the hallways toward his room.

Even though he was no longer in the Head's forbidden wing, he found himself on edge. Everything he learned about the manor only made it seem stranger and more dangerous. What had Finder meant about 'having a duty'? What had he meant when he said he had killed Alex's kind?

Spellbreaker. But the Spellbreakers had died out, hadn't they? Could he be a—

"Webber."

The word cut into his reverie, and Alex stumbled to a halt, feeling his blood freeze in his veins. He turned slowly, and was met with the sight of Professor Lintz. His portly form was little more than a shadow as he stepped forward out of the dark, his eyes narrowed.

"What are you doing out at this hour?"

Alex swallowed, all too aware of the weight of the book against the inside of his jacket.

"Just going to check on Natalie, sir," Alex said. "She's sick, you see, and—"

"And she was sick at the speech. Yes. I was there."

Lintz's eyes scoured Alex with a critical gaze, a thin tongue darting out to wet his lips. That look said it all.

You weren't there.

"I'm patrolling the hallways," Lintz said, shrugging and looking away down the darkened hallways. "Seems some student has been creeping around out of bounds. You wouldn't happen to know anything about that, would you?"

"No, sir," said Alex, hoping against hope that Lintz wouldn't hear the lie in his voice.

Lintz's eyes flicked back to him. "Then what's that you're hiding?"

Alex's jaw locked. His legs tensed, although whether to run or to fight, he did not know.

"Your pockets," Lintz said, gesturing. "Turn them out."

Alex frowned, then turned out his pockets. A few coins, some crumpled notes, and one illicit screwdriver.

Lintz looked at the tool, then reached out and plucked it from Alex's hand.

"You know these aren't supposed to be out of the lab," he said, his tone disapproving.

Alex stared at his feet, praying that the man wouldn't demand to search the rest of him. "It makes me feel safe," he mumbled, hoping this would ring true.

Lintz huffed, then looked back down to the screwdriver.

"Safe, huh?" he said.

With a brusque motion, he handed the tool back. Alex took it with a blink of surprise, looking up at the professor.

Lintz wouldn't meet his eyes. He was looking away again, down the hallway.

"I need to keep patrolling," he muttered. "Get to your room, and stay there."

Alex nodded and darted off into the night. The screwdriver had turned out to be useful in quite a different way than he had ever expected, but he was more grateful than ever to Aamir.

His room was quiet when he entered. Jari and Aamir had already turned in. Aamir lay on his side, while a showered Jari was sprawled over his bed with one bare foot drooping off the edge, his oversized, striped pajamas hanging heavily off his thin limbs. Alex smiled, then went to his desk and retrieved a pair of scissors.

Pulling his pillow from its case, he made a quick incision into the side and stuffed the book inside, carefully fluffing the stuffing back out around it. Reversing the pillow so the damaged end was on the interior, Alex slotted the pillow back into its case, then lay down. It was stiff, but not horribly so. It would have to do.

Alex awoke to the sound of someone hammering on the door. He sat up, rubbing at his eyes as Aamir slid from bed and made his way over to answer it. The door swung open, and Alex had a clear view of a tired, disheveled, and distinctly upset Professor Derhin, holding a shining lamp.

Before Aamir could say a word, Derhin had shouldered his way inside, looking around with hawkish eyes. Jari's eyes fluttered open just in time to see the professor bent over him. He yelped, scrambling against the wall.

"What the hell?" he cried.

Derhin took one more look around the room, his lamp splashing light across the walls.

"An artifact has gone missing from the Head's office," he said shortly. "A book of some value."

Alex kept his eyes locked on Derhin, resisting the urge to check on the pillow in which he had hidden the stolen book.

"A book, sir?" Aamir said, pushing impatiently at his dark curls.

"A book," Derhin repeated. He rubbed at his temples, looking about the room. "You'll need to empty out your dressers. Yes, you too, Petra, come on. I've got three more rooms to do, and I don't want to be up the whole night."

"Happy New Year to you too," Jari mumbled as he rose, tossing the drawers from his dresser into a haphazard heap on the floor. Alex and Aamir unloaded theirs in a more orderly fashion while Derhin looked under the beds.

When the brief search was concluded, Derhin sat down heavily on Alex's bed. Alex carefully controlled his breathing as the pillow he had hidden the book inside slid dangerously toward the professor.

"Look," Derhin said, "I don't need to tell you two this, but for Webber's sake, I'll spell it out. If I catch you with this book"—and here his eyes narrowed to angry slits—"I will end you. As a wizard. As a student. This is not something that should be tinkered with. Do I make myself patently clear?"

The three boys nodded. The air in the room had gone still as Derhin had spoken, and everybody was holding their breath, waiting to see what would happen. Now, however, the professor relaxed, shooting them his normal dopey grin.

"Right," he said. "On to the next room."

Derhin stood briskly, brushing his hands together, then smiled and vanished into the hallway. Darkness flooded back into the room as his lamp was whisked out of sight, and suddenly there was nothing left but the uncertain, worried breathing of three young men.

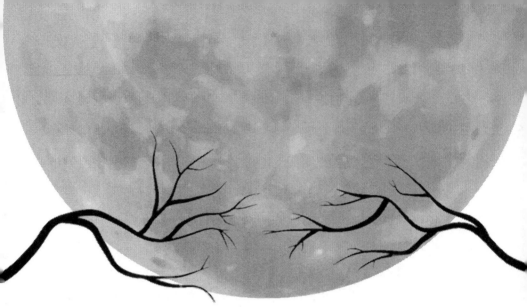

CHAPTER 27

THE NEXT TIME ALEX AWOKE, IT WAS TO THE SOUND of Jari arguing with someone at the door. He rolled over, trying to cover his ears, his body stiff and heavy from the previous night's ordeals. He could feel his stolen book wedged up against his head, and shifted his weight so he lay more firmly atop it.

"He's sleeping," Jari said.

A sharp response. Jari laughed nervously. "Besides," he said, "girls really aren't supposed to—"

"*Alex.*"

Natalie's voice sounded every bit as bad as it had the day before. It was hoarse, but it was undeniably her.

Alex groaned, propping himself up on his pillow. "Natalie? Let her in, Jari."

Jari bowed Natalie inside with a flourish, and she made her way over to Alex's bed. Alex smiled at her, raising a hand in greeting.

"I hear you were sick," he said. "Are you feeling okay?"

Jari looked around nervously as Natalie sat down on the edge of Alex's bed. Alex noticed with some concern that her skin still had that pallid, sickly look to it. In response to his question, she laughed, shrugging.

"I did not throw up on everyone," she said with a twinkle in her eye. "Only a select few."

Alex laughed, but his heart wasn't in it. By the door, Jari let out an indignant noise.

"Not as funny if you were one of the few," he said, folding his arms.

"I thought you could handle it," Natalie said seriously, looking back at him. "I didn't want to throw up on anyone too sensitive. But I am sorry. I could not help it."

Alex smiled. It was just like Natalie to try to spare the sensitive, but he hadn't thought she would actually puke on someone.

"Well, I guess I can't ask a favor, then?" she asked Jari with a smile.

Jari rolled his eyes. "Let me guess. You want to be alone with Alex?" He shook his head. "You two are not subtle. Let me just grab some things, and I'll get out of your hair."

Aamir had already left, presumably studying or practicing magic in the cellar, and Jari was giving the two
of them a pointed look as they sat next to each other on
Alex's bed. Alex just grinned, saying nothing. This was
probably better than any cover he and Natalie could have
thought up on their own.

"We just want to talk," Natalie said. "Really."

"All right. Have fun *talking*, then," he said, rummaging
through his dresser until he found a small, battered book.
On the cover, a woman swooned into the arms of a man
with flowing, golden locks.

"Classy," commented Alex.

"Entertaining," replied Jari. He gave a cheery wave,
then strode out of the room.

The door had barely closed when Natalie rounded excitedly on Alex.

"How did it go?" she asked. "It was horrible sitting in
that stupid little room wondering if you were okay! I am so
glad you are unhurt." She leaned forward and wrapped her
arms around him, pulling him into a brief, tight hug.

"It went okay," he managed, clearing his throat. "I hit a
few spells and got a little banged up, but…"

He pulled his pillow out of its case and drew out the
leather-bound copy of *Nobilitum Mortem*. It looked different here; in the eerie, macabre setting of the Head's office,
it had seemed like a commonplace thing. Here, however,
there was something otherworldly about it. Maybe it was

the letters of the title, etched into the leather as if by an unsteady hand wielding an oversized knife. Or the way the surface seemed to warp and twitch at the touch.

Natalie didn't seem to care. She reached out, hefting the book and flipping it open.

"This is really it?" she asked. Her eyes sparkled with excitement as she looked at the page. "Is this Latin?"

Alex cursed under his breath. "I didn't look inside," he said, taking the book from her and staring at the rows of indecipherable script. He felt a flash of disappointment that this would not be simple.

"Looks like it," Natalie said, taking it back. "Oh, this passage is about corpses." She made a face.

Alex paused. "You can read it?"

Natalie had tilted the book, and was squinting at the fine, handwritten text, glancing from time to time at an illustration of what appeared to be a disemboweled rat.

"I took Latin classes at school," she said absentmindedly. "I am not great at it, but I think I can make sense of some of this."

"That's good," said Alex, wetting his lower lip nervously. "But you need to be careful. Really careful. Derhin came 'round last night and threatened anyone who might have it."

She stood up, holding the book close to her chest like a favorite child.

"I will be careful," she said solemnly. "I just need to do

something *useful*…I'm glad that you are okay."

With that, she turned and headed toward the door. Her cool façade was spoiled only slightly by a fit of coughing that left her leaning against the doorframe. Alex leaned back in his bed, his brow deeply furrowed.

"I wish I could say the same, Natalie."

"Oh," Natalie said, her voice quavering. "You worry too much."

And with a click of the latch, she was gone.

CHAPTER 28

NATALIE QUICKLY BECAME ABSORBED IN *Nobilitum Mortem*, working relentlessly, though not tirelessly. She and Alex moved from their customary table at the library to one that was more private, located in a small reading nook in the darkest corner they could find, where the only illumination came from flickering candles. By their light, Natalie looked half dead, her skin shimmering with sweat, her paling hands flipping page after page, occasionally cross-checking a word against a Latin dictionary she had managed to dig up from somewhere.

Her illness, to Alex's consternation, had not gotten

better. While Natalie had begun to act more or less like herself again, it was clear that she was pushing her health in order to do so. She went to bed earlier, and lasted for less and less time during their study sessions before being too exhausted to work. When Alex pressed her on how she was feeling, she insisted she was fine and wanted to keep working. He knew she was as motivated to figure out the school's secrets as he was, but he also knew she was pushing herself too hard.

Bent over the book, Natalie frowned, looking between it and her dictionary.

"What's wrong?" Alex asked.

"This must be a magical word," she muttered. "It isn't in the dictionary, and I do not know it."

"What's the context?"

Natalie read the sentence in Latin, which was gibberish to Alex, then read it in English. "The 'inmagus' are immune to the gaze of specters, and the magic of the dead cannot touch them." She let out a frustrated breath, brushing a lock of dark hair behind her ear. "Sounds useful, if we knew what it was."

Alex paused.

"I think I know the word you're looking for," he said.

Natalie looked up, her eyes reflecting the candlelight. "What is it?"

Spellbreaker, Alex thought with a thrill of excitement, but didn't say anything. He wanted to confirm his suspicions and find evidence to support them before making an announcement. But this could be huge.

Alex rose to his feet, and Natalie let out a quizzical murmur as he began to walk away.

"I just need to check something," he said, turning to her and walking backwards a couple paces. "Why don't you take a break? I'll be back in a moment."

His feet clattered against the metal grate of the steps as he ascended one of the library's three towers, row after row of books passing him on one side. Looking down through the holes in the steps, he could see the dizzying drop of at least a hundred feet down to the library floor. He watched a student vault the waist-high handrail and sail gracefully through the air, landing lightly with a puff of golden magic. Alex swallowed and gripped the railing more tightly, imagining himself falling heavily through the air and landing with a hideous thud. He did not have the option the magical students did. One misstep could send him to an unfortunate fate up here. He moved on, his steps careful.

The paper lanterns hanging from the web of threads linking the three towers cast a cozy multicolored glow over the spines of the books as Alex perused them. He was in a section of the tower dedicated to the histories of old bloodlines, but he wasn't sure he would find what he was looking for. He stared at the adjacent tower, wondering if perhaps that would have been the right place to begin. He had seen students jump from one to the other on magically enhanced legs, but for him to get there, it would require going all the way down, then all the way back up. That would be both tiring and time-consuming, and he hoped he wouldn't have to check that second tower.

Returning to his search, Alex ran a finger over book after book detailing the lives of ancient magical families. He wasn't even sure what he was looking for, as the Spellbreakers did not merit their own category, and the book he remembered had mentioned them only in passing. Did he expect to find "Spellbreakers" just written on the side, plain as day? They weren't exactly well-known, or even well-regarded.

He thought of the bodies of the people Finder had mentioned, their bones probably still lying there under the ice out in the lake, and swallowed.

On a whim, he changed tact. While he didn't know the family names required to find a Spellbreaker history directly, he could at least look up the history of those who had slaughtered them. Finder's true name was Malachi Grey; that was a sensible starting place. He began to hunt, and within a few minutes had victoriously located a series of books, each labeled "Grey".

It took a few more minutes of searching to find the correct book, and even then he found only a reference. Alex sat on the walkway, ignoring the looks he got from other students who had to turn sideways to edge past him, and read the passage.

Lord Evan Grey was the fifth of his line, and continued his predecessors' hunt with zeal. He gained recognition and infamy for his enthusiastic continuation of tradition of slaying those with anti-magical blood and disposing of their bodies in his lake. While many viewed the tradition as barbaric, he claimed it to be the only way to protect his people from their natural enemies.

He became increasingly reclusive throughout his rule, and few details remain concerning the events at Spellshadow Manor during his residence there. It is certain, however, that he killed several known Spellbreakers, including Loran Steele and Ellen Forte. He married Loraine Brune of Stillwater House, and she bore him a single son, Malachi.

Alex flipped through the pages, hungry for more, but that was it. There was nothing else on the family; it was like they had simply stopped existing after that. However, he'd learned from Finder that sometime later, young Malachi had taken up his father's mantle. Later still, the Head had come to Spellshadow, and its lord had apparently offered his body and soul, his eternal servitude, to the man's twisted designs.

"Why?" Alex muttered to himself, frowning. What could have motivated Malachi to sacrifice himself like that? He was missing something. Something big.

All the same, he had found what he was searching for. Another quick search yielded a tidy stack of books, and he tromped back down the stairs to where Natalie was studying away in her corner. She looked up as he dropped his literary heap on the table, her face breaking into a weary smile.

"You have found many books, I see," she all but whispered, her voice cracking.

"Yep," Alex declared with satisfaction. "But hang on, there's still some reading I have to do."

He opened the first book. It contained details of the life of Ellen Forte, a woman described as having a wicked demeanor and a savage temper, who had been involved in "anti-magical resistance". It only took a few pages before he found the word he was looking for.

Spellbreaker.

After that, it was easy to find more. Spellbreaker blood, he learned, was a rare genetic strand that gave a person the inherent ability to resist the negative effects of magic. The body, he learned, somehow transmuted the magic into cold, leaving the user frigid under prolonged exposure.

I bet you've been so cold, Finder had said.

He continued to read, his eyes growing wider, his hands toying with the tips of the pages in his haste to dig through what was in front of him. An answer. A real, complete answer.

"Natalie," Alex said, his voice fairly quivering.

She looked up, her movement slow. "Yes?"

Alex reached out, putting his hand palm up on the table.

"Burn me," he said.

Natalie gave him a worried, uncertain look. "Alex?"

"Just try it, please? If I'm right, it won't hurt me. Go on."

Natalie appeared too tired to argue, though she looked extremely disconcerted. She flexed her power, managing to form a ball of flame. Alex frowned at the deep red veins that lined it—and the way her hand shook at the effort.

He put his worries aside the instant she bounced the little ball down into his hand. Cold burst from the spot it had hit, a sharp, numbing *pop* that made him wince and grit his teeth. But the pain was worth it. He watched triumphantly as little whirls of frost rose around the spot, feeling the fire pushing against him, hot and cruel, before melting away.

Natalie stared at where a little piece of ice lay in the center of Alex's palm. She looked between him and it, then back to him, her face dumbfounded.

"Um," she said eventually. "I know I'm sick, but that is weird, yes?"

Alex grinned, tipping his hand and letting the little piece of glassy ice shatter against the table.

It was more than weird.

It was the best kind of weird possible.

For that afternoon, Natalie gave up on necromancy. After Alex explained his Spellbreaker theory, the two of them set about testing his powers. In her weakened state, Natalie wasn't able to push Alex's limits very far. She did, however, almost give him a case of frostbite from all the ice that was coating his arm by the time they took a break—it seemed that being able to resist magic and being able to resist cold were two very separate things.

By the evening, however, they had fallen back into their usual pattern. Natalie was curled up with her book propped against her knees, and Alex was reading an anthology of Spellbreaker histories while growing increasingly worried. It seemed that if there was one thing the Head would be less happy to find in his school than a non-magical person, it was a Spellbreaker. Their supposed extinction had been no accident: they had been hunted until none remained.

Or at least, that was how it seemed. That was the strange thing about every book that Alex read: past a certain point, they all cut off. Huge sections of books were filled with empty pages, as unmarked as though all the words had been sucked straight off of them.

"History? That's what you do with your spare time?"

Alex nearly toppled out of his chair as Jari appeared at his shoulder. Natalie had slammed the cover of her book shut with wide eyes, staring at where their friend seemed to have appeared out of thin air.

"At least you have the good sense to look guilty about it," Jari continued.

"What do you want?" Alex asked, annoyed at the rude interruption.

"You."

"Do you need me to leave?" Natalie asked feebly from her corner.

Jari laughed, but his heart wasn't in it. "I was just hoping…you know."

Alex had some idea, and closed his book immediately.

"Aamir?"

Jari nodded.

Aamir had been growing even bolder in his disregard for their lessons of late, going as far as to stop showing up to class. Their professors had begun to shoot dark looks toward his empty chair, and there was something in their eyes that went well beyond the disappointment of a disrespected teacher.

"I know he thinks class is pointless," Jari said, "but he's standing out. Can you come talk to him with me?"

Alex looked over at Natalie, who waved a hand.

"Go," she said with a cough.

Alex gathered his books, depositing them into his

shoulder bag before leaving the library with Jari.

Life at Spellshadow had changed, Alex realized as they walked. Jari no longer continued his odd quirk of leading him by the hand, but walked alongside him. It was strange, in a way. He felt settled in Spellshadow in ways that he never had before. It was easy to fall into the patterns of this place, the consistent classes and the easygoing teachers, and forget the dangers. Perhaps that was the point.

Jari led Alex out of the door into the gardens and along the scattered remains of a path, snow and gravel crunching under their feet. Before long, they came to a little bench by the great ivy-shrouded wall.

Aamir was sitting there, staring down into a steaming mug in his hands. He was wearing navy blue gloves and a puffy coat that for all its bulk somehow made him look smaller. His cheeks were gaunt, his eyes shadowed from lack of sleep. He hadn't even bothered to sweep the snow away from where he sat.

He looked up as Alex and Jari drew closer, and nodded in his solemn way.

"Hello," he said. "I suppose you are here to berate me again?"

"No," Alex began, shaking his head.

But Jari, who did seem to want to berate Aamir, launched ahead.

"You have to start coming to class again," he said.

"Why?"

"For appearances."

Anger flashed in Aamir's eyes, and he rose swiftly to his feet.

"I'm sick of appearances," he said, and his normal calm melted along with the snow around his feet as a ripple of heat swirled off him. Alex took a step away from the raw fury in the boy's eyes. "I'm sick of smiling and playing along. We can't all just go willingly to our graves, you know."

"There's a difference between preparing for the worst and actively calling it down on yourself," Jari retorted, and now there was heat in his voice as well. Crackles of angry electricity danced over his hands, his hair lighting up with sparks.

"Oh, is there?" said Aamir. "Because it seems like I can't do anything that's mellow enough for you. You want me to go to class, do my projects, and graduate like a good boy, isn't that right?"

"You *know* I—"

"You just want me to ride this out and hope for the best!" Aamir yelled, taking a step forward. "You don't care about what happens to us! You don't care about me! All you care about is that everybody is fine and happy and fits into your tiny vision of 'okay'!"

Jari stood very still, but the magical electricity that surrounded him seemed to glow with rage. It flickered, but he said nothing at all.

Aamir, emboldened by Jari's lack of response, continued.

"Have you ever stopped to wonder how it feels for someone like me? Someone looking at that date coming closer and closer?" he cried. "It's January. I'm set to graduate in *May*."

And then Alex saw it. That little date next to so, so many names.

May 7th.

He stood stunned as he realized the implications. Aamir was right—the students who had graduated were not likely off making their way in the world. And what had been written next to Blaine's name? *Not matured enough.* A chill unrelated to the snow ran through him.

Not matured enough for what?

Alex snapped out of his reverie as Jari let out a roar of fury and punched his hand forward, toward Aamir, whose mouth was opening to continue his tirade. While the physical blow fell short of the mark, a bolt of electricity shot from his knuckles and caught Aamir's cheek, sending the boy spinning to the ground. Aamir had barely hit the snow before he was up again, his own hand out, sending a wave of fire tearing through the air toward Jari. The smaller boy ripped it in half with fingers alight with energy.

"Stop it!" shouted Alex, alarmed, but his roommates ignored him.

"You dare tell me who I care about?" Jari said, his voice a frozen ruin of its usual cheer. "You dare tell me what I worry about?"

Jari batted aside another flame, then lashed out with a foot, sending a ripple of burning light through the air. Aamir stumbled back, but seemed to repel the blow, this time with sheer magical force. He snarled, stepping toward Jari, then heaving his fist upward. Mirroring the motion, the earth under Jari's feet snapped upward, smashing into the boy's jaw. Jari was pitched into the air and landed heavily in the snow with a cry of pain.

"Jari! Aamir, stop!" Alex tried again, now stepping toward Jari. "You hurt him!"

"Then show me!" Aamir bellowed, as though Alex had not spoken. "Show me you care! Because honestly, I cannot see it. You don't try to support me. You merely hold me back."

Jari rose shakily to his feet, wiping a line of blood from his mouth, and Alex froze before he reached him, apprehensive, looking up as the air shifted. The sky overhead darkened to an angry gray, and the wind grew sharp and fierce all around them, heavy with the metallic scent of a storm. In response, flames burst into life around Aamir's arms and legs, sending a spiraling column of orange tapers skywards, the heat blistering even at a distance. Alex watched the two glaring at one another.

"Oh no," he whispered.

They lunged at one another, and Alex moved without thinking.

Hurling himself between them, he spread his arms, one toward each of his oncoming friends, putting one hand into the storm, the other into the flames.

The cold took him at once, freezing the spit in his mouth, sending him toppling with a gasp into the snow, which felt warm by comparison. Everything grew violently frigid, and he spasmed, crying out, coughing up ice and snow and rolling uncontrollably back and forth.

If he'd been able to, Alex almost might have laughed. He could wield an incredible force to combat these magical energies, yet it led to him lying helpless in the snow, weakened and frozen half to death by his own legendary power.

His vision blurry with pain, he heard frantic cries above him. Jari and Aamir had extinguished their magic in an instant, and both boys were crouching down over him.

"Damn it," Jari was saying. "He's so cold. Why is he so cold?"

"Move over," said Aamir. "I can warm him up."

"The hell you can. You did this."

"*We* did this."

A silence. Alex felt warmth spreading over him as someone blessedly conjured up a heat source and began to draw it over his skin. His friends' murmuring voices continued to sound out above him as he shivered.

"Why is he so cold?" Aamir muttered.

"I was *just* saying that."

"It's just…he wasn't struck with *ice*. The only thing that would cause this is…"

More silence. Alex managed to open his frost-covered eye-lids. Aamir was staring at him, his hand emitting a warm light, Jari looking between the two of them.

"What?" Jari said.

Alex looked imploringly at Aamir, and flinched inwardly when he saw the understanding in the other boy's eyes. While Aamir didn't stop warming the ice away from Alex's skin, Alex recognized that the look in his eyes might be fear.

"How have you been doing it?" Aamir asked, his voice soft.

"D-Doing what?" Alex asked through his shivering.

"The magic, in class. How?"

Jari's frown deepened. "Hey, what? What are you getting at?"

"Natalie," Alex whispered, letting his head fall back against the snow. It was like a warm pillow against his frigid neck. The edges of his vision were blurry. "Natalie has been helping me."

Aamir's eyes grew soft with understanding, and he nodded. "So that is why you are so inseparable," he said wonderingly. "I thought…but I never would have guessed."

A lick of electricity reemerged to snap angrily between

Jari's brows. "If somebody doesn't tell me what's going on," he said, "I'm seriously going to—"

"I'm a Spellbreaker," Alex choked out.

Jari paused, then looked between Alex and Aamir with sudden clarity.

"No way."

Alex nodded.

"It's the only way he could have survived what he just did," Aamir said, his voice distant. "Even so…" He trailed off.

Jari swore under his breath.

Aamir nodded. "Indeed." His hawk-like eyes seemed to bore into Alex. "We need to talk."

Alex, though uneasy at Aamir's expression, silently agreed. He tried to say something, but there was ice in his mouth, under his eyelids, and he could find no words.

"Give him a minute to warm up," Jari interjected, and Alex felt a surge of gratitude for the boy. "We still need to settle things."

Aamir's eyes grew hot as they darted to Jari. "Don't think I've forgotten what you said," he said, "but I think we have more pressing matters to attend to."

Jari snorted. "What, the matter of Alex being strange and keeping secrets? That's hardly new. I didn't come here to talk to Alex. I came here to talk to you, and the result is that we both nearly killed a friend. *We* need to talk. Then we can talk to Alex."

Aamir hesitated, looking down at Alex's frost-covered body. Alex made an effort to smile reassuringly up at him.

"You two sort things out," he said. "I really could use a minute."

They moved to a place some twenty yards distant. Jari propped Alex up against a tree to keep him from sprawling in the snow, then Jari and Aamir stood, staring at one another with wary eyes.

"I apologize," Aamir said first. "I never intended for things to get so out of hand."

Jari raised an eyebrow. "Are you willing to start coming back to class?"

Aamir's eyes narrowed. "Don't you have something you want to say to me first?"

Lightning streaked the clouds above, and a rumble rolled over the gardens. A light rain began to fall, pattering little holes into the snow all around them.

"Jari," Alex said. "Don't be a jerk."

Jari looked over at him, then released a heavy sigh. "Fine," he said. "I was an ass. I have the social graces of a pole-dancing T-Rex, and I'm sorry. Is that what you wanted to hear?"

A rare smile cracked Aamir's lips. "It's a good start," he said.

"Look," Jari said, "it's not that I don't get it. Please don't think that I don't get it. You're my best friend, and I need you to understand that you aren't the only one afraid about your graduation. I'm terrified of losing you."

Aamir blinked. "To be honest, I hadn't even considered what my graduation might do to you," he said slowly. "You seemed so opposed to my efforts to prevent it that I didn't really think you cared."

"Of course I care," said Jari, stomping his foot and throwing up a little spray of slush that clung to his pant leg. "It's only…If you become a teacher, you're one of them. I lose you anyway."

Aamir stood, stunned. "Jari…"

"Don't do that," said Jari. "Don't condescend to me. You think I haven't been searching for a way out? Hunting for every minute I've been here? I miss my family, Aamir. I miss my brother, my mother, my stupid prank-pulling father. But if I became a teacher, I'd be just as stuck, and what's worse, I'd be responsible for what happens to the students. I'd have to watch."

"I don't intend to just—"

"Do you think any of them did?" Jari snapped, cutting Aamir off. "Do you think any of them were committed to luring pupils to whatever fate awaits them at the end of this road? Something is seriously wrong with this place, and you have to be an idiot not to notice it. The teachers know what it is, but whatever they are hiding is so serious that none of them have ever talked about it, not a single one."

Aamir was silent. Sitting against the tree, Alex stared

at Jari. Feel-good, cheerful Jari, who now stood with tears in his eyes, his hands balled in frustration, his cheeks pink with ire. Alex hardly recognized him.

"I never considered that," Aamir said, staring at his feet.

"Of course you didn't," said Jari. "You didn't listen."

The two stood, staring at each other for a long time. Then Jari spun to face Alex.

"And what the heck is up with you!" he cried, waving his hands in the air. "You're a Spellbreaker!"

"Seems that way," Alex replied.

"I'll put that on the 'things that would have been nice to know' list," said Jari. "Were you ever planning on telling us?"

This time, it was Aamir who came to Alex's defense. "He could have been killed," he said gently.

Jari let out an angry breath, glaring at both of them. "You two are idiots," he said.

Alex and Aamir shared a look.

"To be honest," Alex said, "I only just found out myself."

Jari rolled his eyes. "You find anything good on New Year's?"

Alex's jaw worked as he fumbled for an excuse, but nothing he came up with seemed believable.

Aamir cleared his throat. "You weren't at the speech," he said. "Not unusual, but when Natalie threw up, and you came back late…"

"It wasn't subtle," Jari said.

Alex glanced from side to side, wondering if he should trust them. He knew what Natalie would say—she would want to include them, to help them. "I did get a book," he admitted. "A tome of necromancy."

"Oh good," said Jari. "He's evil. That's nice."

Aamir, on the other hand, wore a puzzled expression. "Why?" he asked.

And so Alex told them the whole story. From seeing Finder that night at the party, to following Natalie to Spellshadow, to the two of them tracking Finder to his lair, and then Alex's daring assault upon the Head's study. The only detail he left out was Elias. He wasn't sure why; he just had a feeling he didn't want to mention the shadow just yet.

At the end, Aamir looked stunned. Jari just looked impressed.

"I think you've covered more ground in months than I have in almost two years," he said, letting out a low whistle.

Aamir seemed stuck on a different note.

"A ghost," he said under his breath. "I thought he was using invisibility magic, but if it's necromantic…I always wondered why there were no books on the subject." He looked sharply over at Alex. "I need to see that book."

"Natalie is using it," he said. "Also, it's in Latin."

Aamir opened his mouth, then shut it.

"Then I'll need to talk to Natalie about it," he said.

Alex looked between Jari and Aamir, hoping against hope that he wasn't about to make a mistake.

"I...can trust you two, right?"

Jari almost looked offended. "We're on the same side," he said, giving Alex a look that said exactly what Jari thought of his intellect at that moment.

"But my people," Alex said. "They killed yours."

Jari's head tilted. "They killed the Greeks?"

Alex gave him a rebuking look. "Wizards."

Jari let out a low noise of amusement. "In case you hadn't noticed, we're all captives here. Even if we weren't, who cares what our forefathers did? You're a friend. Your blood doesn't make you want to kill me, does it?"

"No." Of course not. But they had been painted as natural enemies.

"Then that's that."

Aamir seemed a little more reluctant, but he also nodded. "That's that," he echoed.

Alex looked between them, his gaze lingering on Aamir. The older boy was desperate to survive—was he desperate enough to give Alex up? It could be that turning in a Spellbreaker would save his own neck somehow. But Alex didn't think Aamir would do something like that. He was desperate, yes, but essentially good.

"Thank you," Alex said, and meant it.

They smiled in unison.

"Just get us out of here," said Aamir.

Alex tried to smile, but he couldn't quite manage it. His chest still felt heavy with cold, his limbs stiff.

"I'll try."

CHAPTER 29

ALEX AWOKE THE NEXT MORNING TO THE TRULY strange sight of a small mouse crouching on his chest, its eyes aglow with a crimson light. It scurried in circles, tail lashing, revealing patches of missing fur that exposed shining white ribs. Its tail seemed to hang from it by sinew. It pounced from side to side on emaciated legs, leaving little red paw prints on Alex's comforter.

On instinct, Alex yelled, hurling his sheets, mouse and all, to the floor, where the bedclothes began to thrash, panicked little squeaks cutting the air as Alex sat on his bed in his pajamas, breathing hard in surprise. In his bed, Jari opened an eye, looking over.

"Bad dream?" he asked blearily.

"Mouse," Alex explained shortly, jerking back as the mouse burst from the sheets. Jari let out an undignified cry of terror and flattened himself against the wall.

The mouse sprang back up onto Alex's bed and advanced upon him with glittering eyes. Alex held out a placating hand, as if the creature would listen to sense.

The mouse leapt, and Alex braced himself for the pain of its little teeth sinking into him, but instead he only felt a cold, wet weight drop on his hand as it settled comfortably against the side of his open palm. He looked down, and his gaze was met by eyes like flickering, waning candles.

Lifting his hand, Alex surveyed the animal. It had a bloody hole in its side, and was missing a substantial part of one ear. He lifted it up, rolling it onto its back to reveal a little note tucked against its belly, held in place by a thin piece of string.

He undid the binding and took the letter, the mouse hopping from his hand and dropping back to the bed, sitting obediently while he read.

Alex,

I found this dying mouse in my room, and I had to experiment on something, so…here it is. It's not very pretty. I think it must have been attacked by a cat. I hope it didn't frighten you too much! Anyway, it looks like I got the magic to work. I'm curious about what he will do when his task (delivering this letter) is complete. The book was vague.

-N

Alex looked down just in time to see the mouse give a final, beatific squeal before falling dead on his bed. A little dribble of red drained out of its side.

"She's more cold-blooded than I am," Alex muttered, staring from the letter to the mouse and back.

Jari nodded emphatically from where he was still curled on his bed, his eyes wide.

The door opened and Aamir came in, a book under his arm and a determined look on his face. His eyes swept the room, landing on Alex.

"Ah, Alex. Good, you're awake."

He hesitated, seeing the sheets on the floor, then the dead mouse bleeding on the mattress.

"Hm."

"Don't ask," Alex grumbled. He tried to pick the mouse up by the tail to move it, but the thing came off in his hand. Jari made a retching noise.

"I confess I am curious," said Aamir, a wry smile slanting one corner of his mouth. "But no matter. I came to ask a favor."

Alex threw the tail in the trash bin as Jari made unintelligible noises of protest.

"What's up?"

"I wanted to ask you to train with me, actually."

Aamir and Jari had continued their argument from the previous day in more civil terms after Alex's revelation the previous night. Jari had begrudgingly admitted that Aamir's additional practices might serve a purpose, but he had also convinced the boy to come back to classes. The peace between them was uneasy, but seemed to be holding for the time being.

Now, Alex gave Aamir a questioning look.

"And do you think I would be useful to help you study magic?" he said, one eyebrow raised. "Although my...talents apparently lie in the exact opposite realm?"

"I do."

Alex poked at the body of the mouse, and Aamir made a noise of impatience, his hand shooting out. Little flames engulfed the rodent's body, burning it until nothing but ash remained. Aamir made a second gesture, and the heap of ash blew apart.

"It's *everywhere* now," Jari said in horror.

Alex returned his attention to Aamir with a sigh. "I'm just not sure what I can do."

Aamir looked away, scratching at his cheek. He opened his mouth, then shut it, trying several times to speak but seeming completely unsure about how to proceed.

"It's just..." he said, trailing off and gesticulating. "I, well, my disagreement with Jari—"

"'Disagreement', he says," Jari interjected.

"—has left me concerned," Aamir continued, glaring at Jari, "about what to do in the event that I have to duel someone in the process of taking a teacher's position. I need a training partner."

Alex's brow rose even higher. "You want to have a magical duel with me?"

Aamir made a face.

"I need someone I won't kill," he said.

"Ah," said Alex, then gave him an incredulous look. "You did see what happened to me yesterday, right? I almost froze to death."

In the corner, Jari shrugged. "That was probably because I hit you," he said.

Aamir shot him a look, but nodded. "It probably had a lot to do with both of us hitting you at the same time. If we were to limit your exposure to a single source of magic, I think you would find it much milder."

Alex was silent for a long time. All his efforts to engage his Spellbreaker powers thus far had resulted in him curled up on the floor covered in painful ice burns; he could still feel them, hot and raw under his clothes. On the other hand, he was the only person with this power. If he could hone it, he might be able to make something of it, a weapon the Head wouldn't see coming.

"I can even try to—" Aamir began.

"I'll do it."

Aamir stopped.

"Really?"

Alex nodded. He could feel the cold rippling in his bones. His blood, he knew now. Holding the manor at bay. He didn't need to wonder what would happen if he let himself grow weak.

Aamir took Alex down to the cellar, then stood him at one end of the room.

"So," said Alex, "how are we doing this?"

Aamir looked around, seeming confused.

"It does seem strange," he said. "I mean, I would say we just fight, but you can't really fight back, can you?"

Alex let out an affronted noise. "I could punch you, if that would help."

Heat began to ripple the air around Aamir, and the same mantle of flames that Alex had seen the previous night surged up around the boy's arms and legs, spilling down his chest. His eyes glazed over with sparks.

"You think you can punch me?" Aamir said, amused.

Alex raised his fists like a Hollywood boxer, trying to make himself sound more confident than he felt.

"I think I can try."

Aamir stepped lightly from foot to foot, then nodded.

"I suppose so," he said, settling into a combative stance. "I'm ready when you are."

"Bring it," Alex grinned.

None of the action movies he had watched could have prepared Alex for the speed with which Aamir moved. Alex was lean and tall, and liked to think he was fairly fast on his feet, but when the other boy threw his first line of flames, Alex's feet locked up. He tried to get them to move, but all he could do was watch, petrified, until the bolt of fire connected squarely with his chest. He staggered back a step, his breath erupting from him in a burst of ice and frost as he gasped, falling to one knee.

Aamir was by his side in an instant. "This was a terrible idea. I'm sorry, I don't know what I was thinking."

Alex staggered to his feet, shaking his head. "Again," he said.

Aamir's eyes widened. "No, we should—"

"Aamir."

The two locked eyes, and Alex tried to put the full force of his passion, his determination to help, to *learn*, into that stare. "Again," he said.

Slowly, Aamir nodded.

The next hour was a whirl of pain for Alex as his body slowly adjusted to the nearly unpredictable movements of Aamir's flames, and the ensuing waves of cold that consumed him as they broke against his body. It took him three tries to successfully sidestep Aamir's first blow, and when he did, his euphoria was short-lived as the lance of flame snapped sideways, smashing into his side.

Aamir, in his stoic way, offered no advice. He attacked, his eyes narrowed with concentration as he shot assault after assault at Alex. Before long, the ground was muddy from the ice sloughing off of Alex's body, and the air was hot with Aamir's magic. The two stood, Aamir sweating, Alex shivering.

Aamir jabbed with his fist, sending a bolt of crimson flames toward Alex, who sidestepped, then ducked as it twisted in midair at a flick of Aamir's fingers. Alex kept an eye on the flames, moving back a step as the fire tore into the dirt in front of him.

Before he could even feel proud, an impact from behind sent Alex staggering forward onto the ground, a wave of frost splashing out over his back. He let out a moan as the mud slapped against his face, his body aching. After a moment, Aamir's arm wrapped around his shoulders, lifting him up.

"That's enough for today," he said.

"I can keep going," Alex tried to say, but Aamir shook his head.

"There's valor in training," he said. "There is none in burning yourself out and groveling in the mud. We'll try again tomorrow, if you're feeling up to it."

Alex, though reluctant, admitted he saw his point.

Aamir set about cleaning the grime from their clothes and tending to the icy burns on Alex's skin.

"Anti-magic seems far less useful than I would have expected," Aamir said absentmindedly. "You're still getting pretty hurt."

"I'm not getting pretty dead, though."

Aamir gave Alex a wry look, one eyebrow raised.

"I suppose."

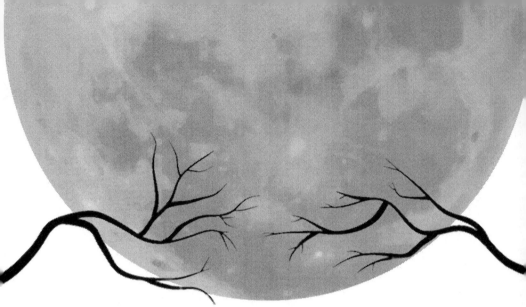

CHAPTER 30

A FTER AN HOUR OF FIGHTING IN THE CELLAR, Professor Derhin's lesson that afternoon seemed unspeakably dull. Alex watched as the man droned on about *Shanna's Twofold Focusing*, all the while playing out the fights over and over in his head, analyzing every movement. He wondered how he was supposed to beat someone who could summon fire out of thin air and direct it with their hands. If only there were anti-magical lessons.

Alex moved through the motions of *twofold focusing*, feeling the warm embrace of Natalie's magic fluttering around him.

There had to be a way to overcome Aamir's advantages. After all, Spellbreakers were notorious for being wizard-killers; it simply didn't make sense that he would barely be able to fight a student who wasn't even fully trained. Perhaps his blood was simply weak, diluted from years of disuse. Or perhaps—

"Webber."

He looked up to see Derhin watching him.

"Sir?"

"Your aura."

Alex looked down, and saw that the magic around him had vanished. He felt the telltale chill on his skin, and almost heaved a sigh of relief when he saw that there wasn't any visible frost on him. He looked back at Natalie, who was giving him a strange look.

"Sorry," Alex said. "Lost in thought."

On cue, Natalie's magic folded around him again, and Derhin nodded in approval.

"Just remember," he said. "It won't do to lose focus. You need to learn to control your energy, not let it wander."

"Alex," Natalie said later that day, "please try not to eat my magic when I try to help you. That is not productive." She sounded annoyed.

They were sitting in the library, looking out the window from their concealed nook. Red slashes of sunset were making silhouettes of the ivy that coiled around the metal spikes atop the wall, creating strange, waving patterns against the light.

"I know, I'm sorry," said Alex a little guiltily. "I don't even know how I did it. Normally my body only nullifies things that are hurting me."

Natalie let out a sigh. "Maybe it is a reaction to letting Aamir beat you up all morning. You shouldn't push yourself so hard."

She was probably right, Alex thought, but what other option did they have? Either he pushed himself a little, or Aamir got killed in battle and Alex got killed for being a Spellbreaker. He couldn't possibly hide that forever, not in a place filled with wizards. Just now, in class, he felt he had come close to revealing himself. Not wanting to upset her, Alex changed the subject.

"Don't you ever wonder where they went?"

Natalie had already turned back to her book. She looked up from where she had scribbled something on the page of translations that always sat out next to her, and lifted her eyebrows inquisitively.

"Who?"

"The myths."

"The…oh, one moment."

Natalie looked interested, but held up a finger. She set down *Nobilitum Mortem*, finishing what she had been writing before interlacing her fingers and giving Alex a look to continue.

"It's something I've been wondering since I came here," Alex said. "Magic is in so many of our myths that, knowing it to be real, I find I must start believing in some of them. When Finder was talking in the Head's office, he mentioned dragons. And if they were real..." He trailed off, drumming his fingers on the tabletop. "I just wonder where they went."

A strange look crossed Natalie's face, and she turned to look once more at where the setting sun had faded to a diffuse orange, nestling among the hills of olive trees that made up today's horizon.

"Once, I watched a house fire," she said. "I thought it would be cool, you know? Mama was always talking about her heroics, so one day I followed a fire truck." She smiled sheepishly. "I know you aren't supposed to, but I was curious."

The sun grew pink, sending spears of light through the gaps in the hills, shining against its halo of low, silver clouds.

"It wasn't what I expected," Natalie said, her expression soft. "It was so loud. The roar of the fire was like a beast screaming in my ear. So much rage and heat, and I just watched. Nobody could do anything. I saw inside a window, and there was an old movie poster in the room, and I watched it curl and burn and vanish. I wondered how many memories I was watching just..." She made a gesture. "Poof. Disappear."

Alex watched her for a long moment as she kept thinking.

"And?" he asked, after it seemed that she wouldn't continue on her own.

Natalie sighed. "I don't know," she said. "I guess I mean, sometimes something happens. Something that nobody expected, and nobody could have stopped. And everything disappears. Life does not always make sense."

Alex thought about all those blank pages in the history books. All the stories that didn't quite end…all the strange *absences* of endings. He thought about them, and he thought of a house, burning.

The sun slipped below the horizon, and the hills vanished with it, replaced by a blank expanse of nothing.

CHAPTER 31

IN TRAINING THE NEXT DAY, ALEX WAS SORE AND STIFF. Aamir, however, seemed every bit as energetic as he had the day before, and it only took a few moments for him to floor Alex again. He let out a wheeze as Aamir sighed.

"You might need a few more days to recover from last time," Aamir said. "This won't be good for either of us."

Alex struggled upright, his limbs aching, his shoulder covered in icy crystals where the other boy had struck him.

"One more try," he said.

"Alex…"

"What?" Alex said, trying to force the warble from his

voice. "You scared?"

Aamir's lips thinned. "You know I am," he said quietly.

He took his position opposite Alex again, and the two boys locked eyes. Fires began to spark around Aamir as he focused his magic, little glimmers of heat popping from thin air all about him. He raised his hands, opening his mouth, and Alex braced himself for the cold.

There was a *crack* as a bolt of fire snapped against the ground between the two boys, and they both jumped in surprise. Natalie stood nonchalantly at the base of the ladder.

"Alex has already been beaten up," she said to Aamir. "But I figured you and I could both benefit from sparring too."

They both gawked at her. Her hair was done up in a bun, and she wore loose-fitting exercise clothes and a pleased grin. She planted her hands on her hips, although Alex knew that was probably also an effort to hide the shake in her arms.

Aamir scowled. "First Alex, who does not know his own limits," he said. "Now Natalie, who is almost too sick to stand."

Natalie waved a hand. "No, I am fine. I have been sick for weeks now. I am used to it."

She coughed, and Aamir glared at the both of them.

"You two—"

Natalie, standing by the ladder, was already closer to

Aamir than Alex had ever managed to get. She stepped forward, and a whip of fire uncoiled from her hand to slap at the ground in front of Aamir, sending sparks flying up into his eyes. He cursed, throwing a hand over his face and staggering back a step.

"Sorry!" she said quickly.

"It is all right," said Aamir a little breathlessly, looking her up and down. "Okay. We will all train together. But I would rather not spar with someone so ill."

Natalie paused, then walked over to the ancient wine rack that still covered one wall, pulling a dusty bottle free and tossing it into the center of the room, where it landed in the dust with a dull clunk. Alex stepped away from it, slumping against the wall and wincing from his icy burns.

"Whoever destroys it wins," Natalie said, pointing at the bottle. "Is this acceptable?"

Aamir rolled his eyes. "We both use fire. How are we supposed to know who hit it?"

Natalie opened her mouth, then paused, her brow creasing.

"Aamir," Alex called from his spot against the wall, "you're supposed to be training. Get creative!"

Aamir glared at Alex, then sighed. The fires around him flickered, then slowly shifted to a shade of deepest blue. Natalie hummed appreciatively.

"You must teach me that one," she said.

"You must teach me that trick with the mouse."

Natalie's eyes brightened. "Did you like him? Alex says he was—"

Aamir acted without announcing himself, jabbing two fingers toward the bottle on the ground. Blue fire tore through the air, and for an instant Alex braced himself for the sound of shattering glass.

Swiftly, Natalie drew in her breath and extended one hand toward not the bottle, but Aamir's fire. It shuddered, grew orange, and halted just short of bottle. Then, jerkily, it began flowing to Natalie, and pooled into a ball over her hand. She smiled at Aamir, whose eyes had gone wide.

"To hell with the rat," Aamir said. "Teach me how you did that."

Natalie gave him an innocent look, then tossed the ball of flames over her shoulder, where it burst upon the floor.

"Break the bottle," she said, her tone teasing, "and I will consider it."

The two quieted as they fell into the competition. While Natalie was able to move Aamir's magic against his will, she lacked much force of her own, and her own magical attempts to break the bottle were quickly slapped aside by Aamir's. Alex watched as the blue flames tore at the orange, a shining, shifting mass of color and heat.

It took Alex what he considered an embarrassingly long time to figure out what was happening. He watched as Aamir's blue fire turned orange and spilled away from the bottle, and Professor Lintz's words filled his mind.

Necromancy is wrong on two levels, he had said. *The first is that it taps on a school of magic which is devoted to ripping the essence out of another person.*

Alex watched as sweat glistened on Natalie's brow and she shoved her hands through the air with rough motions, and Aamir's magic abruptly became hers. He smiled.

With an irritated huff, Aamir changed tactic. He drew his arms wide, then slammed his palms together. A bolt of lightning erupted from thin air just over his left shoulder, tearing the bottle in half before anyone else could so much as blink. There was a spray of red as glass and ancient wine showered the air, and Natalie's eyes twinkled with amusement.

"Tell me how you're doing it," Aamir said, breathing hard.

Natalie grinned through her sweat and fatigue.

"That was my win, no?" she said.

Aamir glared.

Over where he sat, Alex's hand formed the same rough, claw-like position he had seen Natalie using. She was doing something other than using magic. She was reaching into someone else's magic and manipulating it. He knew that he had no magical potential himself, but Alex wondered briefly if his Spellbreaker blood was capable of something similar. He thought back to the class earlier that day. He had accidentally used his powers to snuff out Natalie's magic, even though it had offered no threat to him. He had acted not on instinct, but with purpose.

"I'd like another turn," he said abruptly.

Aamir looked skeptically over at him from where he had been badgering Natalie.

"You do not look ready," he said.

Alex shook himself off, trying to ease the tension from his sore limbs as he got to his feet and moved to the center of the room.

"I have something I want to try," he said.

Aamir sighed, tilting his head toward Natalie. "Can *you* talk any sense into him?"

Natalie laughed. "Not usually. But I would let him try again."

With a dark look, Aamir turned back toward Alex.

"You're both crazy," he said. "And I'm not responsible for what happens."

"Of course," Alex said, taking a wide stance.

Aamir moved, and by now Alex could read the attack fairly well. The way the young man's hands moved, his fingertips flickering, meant fire was coming. The way his palm jutted out meant it would be a spear.

This time, however, Alex made no effort to dodge. He half closed his eyes, letting raw instinct take control as he stepped toward the attack, one hand sliding forward toward the other boy's magic. He felt the cold as his hand entered the flames, but he shut his mind to that. He let his fingers play in the frigid currents of magic, feeling them out, until suddenly something new slipped into him.

Twisting at the center of the flames, it was quiet, calculating, full of knowledge and energy, and Alex knew instinctively that this was Aamir. His magic, his soul, his very being. Alex twisted his hand, and gently pressed the energy to one side, diverting it away from him.

It almost worked. For all his calm, Alex's technique was sloppy; he watched in dismay as the center of the spear of flames shattered in a white explosion of icy dust while the front, like an arrow cut mid-flight, hooked and smashed into his chest. He found himself once again on the ground, gasping, covered in snow, his breath ripping at his throat.

Aamir walked up, thrusting out a hand.

"You all right?"

Alex seized Aamir's hand, nodding, and Aamir pulled him upright.

"You done yet?" Aamir asked.

Alex shook his head.

"Only getting started."

CHAPTER 32

As January dragged on and February drew ever closer, Alex found himself spending more and more time in the library researching the history of Spellbreakers. He stayed up late, sitting up amid the books under the soft light of a hundred paper lanterns, reading and hoping to find answers.

In book after book, however, he met with the same eerie discrepancy. Every time he drew toward what appeared to be the end of magical history, the books would simply stop. Chapters upon chapters of empty pages, the words all vanished as if they had never existed.

Alex let out a groan as a particularly promising-looking

tome turned out to contain the same problem, and jammed the book back onto the shelf where he had found it. He wondered if the other students, or teachers for that matter, would be able to shed some light on the issue, but somehow, it seemed like a bad idea to ask. Standing, he made his way down the steps of the library-tower and back to the little table where Natalie was transcribing a line of Latin onto a piece of paper.

She looked up as he approached.

"Anything?"

Alex shook his head.

"Perhaps you should focus on figuring out anti-magic," Natalie said. "It may help you win against Aamir."

Alex sighed. While his Spellbreaker skills were improving, they were still nowhere near enough to fight a proper mage. Aamir still smacked him around with relative ease.

Natalie, on the other hand, still managed to put up a good fight against Aamir. Her technique, which she called 'grabbing', continued to be a thorn in Aamir's side, and the boy persisted in demanding that she show him how it was done. Natalie, however, seemed delighted to put him off, insisting that he work for it.

"Why do you read so many histories?" Natalie asked, tilting her head. "What are you looking for?"

"Answers," Alex muttered. "To any of this."

"Oh, yes," she said, "answers would be useful." But she

didn't seem to be fully listening, concentrating instead on her magic.

She made a couple quick motions of her hand, and magic flared about it. Then she turned green as a dull red throb ran through the golden fire, and she put her hand back down, panting slightly.

Alex watched with a frown. "I really wish you'd talk to someone about that."

He'd been trying to get Natalie to speak with a teacher about her illness for about a week now, but she was strangely reluctant. Alex was sure at this point it was something magical, but Natalie insisted on pretending nothing was wrong.

"I am fine," she said, wiping at her brow. "I just didn't sleep enough last night."

"You're falling apart," Alex replied, perhaps more sharply than he had intended.

Natalie glared at him. "Don't tell me what I am feeling," she snapped.

Alex held up his hands in surrender, but irritation churned his gut. He looked up toward the library-towers, wondering if there was anything about magical illnesses up there. He was sure there would be.

"I'll be back," he said, rising and departing again. Natalie only grunted at his retreating back.

There was indeed a section on magical maladies, nestled up by the ceiling. Alex found himself standing on a platform high above the rest of the library, scanning through a small collection of books with titles such as *Rotstone* and *Surviving Glithering*. He opened the latter out of curiosity, then shut it instantly upon seeing a diagram inside. He decided that if he ever contracted glithering, he would rather just die. It certainly wasn't what Natalie was dealing with.

He glanced through a few more books, but nothing seemed to have what he was looking for. The things described in the volumes were all sicknesses of the flesh—none of them had anything to do with infecting a person's magic. He sighed, replacing his most recent disappointment on the shelf.

"Alex?"

He turned to see a head of brown hair poking up the stairway that led to his platform, a pair of glasses shining in the lantern light. Ellabell stepped up, giving him a curious look. "What are you doing here?"

Alex lifted his chin in greeting, gesturing to the rows of medical texts.

"Looking for something that might help Natalie."

Ellabell smiled faintly. "You too?"

She walked over, pulling a book from the shelf next to him and opening it, adjusting her glasses with a prod as she skimmed the index. Alex watched her with interest.

"You're here for Natalie?"

Ellabell nodded. "Whatever she has isn't going away," she said in a distant voice, her attention clearly on the book in her hands. "But she's too bullheaded to deal with it on her own, so I figured maybe I could do something to help."

Alex pulled a book of his own down, feeling reinvigorated. As Ellabell reached for another book, Alex said, "Tried that one already."

Ellabell paused, glancing over at him, then nodded.

The two of them worked in silence for a time, occasionally comparing notes. Alex found the quiet studiousness of the girl to be soothing. There were no demands, no duels, no undead mice scrabbling at his chest. Just the two of them, and a silence that was not uncomfortable so much as it was natural, focused.

"You know," Ellabell said as she turned a page, "I'm not convinced she's sick at all."

Alex glanced over. "She's not faking it."

Ellabell made a face. "I know that much," she said. "I meant, I don't know if what she has is natural."

"How do you mean?"

With delicate ease, Ellabell flipped her book shut and swapped it for another, opening to the introduction and beginning to read. "*Let it be understood that this text is meant to help with natural ailments of the flesh,*" she read, "*and not those magical afflictions that one arcanologist might inflict upon another. Those ailments of magic, or curses as they are colloquially known, do not fall under the purview of magical medicine and will not be addressed herein.*" She shut the book again.

Alex considered that for a moment, his brow creasing. "You think someone cursed her? Who would do that?"

Ellabell shrugged. "Lots of people, I guess."

"But why would they do that?" Alex asked, confused.

"Well, she's a natural at magic," Ellabell said. "She's already surpassed most of the upperclassmen in control, and her projects are ambitious, to say the least. That makes her a natural target, unfortunately. Lots of the girls in the dorms are jealous of her. And she seems friendly enough, but she never really clicked with any of us. She's always... well, hanging out with you."

A sinking feeling entered Alex's gut, and he swallowed. "I'm sure she doesn't mean anything by it. And I know she likes all of you."

Ellabell smiled. "Hey, I know she's a good girl—we're roommates, remember? She may not open up to me, but I can tell that none of the things she does are out of spite. Still, if you want to help her, I'm starting to think anti-magic would be the way to go." She sighed. "Which, regrettably, we can't use."

Alex tried to contain his rising anticipation, casually composing his face into a series of neutral lines. "Aamir mentioned you researched it for a time."

Ellabell nodded, sitting down with her back against the thin rail, the dizzying drop down to the library floor at her back.

"I most certainly did," she said. "It was a bad couple of

months when Jari Petra decided he was in love with me."

Alex laughed. "He can be a bit much."

"He filled my room with kittens."

Alex paused. "When you say filled…" he began.

"I mean literally filled," said Ellabell flatly. "I opened the door and was swamped by a deluge of mewling flesh and panicked claws."

Alex burst out laughing, and Ellabell reddened, her glasses flashing. "It wasn't funny!" she said, her hands balling into fists. "It took weeks to get the fur out of everything! I have scars!"

Alex waved a hand, trying to blink the tears of laughter from his eyes. "Sorry, it's just…anyway. You were talking about anti-magic."

Ellabell latched onto topic gratefully.

"Yes," she said. "I was." She drew herself up with a cocky smile that set her glasses askew on her face. "I might know more about it than anyone else in the school, as a matter of fact."

Alex grinned at her. "You were that desperate?"

"*Full* of kittens," she reminded him with a grimace.

They laughed.

"At any rate," she went on, "from what I know, someone with Spellbreaker blood and a great deal of experience would be able to undo a curse. It would be difficult even for them, but possible."

"And, um," Alex said, "how would one go about

something like that?"

Ellabell, engrossed in her topic, hardly seemed to notice the question. Her eyes danced as she began to speak.

"Spellbreakers," she said, "are a lot like mages."

Alex paused, abruptly aware of the cold gnawing at his insides as his blood instinctively fought off the manor's magic.

"They are?"

Ellabell nodded. "They contain a pool of essence. It just isn't controlled by the same methods that normal magic is—our gathering and controlling exercises wouldn't work for a Spellbreaker. Apparently, they operate in an opposite fashion, and the essence they produce cannot conjure realities like ours can." She smiled triumphantly. "What it can do, however, is undo what our magic produces."

Alex paused, weighing his next question. "Then…how would they use that to undo a curse?"

Ellabell deflated, then spoke wistfully. "No idea. I wish I had a real Spellbreaker to study."

Alex let out an awkward laugh. "They're all dead, though, right?"

"That's what the records say."

"Hm. Shame."

Ellabell shot him a strange look. "I have to get going," she said. "I'm supposed to meet someone. It's been nice chatting, though, and good luck with Natalie. If she has been cursed, I hope you can figure out some way of getting rid of it."

Spreading his hands in an innocent gesture, Alex tried to affect a tone of defeat. "Know anywhere I could find a Spellbreaker?"

Ellabell paused as she slung one foot over the rail, her lips pursing pensively.

"No, obviously not," she replied. "Although, there's one other way to undo a curse."

"And that is?"

She moved over, standing on the outside with her hands gripping the metal beam behind her, then looked back over one shoulder as she leaned out over the open air.

"Just kill whoever cursed her," she whispered.

Then she let go, and dropped out of sight.

CHAPTER 33

NATALIE, THOUGH CURIOUS, WAS RELUCTANT TO go to Alex's room, protesting that she really felt fine and he worried too much.

"Honestly, Alex," she insisted, dragging her feet, "this experiment is not necessary."

"I think it is," he said firmly. "Ella said—"

"Oh, Ella!" she exclaimed with a vehement gesture. "Did she talk to you about curses also? That girl is so melodramatic!"

Pausing at his door, Alex turned back to look at Natalie. "She already spoke to you about this?"

"Yes," she sighed in exasperation, pushing past Alex

to flop down on his bed. Rather melodramatically, he thought. "She told me her theory. But who would curse me? I have done nothing!"

"Then what's your theory? I hate to say it, but Ella's fits."

"I'm just sick," she grumbled.

"For over a month?"

"It lingers, yes," she said, sounding uncertain despite herself.

With a sigh, Alex stepped over to the bed. "Look, just let me try this. One way or the other, we'll learn something. You might even be cured."

"That would be nice," she admitted, and turned over onto her stomach, propping her head up on his pillow. "Do you really think this will work?"

"I don't know what to expect, exactly," Alex said, moving to sit beside Natalie and examining her back skeptically. If he was being honest, he really didn't know what to do. He tried to think back to what Ellabell had been saying. Something about Spellbreakers' magic working almost inversely to normal magic?

"I'm about to begin," he told her. "You ready?"

She nodded, and, slowly, he analyzed a procedure he had learned several weeks back in class. It was called *Erandale's Needle*, and it was a focusing technique meant to gather one's energy into a long, needle-like point from their fingertips. First, he attempted the process as normal, and as he expected, he received no result. His fingers pressed tight together, his arm extended, his shoulders leveled, but nothing happened.

"Is that the Needle technique?" Natalie asked curiously, looking over one shoulder.

"Yes. Hang on, though, I have to...concentrate."

He altered the technique, opening his fingers, focusing his energy on his palm. Slowly, he went through the form and corrected it, inverting every aspect. He let his mind unfocus, opening itself to the world around him.

The sudden rush of energy to his fingertips was so abrupt that he almost cried out as he felt a little orb of coldness pulse out of him. He shook his hand, swearing as a disturbance momentarily twirled in the air, then seemed to collapse in upon itself. Natalie lifted her head a little, apparently unable to detect that anything had happened.

"What is it?"

Alex could barely contain his excitement as he spoke. "I just...never mind. I'll show you later."

So, Alex thought. *I was right. A focusing technique for magic can be inverted to create an opposite style of anti-magic.*

Frowning with concentration, he drew his hand into a position for a different technique, one designed to create spheres of magical energy, then corrected it until each element of it was inverted. Then, he let his mind open, becoming expansive and encompassing.

This time, he was expecting the little rush of power, and he could sense the wavering, malformed rod of negative energy that bloomed from his palm. It was gray as smoke, with thin, intricate lines of obsidian lining it like cracks. Looking into the thing, he could almost feel himself falling, drawn in by a sucking, hungry power.

A void, he thought. He wasn't making something. He was making the *absence* of something. He tried to control the little blade as it quaked and shook, but it was like trying to hold sand in his cupped palms. No matter what he tried, his little needle of un-power fizzed and distorted.

Hastily, not wanting to lose it, he dipped the tip down to touch Natalie's back.

She gasped in pain as frost swirled out over her skin, all but leaping away from the touch to sit with her back against the wall, staring at him with wide eyes.

"What was that?" she demanded.

"Sorry!" Alex exclaimed, his anti-magic wobbling out of existence in his dismay. "I didn't mean to—"

"That *hurt*," Natalie interrupted, rubbing at her back with a pained expression. "Is that what it feels like whenever someone hits you with a spell?"

"I guess it must be. Are you okay?"

She pursed her lips, then rolled forward, lying on her stomach once more.

"Of course I am okay. Try again," she said.

Alex hesitated. "Are you sure?"

"If you can endure this for hours on end," Natalie said, "I can deal with it for a few minutes. Go ahead."

Alex reluctantly summoned the void again, the effort of it sending an unexpected tremble up his arm, then lowered it against Natalie's back once more. Cold tendrils snaked from the spot, but this time Natalie just gritted her teeth, twisting his sheets in her fists and cursing fluently under her breath.

Moving quickly, Alex opened his mind and let himself breathe in the sensations of Natalie's essence moving against his own. It was delicate, passionate, with a restless compulsion toward movement that was unable to stop. He almost smiled in recognition.

And then something else touched him.

A sinister malevolence brushed his essence, and both he and Natalie drew in sharp breaths. He could sense the way it coiled around her, like a snake with its fangs sunk deep into her, squeezing. At his touch, it seized up, tightening its hold, and Natalie groaned.

Alex examined the foreign power. It was strong. Much stronger than either Aamir or Natalie had felt, and…cold. It had a calculating, sinister strength to it. If he could change his essence to a blade, he might be able to cut Natalie free, but…

"Alex," she said, "whatever you are doing, I think—"

She cut off, gagging and convulsing as a throb of red pierced her magic.

He abruptly withdrew his anti-magic, recalling Ellabell's words.

It would be difficult, even for them.

Natalie was limp on the bed, panting.

"Are you okay?" he asked, looking at the swaths of ice now covering her back.

"I am fine," she groaned irritably. "I just want to lie here for a minute, please."

"Well," he said with a shaking voice, "I think we can say for sure that you're cursed."

She moaned, pushing her face deeper into his pillow and letting her arms hang over the sides of his bed.

"And I'm afraid I can't remove it," Alex said ruefully. "Not without a great deal of practice."

"Wonderful," Natalie mumbled dismally into the pillow.

She rolled to a sitting position, then rose from the bed, dusting off her clothes and gathering up her book. Alex watched her in disbelief.

"You can't be getting back to work?"

"Of course I am," she said indignantly.

Alex smiled. "If you're sure, I won't try to stop you. I'll stay here and practice. Maybe I can fix it." He sounded uncertain even to himself.

"Yes, practice. I'm sure you will figure it out," she said, and strode out the door, leaving him sitting alone on his bed.

"That went poorly," said a voice.

Alex didn't even need to look to identify the speaker. A coldness ran against his back as a shadow pulled itself up from the ground, congealing into the shape of a young man sitting next to him on the bed.

"Elias," he said cordially.

"Alex," replied the shadow, with a hint of amusement. "How have you been?"

"We got the book."

"So you did. Although you're making rather slow progress." He laughed, shaking his head. "To think you don't even speak Latin. For shame."

Alex shot a glare over at the young man, only to find himself shuddering as he stared into jet-black orbs where whites and pupils should have been, and an open mouth that held nothing but darkness.

"What can I do for you this time?" he asked.

Elias looked affronted. "When have I ever asked you for anything?" he said. "I've always been the one to help you, have I not?"

"Equal parts helping and taunting," Alex retorted.

It was true that the shadow had only ever acted to Alex's benefit, but something about it felt wrong. He felt like he was being strung along in the creature's presence, and he couldn't help but feel vulnerable. He didn't know what he was to the creature, but he was relatively certain he would not qualify as a friend, whatever Elias said.

"Well, then, I suppose I should start helping you," Elias said. He lowered his voice to a mocking whisper. "Seriously, though, did you only just now figure out that she was cursed? I thought you were letting her suffer on purpose for some reason."

Alex got to his feet, his eyes dangerous. "You *knew*?"

Elias held up his hands in mock surrender. "Not only do I know, I know who did it," he said.

Alex's voice caught in his throat. He let out a soft noise of frustration, trying to keep his demeanor polite.

"Who?" he asked through gritted teeth.

"It doesn't matter," said Elias. "You can't do anything about him. He's well beyond you."

"The Head?"

"No," Elias said, "but now we're deviating from the point. I wanted to give you something."

Alex felt his mouth collapsing into a thin line, but he nodded curtly. He already knew there was no point in trying to persuade Elias. "What is it?"

"Well, the other day, when you broke into the Head's study, you left some holes in his defenses in your wake," the shadow said with glee. "So I took the liberty of acquiring something for you. I thought you'd find it interesting." Ah—was that why Elias had wanted Alex to break in, maybe? So he could steal things too?

Elias plunged a hand into his own chest, seeming to rummage around in the vicinity of his ribcage, then pulled out a battered book bound in fading green paper.

"Just a little present," he said too casually.

Alex picked the book up, looking over the cover with interest. It had a title embossed in golden letters.

Historica Magica, it read.

"A history book?" Alex said, turning it over in his hands.

"A rather bland one, I'm afraid," said Elias. "Although I think you'll find it interesting regardless."

Alex opened the book, flipping through it uncertainly. It wasn't until he neared the end of it that he stopped, his mouth slightly open. There were words on every page. No holes. No missing details. He rifled through the pages, moving quickly in his excitement, looking over at Elias.

"Is this—"

"Yes," said Elias, with more than a hint of amusement. "Although it doesn't have all the answers you are looking for, it has some of them."

Alex was silent for a time, the shadow sitting beside him seeming content to simply relax into the absence of words. Eventually, however, Alex found he couldn't hold his tongue.

"*You* have all the answers, though, don't you?"

Alex wasn't looking, but he could hear the inky smile in Elias's tone.

"Of course I do."

"Then why—"

"Why bother helping you at all?" Elias said, his voice lazy. "Why feed you breadcrumbs when I could just stuff the whole loaf in your face?"

He laughed, and the sound chilled Alex's blood. It was a jackal's laugh, high and keening, and it cut out with the abruptness of a breaking window.

"A bomb should only be armed once its user is sure it will hit the mark," he said, his voice creaking with laughter.

Alex drew in a long breath. He knew that outbursts and overt maneuvers would get him nowhere; whatever game Elias was playing, he played it on a level that Alex could hardly fathom, with information Alex didn't have. Alex couldn't turn the tables on his fickle ally just yet. He had to bide his time.

Setting the book gently down to one side, Alex nodded to the shadow.

"Thank you for the gift," he said.

Elias almost seemed disappointed by the response, but shrugged it off. "Out of curiosity, who do you think cursed her?" he asked.

Alex felt the hairs on the back of his neck rising.

He's trying to get under your skin. He wants you rattled. He wants you indelicate.

"Only just realized that it was a curse today, as you rightly pointed out," Alex said, shrugging.

The shadow leaned forward.

"I'll give you a hint," he said.

The room seemed to grow colder, and Alex shivered in spite of himself. The edge of Elias's form was fuzzing, spreading out into a black haze that stole the light, eating it up and growing fat with its luminosity. The young man's head vanished, and in an instant, there was nothing but a voice, lingering in the air.

"He tried to kill me, too," Elias said.

And then he was gone.

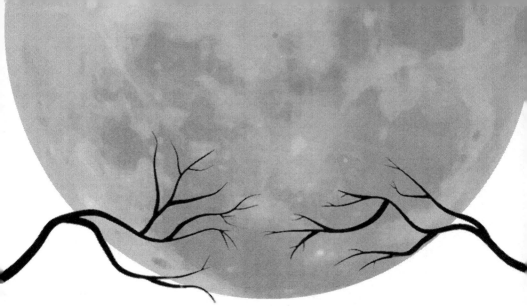

CHAPTER 34

To Alex's immense irritation, Elias's words proved true. The *Historica Magica* was a repetitive slog through a blitzkrieg of facts that rivaled the dullest sections of any reference book, reading more like an enormous index. It seemed to be entirely dedicated to family genealogies, technical descriptions of old magical homes, and recreations (without embellishment, of course) of marriage certificates. It was, in short, an exacting description of the driest facts concerning magical life.

However, it wasn't entirely useless. After putting a false cover on the book to make it unrecognizable, Alex took it to the study hall, finding a large, soft chair in a corner by the fire and settling in. He traced the family lines, and as he did so, his mind dismantled the patterns, names, and ideas. They slowly began to fit together into something that resembled a picture.

The most obvious, and perhaps most expected, fact he found was a sudden rash of deaths in the magical families in the same generation as Malachi Grey. It seemed that almost every family line ended abruptly there; the ones that did not seemed to die out within a couple more generations. Alex was almost relieved when he finally found a footnote on a date of death which read: *the last of the major lines.*

So they had all died out. All his people were officially gone. It didn't say explicitly that Malachi Grey had killed them, but at least he had that detail for certain. But why hadn't he killed Alex? Alex had been completely helpless in the Head's office, completely at the ghost's mercy. And he had spared him. The question had been plaguing Alex ever since, but he could not think of a satisfying answer.

He continued to search the book for a time, but the warmth of the fire and the soft fabric of the chair lulled him, coaxing his eyes slowly shut. He tucked the book closer to himself, hugging it to his chest. He would just rest his eyes for a moment, and then he'd go back to reading.

It would only be for a moment.

"Hey."

Alex blinked his eyes open, shaking his head as he came to, hands scrabbling over the false cover of his book. He looked around with wild eyes for a moment before he saw Ellabell, a little smile on her face, her head tilted quizzically. She had pulled a chair over beside his, and now she was watching him with a raised eyebrow. He shoved the *Historica Magica* farther out of sight and let out an uneasy cough.

"Hey," he said. His head was still fuzzy with sleep, and his speech didn't quite sound right. He cursed inwardly. He should have picked a little wooden chair with wobbly legs, impossible to get comfortable on.

Ellabell's eyes darted to where he had shoved the book out of sight, but she didn't ask after it. Instead, she said, "So, did you figure out if my roommate is cursed?"

Alex shuffled up in his chair, trying to sit up straighter. "I think she might be," he said.

Ellabell nodded with a sigh. "That's my conclusion as well. I've been poking around trying to see if there are any rumors about someone pulling that sort of stuff, but so far no luck. Professor Lintz actually thinks she cursed herself."

Alex frowned. "Why would he think that?"

"He says a lot of really talented young mages push themselves too far and accidentally put a curse on themselves," she replied. "Something about how, if you draw upon too much magic when your body isn't used to it, you can *scar your soul*."

She said the last with a little hokey wave of her hands. Alex raised an eyebrow. "Do you believe him?"

"I believe him as far as I can throw him," she said, lifting one arm. That would not be far: Lintz was a large man.

"Anyway," she said, her arm flopping back down to her side. "Natalie was looking for you. Said she was going for a glass of wine and wanted you to come." Ellabell puffed out her cheeks, and Alex smiled. Of course Ellabell knew there was nowhere to get a drink on the manor grounds, but she didn't seem like she would question it.

"Got it," he said, rising to his feet. His arms and legs, comfortable and warm in the chair and still littered with icy burns from the last day of practice, seared in protest. He shook the feeling off, making sure to keep his book out of sight.

Ellabell nodded amiably, but there was a strange light in her eyes. It wasn't friendly, but neither was it antagonistic.

"You don't need to take such pains, you know."

Alex looked back at her. "Oh?"

She laughed. "It's just..." She looked covertly from side to side. "We've all got secrets here," she said.

Alex nodded, uncertain what she wanted.

"Even me, Alex," she said. "And even you. I don't know what the teachers were looking for the other week, and I don't know what that book you're hiding under your shirt is, but if you think nobody has noticed, you're insane. It's more that…well, we respect each other's secrets here."

She said the last with a smile, brushing a brown curl away from her glasses. He gave a slight nod, then turned sharply away.

How much did she know? She admitted little, but she could have been lying. And if Ellabell had noticed, then others had more than likely noticed too.

He needed to be more careful.

CHAPTER 35

ALEX LOWERED HIMSELF DOWN INTO THE CELLAR just as Natalie seized a bolt of Aamir's lightning and redirected it into the ceiling. There was a low *whump* in the dirt, and the whole room shook for a moment. Natalie cheered, and Aamir, whom they all had learned was something of a sore loser, scowled.

"I did it!" she cried, doing a graceful little twirl, then steadying herself, looking queasy. "I told you I could!"

Aamir continued to glare at her. "That was luck," he groused, although he didn't sound entirely assured. He turned, and, seeing Alex coming down the last rungs of the cellar, he waved. "Alex! Finally decided to join us?"

Alex smiled. "Seems like you two are having fun on your own."

Natalie spread her arms wide with a proud grin. "Aamir is having fun getting beaten."

Aamir rubbed at his brow. "You still haven't even managed to destroy the bottle once," he said.

True to the older student's word, a new bottle of wine had been set out, and now it stood at the center of the floor surrounded by burns and cuts of dirt. Natalie seemed unperturbed by her failure to achieve their real objective, however.

"No, but now I can grab your lightning out of the air!" she said, miming a grabbing motion toward Aamir, who sidestepped with a roll of his eyes. Natalie paused, then doubled over coughing.

Aamir turned to Alex.

"The girl should not continue," he said. "She is not well, and I would not feel good pressing her any further."

Natalie made a noise of protest, a fiery aura bursting into life around her shoulders, but Alex nodded.

"Did she tell you about her condition?"

Aamir inclined his head. "About the curse? Yes. Horrible business." He looked over at where Natalie was now standing with her arms folded, indignation all over her face. "I was also cursed in my first year," he went on. "Took about four months to fade away. It is a nasty affair."

Alex gaped. "You were cursed too?"

Aamir raised an eyebrow at Alex's surprise, then shrugged as if being cursed for four months wasn't a big deal. "I am told that I pushed myself too hard. Personally, I suspect that someone did not like me performing at the level that I was. I have kept my progress to myself since then."

Alex stood in stunned silence. The pieces were starting to fall into place. He walked over to the bottle, lifting it and carrying it back over to the rack. Slotting it in, he ended the challenge between Aamir and Natalie.

"I'm ready when you are," he said, hoping this was true.

His efforts the previous day had been lackluster at best. He had learned how to reach into Aamir's magic and divert it, but the art was inaccurate, and the fact of the matter was that reaching into a fire still hurt, even if it only hurt his hands.

Natalie stalked over to a corner and sat down against one wall as Aamir took his position opposite Alex. As was usual, he took his time building up his power, his fingertips flickering with budding flames. He closed his eyes, drawing in a deep, calming breath.

Alex felt a surge of annoyance. He knew the other boy was taking his time to be kind, to give Alex a moment to prepare himself. Part of him appreciated it, but another part, the part that he was ashamed to admit had been frustrated by magical failure after endless magical failure for months now, hated being condescended to. Aamir assumed he would win and Alex would lose, and what was worse, he was probably right.

Alex planted his feet in a wide stance, staring at Aamir, his jaw set.

Then Aamir's palm came whipping out, and with it came the fire. In his irritation, however, Alex was too focused on Aamir to watch the flames spearing toward him. Moving on instinct, he dodged to one side, using Aamir's outstretched hand as a reference for where the flames would go. He saw the boy's hand flatten, then make a small movement to one side.

On an impulse, Alex stepped forward, and felt a light chill as the flames coursed behind him. Drawing an excited breath, he continued to watch Aamir's hand, trying to read it. He ducked the next waft of fire, sidestepped another, and then bounded forward toward the older boy.

Aamir blinked in surprise, and with finality he brought his other hand around, a second bloom of fire flowing into existence. Alex hesitated, his eyes darting between Aamir's hands, trying to follow both movements at once.

Cold smashed into him from both sides as his head tried to dive forward and his body tried to pull back. He spun, falling to his knees amid a shower of icy dust. He coughed, spitting up snow as he cursed.

"That was…better," Aamir said, his voice soft with surprise. "What did you do?"

Alex struggled to his feet, shaking himself free of his sudden, chill-induced tiredness.

"Just trying something new," he said. It wouldn't do to give away his meager strategy, would it? Dodging attacks wasn't the most impressive thing, but it would be useful in an actual battle.

For the next half hour, Alex practiced watching Aamir's hands, and before long he could identify several different spells and command signs. Thankfully, he already knew a number of them from when he had been helping Natalie with her pyromancy, but now he learned others. The swift, jabbing fingers of lightning. The firm swipes of water, and the rooted, swaying motions of anima. For the first time, he saw sweat on Aamir's face as he attempted to strike Alex, who bobbed and tumbled between the bursts of magic.

When Alex grew exhausted, he taught Aamir and Natalie what he had learned, having each demonstrate a spell so the other could follow it. While neither of them took to the art as naturally as Alex, it wasn't long before their duels over the little bottle of wine took on a more delicate, dance-like approach. They stood, trying to keep one eye on each other and one eye on the bottle, Aamir dancing his magic away from Natalie's gasping motions, parrying her blows, then making desperate assaults. Alex, seated against the wall, thought it looked rather beautiful.

Tuning out the rush of fire, Alex stared down at his hands. They were shaking, red with frost, and he noted with consternation that his left hand was actually bleeding where the skin had dried and split. He sucked at the wound, thinking.

When he had been with Natalie in his room, he had been able to focus his anti-magical energy into a wand of sorts. When it had turned magic to cold, the ice hadn't been on his person, and therefore it hadn't hurt him. He considered that, then drew himself into the first pose he had ever learned: *Alaman's Inner Enlightenment and Fire.*

The pose was meant to make a pillar of energy coming off the creator, so when Alex inverted it, he assumed he would get a downward push of energy. Rotating his arm, he mixed in *Gren's Stalwart Shield,* opening his palm and trying to picture a blade of anti-magic spearing down into the ground.

A rush of cold, and a burst of power. Alex staggered back against the wall as a wavering, sloppy blade seemed to slide from under his skin, glittering silver and swirling like stardust in the air. The other two, each with their eyes intent upon the other's hands, didn't notice as he lifted the eerie weapon, trying to give it a swing.

It blew apart the instant he tried moving it. Alex let out a huff of disappointment as the blade dissolved into the air. It seemed that controlling anti-magic was a finicky process, made all the worse by his complete lack of any knowhow on the topic. Drawing in his breath, he tried to form another blade.

This time, he managed to focus on it enough to bring the weapon around to his side, although the tip drooped like a depressed sunflower. He strained his mind, fingers moving in delicate motions that massaged the void. He realized on some level that his ability to form the blade would be meaningless if it required this much attention; to take his eyes off of Aamir in a fight, even for an instant, would result in a swift and painful loss. However, he focused on holding the blade together until it broke, spilling to the ground in a silvery cascade, onyx lines breaking to dust on the air.

A crash of glass sounded. A spray of red cut the air as Aamir finally managed to sneak through Natalie's grasping magic with a line of fire and slam the little bottle into the dirt. He let out a triumphant sigh, a victorious grin quirking one corner of his mouth.

Natalie, rather than sulking, clapped excitedly.

"Nice one!"

Aamir gave a slight but gracious bow. "Thank you."

"That," said Natalie, dabbing at her brow, "was your first time to break the bottle with fire! I think that is your win."

Aamir's eyes brightened. "Then you mean—"

"Yes," Natalie said. "I will teach you to grab. Of course. But first, I think we should check on Alex; he has looked poorly for some time now."

Alex started. It seemed that one of the duelists *had* been paying enough attention to her surroundings to notice Alex's experiments.

Aamir, on the other hand, just looked perplexed. He looked over at Alex, who just shook his head.

"Just messing around with anti-magic," he said.

Eyes still bright with his victory, Aamir set his stance, energy gathering as Natalie retreated to the wall. "Want to test it?"

Alex smiled in response, inwardly praying that he wasn't about to end up on the floor again.

Aamir's attack came in a savage hook, an arc of flame that cut out to Alex's right before launching itself in at him. Alex moved his hand toward it, altering his stance. *Meron's Blade.*

A shield of anti-magic surged out from his wrist, and he felt a dull impact as the fire spilled over it. He gritted his teeth, but the cold didn't come. The ice and snow flared around his shield in a great explosion of white that left Alex temporarily blinded. He cursed, waving a hand, trying to see Aamir through the surge of snow. He had just gotten sight of the boy's hands again when a bolt of lightning carved the air between them. Alex's shield imploded in upon itself as he tried to bring it around, and he hastily ducked.

Aamir's magic seemed to erupt around him, and Alex rolled haphazardly to and fro, trying to get into a position where he could summon another anti-magical weapon. Aamir, however, did not seem willing to give him that chance. He launched assault after assault, each seemingly designed to keep Alex on his feet and moving, unable to concentrate.

An attack slammed down at Alex from above, and he only just managed to produce a pulse of anti-magic that turned the sundering flames to snow. Aamir laughed, crouching lower in his stance before throwing himself forward, his eyes ablaze with glittering sparks as his leg snapped out, sending a wave of fire rolling off it.

Acting on an impulse, Alex stabbed his hand down. *Gren's Stalwart Shield*, he thought as the blade speared out of his hand in a fount of cold, and then he carved upwards.

As expected, it broke halfway through the swing, but the flecks of anti-magic still took the brunt of the fire, turning the air into a swath of steaming mist and sending a spray of water over Alex's face. This quickly chilled as the remaining flames broke over him. He cursed, waving his hand and trying to clear his eyes, and as he did so, he felt a burst of cold catch him in the midriff. He was thrown to the ground, landing hard on his back with a grunt of pain.

He lay there, breathing hard, and heard the approaching feet as Aamir walked over to him. Aamir knelt, and Alex wiped the ice from his face to see the boy's exhilarated expression. He was not smiling, but his eyes were bright, his chest heaving up and down.

"My win," he said.

"Not yet," Alex snapped, jumping up. "Again." Aamir's smugness was intolerable, and Alex wasn't ready to give up.

"Are you certain?" Aamir laughed.

"Yep," Alex said shortly, and immediately bowled straight into him, all his frustration, his rage, his helplessness pouring out of him, directed at his friend.

Aamir gave a yelp of surprise, and Alex saw a hand snap out, fingers forming the sign of lightning. Concentrating his void into one hand, Alex slammed it into Aamir's palm, disrupting the nascent spell and sending a wave of icy crystals over both his and Aamir's skin. Then, without thinking, Alex brought a hand around and punched Aamir in the chest, putting the other boy on his back with a gasp. Aamir's eyes flashed with exhilaration as he brought his other hand around, and once again Alex pinned it down.

The two of them lay like that for a long moment, panting, their hands pressed together and covered in frost. Mud coated both of their clothes, and Alex was bleeding from the corner of his lip.

Aamir opened his mouth. Alex hesitated.

And then a cold, precise voice split the silence.

"What, exactly," it said, "is this?"

All three of them turned. They had been too intent on the fight to notice that the trapdoor had opened, and someone had let himself in. Alex had to look twice to recognize the man who stood there, straight-backed and proud.

Professor Derhin looked at the two of them, sprawled on the ground, and shook his head in derision. His eyes were deep and laced with eerie anger, his hands folded primly behind his back as he took a measured step into the room.

"Brawling like commoners," he said, shaking his head. "I had heard disturbing rumors, Nagi, but I hadn't expected to find this." He laughed. "Tell me, when you challenge a teacher, do you expect to punch them out? I might have expected this sort of behavior from a weak novice like Webber, but from you? I had higher hopes."

"Challenge?" Aamir said, keeping his tone carefully neutral.

Derhin gave him a scathing look. "Do not insult me," he said. "Do you think that any of us failed to notice what you were doing when you vanished from class? You thought any one of us would be so negligent as to just give up our position?"

Aamir's back straightened, his hands balling into fists, but he said nothing.

"Your little friend Petra could only cover your tracks so much," Derhin continued. "He's smart. Smarter than you."

Aamir was shaking now with fear. Alex moved to step in front of his friend, but Derhin held out a hand.

A coil of magic curled around Alex's neck, and he halted in his tracks. The magic wasn't hostile yet, so his body hadn't responded naturally. If he had wanted, he was sure he could have ripped the little tendril away, but the resulting ice would certainly reveal him as a Spellbreaker. He drew in a shallow breath, feeling the force of the professor's magic against his neck.

It was a sinister malevolence, coiling tighter and tighter around him, and all at once his suspicions were confirmed. There was only one group of people who had the skill, potency, and perverse motivation to curse both Aamir and Natalie. And there was only one who felt like *that*.

He stared at Derhin, breathing steadily to control himself, and held perfectly still as the professor walked up to Aamir, his usual awkward gait replaced with an unconcerned stride.

"So who were you going to challenge?" he asked. "Lintz? Esmerelda? Renmark?" A smooth smile rolled out over his lips, his tongue flicking out to wet them.

Aamir glared up at the professor, and Alex felt panic boil up inside him.

Don't say it, he thought frantically. *Don't say it, don't say—*

"You," Aamir said.

The smile on Derhin's mouth widened into a feral grin.

"Me," he said, almost seeming to savor the word. "Yes, I suppose you would. Stupid Professor Derhin. Untalented, unassuming, and clumsy to boot."

For the first time, Aamir hesitated. Alex could have kicked the boy. Only Aamir could have been bullheaded enough to not notice the malevolence flowing off the man. To not have heeded Alex's warning!

"One week," Derhin said.

Aamir jumped, blinking.

"One week, sir?"

Alex heard the boy try to bite back the honorific, but it spilled out anyway. Derhin noticed as well, and he refolded his hands behind his back with a smirk.

"That will give you some time to continue your training, won't it?" he said, glancing between Natalie and Alex. "Even if your choice of opponent is…lacking. We'll go with what you trained for. One week, on the lawn. I'll inform the Head."

Alex's irritation with Aamir's overconfidence and condescension dissipated as the older boy was threatened with a much crueler, much more dangerous version of the same.

He turned, and walked to the base of the ladder. When he reached it, he looked up, and with a little hop, he shot up through the open hatch, leaving only a ruffled burst of dirt in his wake.

The slip of magic around Alex's neck vanished, and he heaved in a deep breath, turning on Aamir.

"Are you *insane?*" Alex breathed.

Aamir's face was blank.

"I am not sure any other teacher would have been better," he said.

Alex scowled at him. "I told you not to pick Derhin. I said—"

"Look," Aamir interjected, his voice cracking. "What is done is done." He looked down at his feet, and Alex could see his chest moving, his breathing a little too rhythmic to be natural. With a sudden movement, Aamir turned toward Natalie, who had remained uncharacteristically quiet for the whole event. Now she looked up at Aamir from where she sat, her eyes distant.

"Chevalier."

Natalie started at the formal address, rising to her feet. "Yes?"

"Are you and Alex still planning to destroy Finder?"

She nodded uncertainly. "I am figuring out the magic, little by little," she said. "I am not sure I understand it perfectly yet, but—"

"You have one week," Aamir said with finality. When Natalie's brow furrowed, he explained, "When Professor Derhin and I duel, the whole school will be in attendance. It is the perfect distraction for whatever mischief you want to get up to."

Alex frowned. "Aamir, no, we'll be—"

"Exorcising the bastard who dragged me into this," Aamir said through gritted teeth.

A silence fell over the room. Alex stared at Aamir's clenched fists, at where the boy's eyes were glittering with frustrated tears.

"I think I can make the duel last long enough to get you a window," he said. "Use it. Please."

Alex's eyes narrowed. "You'd better not be planning some sort of noble sacrifice."

Aamir drew in a deep breath, then turned to Alex, a wavering smile plastered to his face.

"I just meant that I wouldn't beat him *too* fast," he said with forced nonchalance.

He looked over at Natalie. "I think we know who is cursing you now, at least."

Her eyes widened, and he thought he saw her pale ever so slightly. "You don't mean…But why?"

Aamir was staring at the ladder. "Because he does not want the students to be too powerful," he said wonderingly. "He does not want them to thrive. If they do, they might grow strong. And if they grow stronger than him…"

"They could cast him out," Alex finished, nodding. "So he gets rid of his enemies before they have a chance to know their foe."

The group sat in silence, absorbing the information. The whole room felt cramped. It was as though there were something else in the cellar with them, slithering around them, slowly wrapping its coils tighter until it crushed the life right out of them.

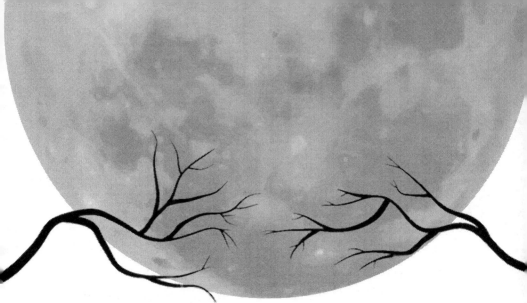

CHAPTER 36

IT SEEMED IMPOSSIBLE TO EVEN IMAGINE HOW complacent they had been. Alex thought about the days spent sitting by the fire, reading the *Historica Magica* or researching some other, more insignificant topic. He thought of Natalie reading her leather-bound tome of necromancy, the curse paling her face by the light of their candles. He thought of his training with Aamir, never too fast, never too rough.

Everything had changed now. Jari had seized Aamir by the shoulders at the news of the duel and dragged him away. When Aamir had asked where they were going, Jari had responded: "Training your stupid self."

The two hadn't been in class since. It had been two days, and Alex had only seen them when they came back to the room, exhausted and covered in mud. Their living space had begun to smell like a sty, but none of them really noticed. Alex woke once during the night to see Jari lying with his eyes open, staring at the ceiling. When he noticed Alex's stare, he rolled away, his shoulders forming a small but solid wall.

If Jari blamed Alex for what had happened, Alex couldn't fault him. Every time he thought of Aamir, his gut twisted. If he had been more careful, maybe they would have noticed Derhin before he saw them brawling and talked their way out of things. If he hadn't agreed to train with Aamir, maybe it could have turned out differently. If he had just taken Jari's side and told his friend to lay low and go to class, he wondered if he would still need to feel like this.

Unable to focus, Alex took to sitting with Natalie in the library as she pored over her book. He had taken her notes and perused them, occasionally asking a clarifying question or requesting help with her flowy handwriting. His thoughts were mostly on Aamir, though, and he wished more than anything that he could be of some help to him.

"Do you know what a 'source' is?" he asked, pushing a page toward Natalie.

She glanced up, pinning the page Alex was looking at

under one finger and pulling it toward her. She frowned, shooting him a disbelieving glance.

"It is explained on the page you just read," she said, pointing.

Alex looked, then sighed. It was indeed. He was finding it so hard to focus.

Source: a central item used as a focus for a spiritual summoning. Usually, but not always, the corpse of the deceased.

"Can't believe I missed that," he muttered.

"Neither can I," Natalie replied, her eyebrows drawn in concern.

He sensed she was about to ask how he was feeling, so before she could, he said, "So it sounds like we might need Finder's body. Where do you think it is?"

"I don't know," she murmured, looking a little panicked. "We should have had more time to look!" she burst out, and rubbed the bridge of her nose with both hands, calming herself.

"Well, his body wasn't at the altar," Alex said. "The Head might have it in his wing."

Natalie nodded, then stopped.

"No, I do not think so. Necromantic sources give off distorting waves of magic." She raised her arms, wiggling her fingers in the air, presumably to illustrate distorting waves. "Little things, like that mouse I made, would not be too bad. But something big, like Finder's source, would really mess up anything around it. I do not think the Head would keep it anywhere it could interfere with someone's magic. If he had it in his office, someone would notice."

Alex stroked his chin. "That leaves us with…"

"Everywhere else, yes," said Natalie with a hopeless sigh.

"But the only place that's far enough away from everyone *and* has a protective golden line," said Alex, realization hitting him, "is the crypt."

"But we didn't see a body there. Unless…"

Alex remembered the three-eyed skull. "Unless it's actually beneath the statue…It must be the skull."

They stared at each other.

"But of course it is the skull," Natalie breathed. "What else could it be?"

As Alex considered her question, his optimism ebbed. It could be any number of things, actually. It could be buried anywhere else, even somewhere far from the manor, protected by something they weren't familiar with…He rubbed his face. With Aamir's predicament playing incessantly at the back of his mind, he was finding it so difficult to think in a straight line. His brain felt foggy, crowded.

He rose to his feet. "I need some fresh air," he told Natalie. "Just give me a few minutes."

"Okay," she murmured. She gave him a worried frown, then sunk her head back down to her book.

Alex gathered his things and left the library. He drew

several stares as he walked through the manor, but nobody thought to stop him. It was common knowledge by now that his friend had been called to a duel by Professor Derhin, and whispers gathered in his wake.

"…They were caught fighting…"

"…Probably encouraged him…"

"…Idiot rookie…"

He tried to ignore them, hurrying down the hallways and toward the garden. Fresh air. He just needed some fresh air.

The sky beyond the windows today seemed bent on expressing Alex's mood, with curls of lightning rolling through black clouds that hung low over jagged peaks coated with ice and frost. Sleet clattered against the windows, the noise loud enough to block out the sound of Alex's footsteps as he walked. When he eventually reached the door that led out to the front lawn, he opened it into a flood of icy pellets.

Alex almost laughed. After all his training, the natural cold seemed to roll right off him. Compared to the icy waves of breaking magic, the sleet was nothing. He stepped out into it, his jacket flaring behind him.

In the end, it had been Aamir who had been training *him*. Alex had been so focused on improving himself and beating the other boy that he hadn't even registered how little Aamir had probably benefited from their mock duels. The only time Aamir had seemed even remotely pressed had been their last encounter, and that had ended in abject disaster. Jari's face when he had learned of the duel, that twist of surprise and scorn, lingered in Alex's mind as he walked through the storm, his hair filling with little white shards of ice.

What had he thought he could teach Aamir, anyway? How to fight a Spellbreaker? Alex laughed aloud at the thought. He was part of a dead line; as far as he knew, he was the only Spellbreaker to have emerged in decades, maybe even centuries. He was no help.

Quickening his pace, Alex found himself at the front gates of the manor, staring up at the great iron bars. With his increased training, he could now feel the throb of the magic that locked the great portal; it stifled the air, its presence cold against his skin.

Alex swept out his hand, willing his energy to flow with all his might, and the hazy outline of a blade appeared at his fingertips. With a curse, he swiped it at the gate.

His attack caught on the ivy coating the metal and simply exploded. Ripples of magic burst out, howling through the air past him, leaving icy white slashes across his face. He growled, reforming the blade and taking another swing, then another. Each time, the weapon broke harmlessly.

He should have done more, done better. He should have had this anti-magic figured out by now. He should have had a grip on what was going on in this prison of a school. If he had tried harder, he could have even saved

Natalie before she'd reached the end of Spellshadow Lane, could have prevented all this mess. If he had been smarter, quicker…

Alex smashed yet another sword against the ivy, and watched as the blade tore asunder, shards of ice spearing into the snow all around his feet. He swore again.

Natalie had been so vibrant before coming here, so alive, so exuberant. And now? Now she was hopeless, dejected, all but friendless, and cursed—always feeling ill, always coughing and trembling. And here he was, the only one with the power to break that curse, but he wasn't even capable of that.

He let out a long, steaming breath through his teeth as he strained to draw another blade, smacking it weakly against the gate. It collapsed into chilled flecks in his hands. The hail had slowed, growing fatter and softer until it became snow, drifting down to land softly on his hands and legs.

What did he think he was going to accomplish out here? Was letting Natalie lead the fight against Finder the best way forward? Of course not. He needed to head back. He should be the one battling these impossible forces, battling Finder, escaping the Head…

He had briefly searched for the Head in the records of the *Historica Magica*, but it had not surprised him that, even in the meticulously detailed annals of the old book, the man had not appeared. He was like a wraith, the patron deity of the school. Alex supposed he could be any number of the several wizards who had lacked a date of death, but narrowing it down was impossible. Also, those men had all lived hundreds of years ago. If the Head was truly one of them, then the man was not only powerful, but ancient. Alex wondered what hope they had of defeating such a man. They could wound him, of course. They could take his resources and harass him, but Alex found it hard to believe they had enough time. In five days, Aamir would likely be killed by Derhin…

Lost in dismal thoughts, Alex barely noticed when someone crept up behind him and touched his arm lightly. He spun, wide-eyed, and saw Natalie.

"I needed some fresh air too," she said quietly, sniffing and lowering her eyes to the ground.

Although Alex had initially wanted to be alone, he felt glad for her company now. Her arrival helped draw him back to the present, which, however stressful, was better than being lost in his head, blaming himself for things he couldn't change.

She drew closer for a hug, and they both stood still beneath the snow, their gazes drifting to the ivy-ridden gates. It was hard to fathom that just a few feet away lay escape, freedom—something Alex had taken for granted his whole life and now, something he would risk losing his life to obtain.

Feeling the press of time acutely, Alex cleared his

throat. "We should go," he said hoarsely, detaching himself from her and turning back toward the manor.

But Natalie remained where she was, her eyes lingering on the gates. "We will see the other side of them again." She whispered so softly, she spoke more to herself than Alex. Her gaze hardened, anger sparking. "They cannot keep what is not theirs."

A few more seconds passed, and then she stepped away, letting out a breath—her eyes still not meeting Alex's as they trudged back.

As dangerous a time as they had ahead of them, Alex felt that blowing off some steam had done him good. His head felt sharper, clearer, now. He even felt his spirits lifting a little as he returned to the conversation he and Natalie had been having before he broke away. That skull… It was very possible that it was Finder's.

His mood stopped lifting abruptly, however, as he spotted a figure leaning in the manor's doorway. Jari. He wore a bitter expression as he watched the two of them approaching him, his hands stuffed sullenly into his pockets. He was chewing on his lip, his clothes tattered and streaked with mud, his hair slightly on end.

"Having a nice walk?" he asked as they drew closer.

Alex regarded him cautiously. "What is it?"

Jari grunted.

"How's Aamir?" Natalie pressed.

Jari shook his head. "Not strong enough," he said. His

eyes narrowed. "But he tells me that you know some inter-esting techniques. Both of you."

Alex smiled. "Natalie sure does."

Jari shoved himself off of the doorframe, coming to stand in front of the two of them.

"He also tells me," he said, his eyes sliding away to rove over the gates behind them, "that I am being a bad friend to the both of you. That you shouldn't be blamed for his encounter with the professor."

Alex remained quiet, watching the short boy.

Jari let out a long breath, running a hand through his golden hair and rocking from foot to foot.

"I'd meant to start practicing with him sooner," he said. "It's just...life got in the way. I thought..."

"You thought you had more time," Alex and Natalie finished for him in unison.

He smiled weakly. "Something like that."

The three of them stood there, uncomfortably re-garding one another as the snow continued to drift down among them.

"Long story short," Jari said, "I'm sorry. Not only that, but I'd like for the two of you to join me in training Aamir. I'm getting worn out doing this day in and day out."

Alex stretched, still feeling the aches and sores from when he had last dueled with Aamir. "It takes it out of you, doesn't it?"

"No kidding," Jari chuckled. He shot a pleading look

between the two of them. "So you'll come?"

"Of course we'll come!" Natalie replied, giving him an affectionate squeeze on the shoulder.

Jari sighed and led them through the grounds toward the cellar, and for a moment it almost felt like the early days at the manor. Everything seemed fresh and new somehow, the falling snow casting a cold, white shadow over the familiar scenes. The abandoned gardens. The disused statuary. The gnarled trees, their spidery branches hanging heavy with the winter's ice.

Jari kicked the trapdoor twice before entering, and Alex felt the familiar warmth of the place rush up to greet him. Aamir's fire practically turned the place into an oven at all hours.

Aamir himself was sitting against the far wall, looking anxiously down at his hands. His head shot up as he heard them descending the ladder, and a smile broke out over his face when he saw Alex and Natalie.

"You came," he said.

Natalie grinned. "Still have to teach you to grab, don't I?"

Aamir was on his feet in an instant.

"Yes," he said, "you do. Show me the form of it now. I want to get started."

He all but dragged Natalie away, leaving Alex and Jari standing awkwardly by the ladder.

"Well then," Jari said.

Alex watched as Natalie began to walk Aamir through the forms, her hands in the claw-like positioning that Alex had seen so many times before. Aamir was nodding, his own hands mimicking the motions.

"He's going to be fine," Jari said, staring at their friend.

Alex continued to look on as Aamir's brow furrowed with concentration, his hands moving in intricate patterns. He didn't want to tell Jari how powerful Derhin was. How the touch of the man's magic had felt like having the breath crushed from him.

"I know what you're thinking," Jari said. "Derhin's a teacher, and Aamir, for all his talent, is a student. I know." He kept watching his friend, and a little smile slipped onto his lips. "I know all of that is true," he said. "But still. He's going to be fine."

Natalie summoned a ball of fire, lifting it into the air between her and Aamir. Aamir thrust out his hand, his fingers grasping, then closing. The fire wavered, slipping an inch or two toward Aamir. Natalie smiled, saying something with an encouraging nod.

"He's going to be fine," Jari repeated.

It was as though the words were a mantra, and repeating them would make them true. Alex thought again of Derhin. Of the power the man wielded. He thought of the feeling of having his neck crushed by the man's magic, then looked at Aamir again.

Alex joined in the prayer. "He's going to be fine."

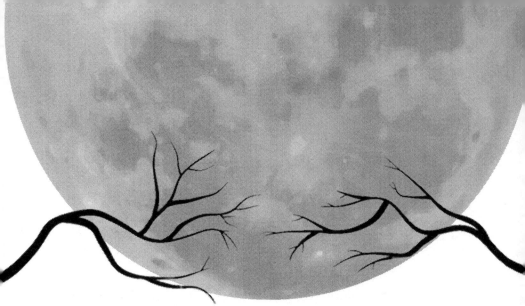

CHAPTER 37

THE DAYS MELTED BY IN A SNOWY WASH AS THEY trained. All four of them stopped attending class, a fact that earned them stern looks from their teachers in the hallways, but other than that garnered no repercussions. Each of them threw themselves into their practice with vigor—Alex and Natalie trying to continue formulating a solid plan for Finder on the side.

Alex's anti-magic conjurations were getting better, but they were still far from perfect. He had to focus too much, and it inevitably came down to a choice between concentrating on his enemy's hands and holding his own energies together. He was pleased to note his improvement, but frustrated that he still ended up losing.

With her curse hanging heavy around her shoulders, and Aamir having developed a firm grasp on the basics of grabbing, Natalie's success against the older student dwindled to almost nothing. Her endurance was poor, and her magic was weak. She spent most of their practices sitting against the wall with Alex, who was glad she was finally resting a little.

Then there was Jari. Aamir had always said the small boy was good, but Alex had never fully appreciated the statement until he saw him spar. Jari stood, his body held sideways to present the smallest possible target, one hand slotted behind his back and the other held out like a fencer's foil in front of him. His hair glowed with crackling power as his fingers snapped one way then another in a blur of magical signs, sending spell after spell raining down on the bottle, and Alex noted with surprise that Aamir struggled to keep up.

A crack of glass, and the bottle at the center of the room spun, a small hole in its side burbling with fizzing wine, the sickly smell of scorched grapes floating into the air. Aamir smiled weakly, then slumped down to a sitting position, panting. Jari flicked a couple stray bolts of lightning from his fingertips.

It was the night before the duel. So far, none of them had actually mentioned the fact, but it hung heavy over the room. They had been talking less, concentrating more.

Now, however, it was growing late and they would soon be forced to sleep, or face the dawn unrested.

Jari made a hand sign in Aamir's direction, and the boy's hawk-like eyes caught it, squinting in the gloom of the cellar.

"Anima, strong, ground to my left."

Jari smiled, then changed the sign.

"Lightning, straight to the face."

There was a chime that seemed to roll through the room, and Jari's watch began to emit a faint light. He didn't even look down, flipping his hand into a new position.

Aamir, however, did not answer. He was staring at the watch.

"Jari…"

"What's the sign?" the younger boy responded.

Aamir sighed, then looked at the hand. He blinked, a smile sliding over his face as he saw what the other boy held toward him: a thumbs-up.

"Time for bed," Jari said.

On the way back, Jari drew Aamir ahead by the arm, and the two of them spoke in hushed whispers that were masked by the wind as it whooshed through the bare branches of the toppled trees. The two boys walked, their long gray coats tumbling behind them in the wind, and for a moment Alex thought they were the very picture of modern magicians.

Beside him, Natalie was muttering to herself too, her hands making signs he didn't know. Alex noted with interest that the spells she was practicing took both hands, one fluid and wavy, the other stiff and harsh.

"Necromancy?" he asked.

Natalie shot him a small smile.

"Have to make sure I have it right for tomorrow."

Alex nodded. "Did you get enough practice? I was worried that you wouldn't have time, what with training Aamir."

Natalie shrugged. "There is no way to know, is there? We'll find out tomorrow."

They walked in silence for a time, Natalie continuing to mutter and flex her hands.

"So," Alex said as the wind cut a cold line across his cheek, "what's our plan tomorrow?"

"We have already gone over it at least a dozen times."

"Humor me."

Natalie sighed, but she settled into the discussion with an ease that would have been impossible for someone who hadn't already been thinking on the topic. "We go to the crypt," she said. "Odds are very good that the source will be in there, possibly the skull. We sneak in, locate it, disenchant it, and get out."

Alex nodded. "For my part," he said, "I'll take care of any traps and wards set on the crypt. My anti-magic should be able to dismantle spells rather than trigger them, so if we're careful, we won't sound any alarms…Should be a clean trip in and out."

As they walked, Alex tilted his head back, staring up at the mess of stars that washed over the sky. He picked out constellations, slowly building a map of the cosmos high above.

Natalie looked up as well, her brown eyes soft in the moonlight.

"It is like they are putting on a show for us," she said.

Alex frowned. His complex web of patterns and lines wavered, and for a moment he saw the stars.

"A show?"

Natalie smiled and moved a little closer to him, wrapping her arms around herself in an effort to keep warm. "They look a little like fireworks, do they not?" she said.

Alex squinted, and then he saw it. Like a thousand fireworks exploding in frozen water, deep and distant, halted in mid-blast.

"I was just mapping them," he said with a frown.

Natalie laughed. "Of course you were."

He helped her over a large tree that had been thrown across the path, her hand soft and warm against his palm, and led the way back toward the manor.

"Do you really think we can do this?" she asked in a quiet whisper. It was the first time she had allowed herself to show true doubt in a while.

Alex looked back at her, studying her face. For a

moment, all he could see was her eyes, sparkling in the night. She seemed taller than usual, her dark hair tied back in a bun that left only a few long locks to hang loose over her face. They fluttered in the wind, the wooly coat around her neck ruffling.

He smiled. "Only one way to find out."

With all the anticipation, stress, and worry churning his gut, Alex had a horrible time getting to sleep that night. He stared up at the ceiling, where Jari's New Year's fireworks had never quite faded. He found himself making constellations of the swirling sparks as they fell into place, his hands moving from one anti-magical position to the next, until he finally drifted off.

By some quirk of fate, all three of them woke at the same time. Jari rubbed at his eyes, and Aamir just stared at the ceiling with a distant expression. Alex sat up, propping his back against the wall. He felt stiff, but wide awake.

They dressed in silence and made their way to the mess hall. Everywhere Aamir walked, the conversations died as students stared at him. Whispers followed him like the wake of a plague boat coming in to harbor. When they reached the buffet, Aamir took only few pieces of toast with a single sad dollop of jam. Jari, on the other hand, mounded a plate so high with food that Alex had to wonder what the small boy was planning to do with all of it, because it certainly wouldn't fit in his stomach.

They ate in silence until Natalie walked up, practically dropping a half-full plate onto the table. She had deep shadows under her eyes, and she fell into her chair in a way that suggested she had died and resurrected herself, mostly. He knew how she felt, and gave her a weak smile.

Their meal continued uninterrupted for a little while until a boy that Alex recognized as a second year named Ryan Cross scurried up to them. He had a thin face and gangly arms, and he seemed to vibrate as he stood before them, his hands smashing together in a nervous series of movements as his eyes carefully locked on everybody except Aamir.

"Excuse me," he said in a cracking voice.

Aamir's head swiveled toward the boy, who swallowed audibly.

"I, uh," said Ryan, his mouth working furiously, his teeth pulling his upper lip into his mouth. "I'm supposed to tell you that you'll be needed on the main green in thirty minutes for your d-duel."

His voice tripped over that last word with a mixture of fear and excitement. Aamir, still staring at him, only nodded.

The boy nodded back, the motion swift and sharp,

then hesitated.

"Uh," he said.

"Go on," Natalie encouraged him, her voice kind but firm. "It's okay."

Ryan looked gratefully at her, then finally locked eyes with Aamir. He gave a short but respectful bow. "Good luck," he said. Then he turned and skittered off out of the dining hall door.

The whole room had gone quiet as the conversation took place, and now the other students in the room were openly watching Aamir.

"All right," said Aamir under his breath, and turned back to his toast. He had only finished one slice, but he made to shove the plate away from himself. Jari caught it, holding it in front of his friend.

"Finish it," he ordered.

"I'm not—"

"Finish. It."

Jari's voice brooked no argument. Natalie swallowed a mouthful of cereal, then looked at Alex.

"Should we go get ready?"

Alex nodded, and the two of them rose.

"We'll walk out to the grounds with you," Alex promised as they went.

Aamir gave him a stiff nod.

Their preparations were short. Alex retrieved his

screwdriver and slotted it into a pocket while Natalie shoved *Nobilitum Mortem* into her coat. They both donned dark cloaks, and Natalie even slipped on a pair of black gloves.

"If you're going to commit a crime," she said, "you might as well look the part."

She put on a dark silk scarf, drawing it up over her nose, then giving a little twirl.

"How do I look?"

A little laugh forced its way from Alex's mouth.

"Beautiful," he said, then returned the spin. "And me?"

Natalie gave an approving nod. "Very dashing. The image of a criminal."

They met Jari and Aamir outside Alex's room. Aamir was dressed as normal, and Jari stood at his side with a nervous expression on his face. As Alex and Natalie approached, he gave a little wave.

"Come inside for a moment," Aamir said.

Puzzled, Alex and Natalie followed him into the room. Alex let out a strangled yelp when he nearly ran face first into a mirror image of himself standing in the doorway. Natalie gasped in surprise as she encountered her own doppelganger.

"What—" Alex began.

Aamir smiled at him.

"You'll waste time walking with me," he said. "And people will notice if you disappear. You need to be present at the duel. Jari agreed to make these two to come with us. You'll go straight to the crypt."

Alex frowned. "No, Aamir, we'll—"

Aamir made a firm gesture that cut Alex off mid-sentence. "No," he said, his lips twisting in a sad smile. "No. I appreciate the offer, but this is how it needs to be."

The two young men stared at each other for a long time. Alex could see the fear in Aamir's eyes, the tremble in his hands. He stepped forward, putting his arm around Aamir's shoulders, and pulled his friend in for a hug.

Aamir tensed for a moment, then relaxed, his own arms encircling Alex to pat him on the back. Alex could feel Aamir's heart fluttering against him like that of a bird, his lean body tight.

"I want to hear all about your victory afterwards," Alex said with assurance as he stepped back, a hand still on Aamir's shoulder.

Aamir smiled. "I'm sure Jari will do it better justice than me."

Then Natalie slipped her arms around them both.

"We want to hear it from *you*," she said.

Aamir, his eyes glittering, nodded.

They parted ways, Jari and Aamir walking in one direction with the clones, and Alex and Natalie taking off in the other. Natalie drew her scarf up over her face again, and they set off at a brisk pace, toward the hallway that would exit the manor near the cemetery.

A silence fell over them as they made their way through the hallways. Any students who would normally have been in this part of the manor had long since vacated it, heading toward the lawn in an effort to get the best view of the action. The teachers' offices were located at the front of the building, so they wouldn't encounter any of them either.

This was no place for students; this was the Head's realm. Soon they would be over that golden line once more, into the eerie magic of the man's private space. Alex slowed their pace slightly as they approached a small wooden door carved with the images of trees laden with vines.

She looked over at him, her eyes sparkling over her scarf, and he nodded. Natalie shouldered the door open a crack, then spilled herself out onto the grounds.

The sky was a bloody crimson that morning, slashes of gold and fiery orange cascading out over the few low-hanging clouds. With the sun at the far end of the manor, however, the building threw long shadows over the frozen grass, and Natalie sank into them as she began to make her way toward the old crypt.

The trip felt much too short, ending well before Alex felt he had gotten the chance to steady himself for what was to come. But there was no other way. Natalie halted abruptly, Alex forced to stop rather suddenly to avoid running face-first into her. She held up a cautioning hand, crouching low, and Alex mimicked the movement, peering around for a better look at what she was seeing.

The little graveyard was just as he remembered it. The smooth, weathered headstones were just visible amid the shadows of the manor, standing before the gaping maw of the entrance to the catacombs below. Alex was about to ask Natalie why she had stopped when he noticed something. A shadow, kneeling before one of the graves. He caught the glitter of pale white skin, and felt his whole body go cold.

The Head rose, his long robe tumbling about him like a storm cloud, and they immediately dropped to the ground, flattening themselves and exchanging quick, nervous looks. The two lay still, praying that their cloaks would keep them hidden in the dark. The Head stood in front of the graves for a long moment, looking out toward the main walls, his hands moving to clasp at his back. He let out a long sigh that was clearly audible over the whistling of the morning wind.

Then, with a twist of his cloak, he was gone.

Natalie and Alex stared at the empty air, stunned.

"Invisibility?" Natalie said in a hushed voice.

Alex shook his head. "I don't think so."

"It does not make sense," Natalie said confusedly. "Magic follows rules. It is like sculpting. How can you sculpt yourself out of existence?"

Alex did not know what to think, but it certainly

seemed like the Head used magic differently from other people. He rose to his feet, approaching the stand of stones to see what the man had been looking at. Natalie, uncertain, followed in his wake.

"Why was he here?" she asked, moving up alongside Alex as it became clear that the Head was no longer present.

Alex was looking down at the grave that the Head had been kneeling in front of. Its surface was blank; it looked no different from any of the other graves in the little stand of stones. And yet, the Head had chosen this place to kneel.

"I don't know," he said, frowning at it in contemplation.

Natalie stared down at the stone for a time, her brow twisting in puzzlement. Then, she shook her head.

"We do not have time for this," she said urgently.

As one, they turned to look at the gaping hole in the side of the manor. Even from where they stood, Alex could see the golden line shimmering in the dark; as they approached, it only grew brighter. It seemed dazzling, powerful, full of light and energy, and Alex drew in a long, steadying breath as he looked at it.

"You ready?" Natalie asked eventually.

Alex swallowed, then nodded. If all went to plan, this time he would not end up on the ground with ice and snow spewing from him. He held out his hand, twisting it, emptying his mind. There was a rush, a surge of cold down his arm, and then a long, thin blade slipped from his hand, wobbling and distorting in the space in front of him. So far so good. Carefully, straining to hold the weapon in place, he reached out and drew a quick slash over the golden line.

The second his blade touched the line, Alex knew something was wrong. The line fizzed and hissed, and then in a burst of cold it erupted into icy shards. He staggered back, but saw with horror that the ice was whipping toward him, slipping up through the void toward his fingertips. A slicing blade of frost crested from the tip, and Alex saw, as if in slow motion, the thing whipping toward his neck.

Natalie's hand crashed into the ice in a blaze of fiery sparks. The shard broke apart, the blade of ice spinning to shatter against the wall as other such blades speared into the veil of flame that Natalie had cast in front of them, then melted as they succumbed. She was panting, pale, her eyes wide as she surveyed the scene in front of them.

Alex looked aghast at the jagged hooks and blades of ice that curled up from the floor. His hand shook, and the blade of anti-magic he held dissolved.

"Security seems to have been improved," he said, more nonchalantly than he felt.

"It chased you," Natalie replied, her face worried. "How could it do that? Your anti-magic, should it not...?"

Alex looked down at his shaking hand. The magic here hadn't just been effective against him—it had been designed to kill him. Specifically him. He turned, staring toward the distant lake where the lords of Spellshadow Manor had been dumping Spellbreaker bodies for centuries. He felt a surge of sorrow for his dead people, murdered and unceremoniously disposed of, and fervently hoped he would not join them.

"Let's just go," he said softly.

Natalie took a minute to burn the ice from their path, working with a precision and quickness that belied her weakened state, and Alex took point as they descended into the depths.

The strength of the golden line wasn't the only thing that had changed since their first visit. First and foremost, there was the intense cold. It grew as they descended, reaching a pitch where Alex could feel his bones stiffening and creaking as he walked. It was uncomfortable, but not entirely surprising. He looked over at Natalie, but she seemed unaffected.

"Magic," he muttered. "Strong, too."

Natalie looked over at him, then nodded.

Next, there was the ivy. The plant, previously absent from the underground resting place of the lords of Spellshadow, now hung heavy on every wall. It lay still, for the moment, but there was something predatory about it. Like it was lying in wait somehow, attentive to their progress.

"Don't touch the ivy," Alex said, finding his voice

hushed to a whisper.

"Was not planning on it," murmured Natalie, giving it a wary look.

As they drew past the tall statues of the old lords, Alex thought they looked somehow more decayed. The statue of Gifford White, previously laced in ice that looked like lightning, now dripped with loose-flowing water, his outstretched hand looking more placating than powerful, his eyes forlorn. The skull on the plinth before him was browning, missing teeth.

Looking around, Alex saw that all the statues were in a similar state. The gemstones had fallen from the eye sockets of the lords, giving them hollow, endless stares. Alex swallowed hard as they made their way toward the end of the hall. He just had to keep moving, he told himself, trying not to look at where gray ivy had wrapped itself around a female statue's neck like a noose.

All the same, when he saw Finder's statue, he stopped, and could not tear his eyes from it.

The tall statue's shoulders had hunched, his muscles atrophied down to nothing more than spindly limbs under a too-large hood. Bony fingers stretched from under a cloak of marble, his golden eyes reduced to burnished holes in the shadows of his garment.

Under him, upon his plinth, sat the skull, with the hole carved into the forehead that looked like nothing so much as a third eye.

Alex felt another wave of magical energy spill over him, shivering against it.

"There it is," Natalie said, putting an unconscious hand on Alex's shoulder.

Alex nodded, stepping forward. He could feel the raw magical power of the skull as he reached out, his fingers slowly wreathing themselves in white frost as they inched closer and closer to the source of Finder of Spellshadow. Even through the cold, he could feel the strength of the magic. It burned a hole in his defenses, and through it he could feel…something.

The feeling cut off when Natalie let out a scream.

Alex spun, his heart in his throat, and there he was.

Malachi Grey stood between the two of them, one hand outstretched toward Natalie, who was struggling, her hands scrabbling at gray-gold lines of ghostly magic wrapping around her. She gave Alex a desperate look, her fingers twitching in feeble attempts at making magical signs as Malachi twisted his power tighter.

Alex acted on instinct born of weeks of training with Aamir in the cellar. Stepping forward, he cleared his mind, a swirling hole of anti-magic forming in his palm as he thrust it toward the ghost.

A rumble ran through the room, and Malachi let out a cry of pain as he spun, the ghostly coils around Natalie coming undone in an instant, his empty eyes searching for his new assailant. He looked down, and his eyes lingered on the icy water dripping off him like blood to pool on the floor.

"Spellbreaker," he whispered, the word like a holy oath. "So you're really here."

Alex skipped back a step, feeling the cold emanations of the source at his back. With his current skill, he wouldn't be able to exorcise a ghost, but Natalie had fallen to her knees, one hand at her throat as she sucked in hungry, frantic breaths.

He had to buy her time.

Finder rolled forward in a powerful movement, his hand coming up in a sign that Alex didn't recognize. With a boom like thunder, a wave of force that covered the width of the crypt rolled toward Alex. He held up a hand, expecting to feel the familiar wash of cold, but instead he found himself slammed to the ground, sprawling head over heels across the floor.

"I may not be able to see you," Finder said, "but my family has been killing your kind for longer than you could ever know. If you wish to destroy me, you'll need to work at it, child."

Destroy me.

Alex scrambled to his feet and bolted for the skull atop Finder's altar. A second blast nearly knocked him back to the ground, but he managed to keep his feet, his hand outstretched. He felt his fingers plunging through the cold energies of the source, then closing around yellowing, strangely soft bone.

Magic erupted into Alex's mind, and he let out a shout as light poured into him. He could feel himself lifting, being thrown like a ragdoll as time and space themselves came undone.

"My lord."

Alex blinked the sparks from his eyes, bringing his vision into focus. He was lying on the lawn of Spellshadow Manor, before the great gates. Something had changed, though.

There was no ivy.

The midday sun hung lazily in a blue sky, its light falling over beautifully tended gardens, lined with statues of proud, powerful wizards. On the main path that led to the door, two men stood facing one another.

Alex knew Finder at once, although this version of the man better reflected the statue in the crypts below Spellshadow. He had broad shoulders, his hood thrown back to reveal a square jaw and a thin bristle of black beard beneath stern, commanding eyes.

The other figure was shorter, and it took Alex a moment to recognize the dark robe, the long fingers and pale skin. To say that the Head looked younger would have been a gross understatement. He stood straight-backed, his legs no longer slouched into an elder's limp. His hands at his sides were still pale and spindly, but strong with youth.

"I am sorry I did not invite you sooner," Finder said.

The Head shook his head.

"Many did not invite me at all, Lord Grey."

Malachi looked about the grounds, his eyes distant. He made several uncertain movements of his hands, as if he hoped to pull the right words out of the air, but when that seemed to fail, he spoke anyway.

"I saw Proignius devoured," he said. "I had never thought…"

The Head let out a low breath, and Alex thought he could see the man's features twisting sadly.

"Yes," he said. "I think we had all thought the old beast immortal."

A silence hung over the two men. The Head watched Malachi in anticipation, his stance never wavering.

Malachi, on the other hand, was shifting from foot to foot, his breathing uneven, his hands shaking.

"I'm sure you know of my talent," he said eventually.

The Head nodded. "They call you 'Finder.' They say you can locate any with magical talent, no matter how they try to hide."

Malachi nodded, licking his lips.

"I believe I can, my lord."

"And you would do that for me? Even knowing what would happen to them?"

Malachi had grown pale, shoving his shaking hands into his pockets.

"I would," he said in a voice that was little more than a whisper.

The Head nodded, and held out a hand, palm up. Malachi, however, did not take it. He looked at it with a detached, somber air, bringing up a hand to run through his dark curls.

"This is the only way to stop it, isn't it?" he said.

The Head nodded.

Malachi shuffled from foot to foot, staring around at the high walls of Spellshadow Manor, at the elegant statues and beautiful gardens. He drew in a shaking breath.

"If I hadn't invited you here," he said, "you would have come anyway."

There was certainty in his voice. Dread mixed with respect that hung on the air, sure as a promise. The Head did not move, simply continued to hold out his hand.

"You came for all of them," Malachi said.

Finally, at long last, the Head spoke again.

"What I offer is not a choice," he said, his voice coming out as a growl. "It is an inevitability. It is the fate that will one day come for all who bear magic in their veins."

Malachi Grey, Finder of Spellshadow Manor, nodded. He reached out, his hand hovering over the Head's.

"How did it come to this?" he asked.

The Head considered the question. A wind whipped at his cloak, sending it spinning back from his black trousers, his eyes gleaming under the hood.

"We walk in dreams, friend," he said eventually. "It was only a matter of time before a nightmare followed us back."

With a sharp motion, he brought his hand up against Finder's. Their palms met, and it was as though a bomb detonated from the spot. The shockwave tore across the grounds, throwing trees to the dirt, sending sprays of gray erupting into the air. Statues sundered in place, chunks of stone crashing down to the ground, and at the center of it all stood the two men.

Alex flinched away from the explosion, squeezing his eyes shut. He knew now that he was in a memory, in the past, but fear struck through him all the same.

Malachi's eyes were wet with tears, but he did not run. He stood, resolute, as wisps of magic ran up and down his body, then whirled into his skin, his eyes, his mouth. His head tipped back, and silver light poured from him as he let out a silent howl.

Alex watched in a mix or horror and awe as what made up the man slowly frayed away, the flesh and clothes disintegrating into ash, leaving nothing but a silvery, indistinct form that stood before the Head.

Bonds of red lightning crackled around the outline as bones began to fall from the whirling ash and clatter to the gravel. The Head stared into the vortex of power, then extended his other hand, his fingers pushing their way through the dust and debris. His hood flew back, revealing a young man with white hair and eyes the color of a sea at storm. His teeth were bared, his fingers moving in gestures so infinitely complex that Alex couldn't even begin to guess at their meaning.

With a noise like a massive blanket falling over the earth, the storm halted. Dust, trees, and pieces of statues fell to the ground, and the Head was left standing in a desolate field. In his hand was a skull, his thumb pushed through a hole just between the eyes.

The world came back to Alex in a whirl of light and shadows, and he staggered, gasping as he tried to regain his bearings. In one frost-wreathed hand he held a skull with three holes where the eyes should have been, and in front of him stood a man.

Finder drew back his hood to reveal a gaunt mask of what had been. His black curls fell in lank waves over hollow cheeks, his handsomely square jaw now knobby and worn. He stood there, staring at his own skull in Alex's hand.

"I am Malachi Grey of Spellshadow Manor," he said, and his voice was the rasp of shovels turning grave dirt. "I exist to serve the Head of Spellshadow. I find those with magic, and I bring them to this place."

Alex was shivering. Behind the figure, he saw Natalie regaining her feet, her hands beginning to weave a delicate, silver web of magic onto the ground around her.

"Why?" Alex asked. "Why do you bring them here?"

Finder rocked from foot to foot, his face sad, his expression lost.

"I am Malachi Grey of Spellshadow Manor," he said, ghostly magic flooding the air around him. The gray ivy shuddered, lifting off the surrounding statues to dance in the air. "I exist to serve the Head of Spellshadow. I find those with magic, and I bring them to this place."

Finder reached out, ghostly light pouring from his hands to wash over Alex in waves. Alex gritted his teeth, raising one hand against the magic, and prepared himself to fight.

CHAPTER 38

WHILE FINDER COULDN'T SEE ALEX, HE HAD NO difficulty seeing the skull frozen to Alex's left hand. Clearly using the yellowing bone as a reference, the ghost swept forward, his hands slashing and whirling in the air. Alex tried to keep up, but the master wizard's motions were too quick, his magic too powerful, and the young man felt the air burst from his lungs as he was smashed against the back wall. Loops of ivy draped over him and immediately began coiling about him, attempting to hold him in place. He thrashed frantically, trying to break away, his eyes on the ghost of Malachi Grey.

"I am Malachi Grey of Spellshadow Manor," the ghost roared over the howl of his own magic, the room shuddering with power, cracks spreading over the statues.

Alex managed to struggle free of the ivy, shoving himself away from the wall and back to his feet, darting to one side as the ghost leapt through the air, planting a fist into the earth where Alex had been a moment before and splitting the marble open. Steam rose from the chasm as the ghost's eyes came around, magic whipping the air as he rallied for another attack.

A little way back down the hall, Natalie continued to weave her spell. An arcane circle of light gathered around her, glowing shards of silvery magic rising up around her like petals, her face lined with sweat. Alex could see the red lines of the curse throttling her, but Natalie forced her way through, her teeth gritted as she moved her hands in soft, fluid motions.

A dull impact caught Alex in the stomach, and Finder let out a sigh of satisfaction as Alex was thrown to smash against the side wall. He felt something deep inside him let out a *pop*, and he gasped, clutching his side as his eyes blurred with pain. Frost coated the wound, but it seemed that Malachi was employing a type of magic that his blood wouldn't wholly defend against.

"Got you," the old wizard said, flexing his fingers. He rose to his full and considerable height, black hair floating about his head. "I should have done this sooner. It has been so long since I had the privilege of hunting one of your bloodline," he said.

Alex let out a cough, his whole body tingling with pain. He brought a shaking hand out in front of himself, and a shivering blade of anti-magic wobbled into existence. He stared at the tremulous blade and knew he wasn't going to win this fight.

But he didn't have to; all he had to do was buy time.

"You just hunt wizards now," Alex spat. "Isn't that right, Malachi Grey? The infamous Finder, turned upon his own."

Malachi stiffened, and something in his features distorted. His face grew hazy and indistinct, his hands clawing at the air as he let out a soundless moan of anger, his whole form shuddering.

"I do what I must," he said, the words smooth with practice. "I protect the world."

"You kill young men and women," Alex snapped, taking a step forward, kicking away a strand of ivy that attempted to encircle his foot.

Natalie's magic had begun to let off a dull hum, but Finder didn't seem to hear it. He moved forward, his focus on the skull in Alex's hand.

"I am Malachi Grey," he said softly.

"Of Spellshadow Manor," Alex finished. "You hunt down your kind for a heartless master, and you deliver them to their graves."

The ghost snarled, shaking his head, bursts of magic tearing the air around him.

"I find those with magic—"

"*And kill them.*"

Alex's words hung in the air. Silver light blazed in a bonfire around Natalie, who was going through a complex series of hand signs, the ivy unable to pass into her circle of power. Finder's head hung low, his hands limp at his sides.

"You don't know," he said. "You don't know the choice I had to make. The choice that haunts me beyond my death."

His head came up, and now his eyes had vanished, replaced by maggot-worn holes, his hands little more than bones. "Are you so noble?" he asked hollowly. "Do you think you are stronger than I am? Smarter? I have waited all my death for one to kill me for my sins. Will it be you? Do you have a better solution?"

Alex hesitated. His blade of anti-magic was fizzing as it pressed against Finder's magical aura.

"Solution to what?" he asked, uncertain now. Why *were* the students being killed? Would he finally have an answer? Not if he killed Finder now...

Finder reached out, his pale hand closing around Alex's sword. Frost hissed and popped into the air, a stream of ghostly snow pouring to the marble floor.

"A solution to what we made," replied Finder.

Alex opened his mouth, but Finder spread his hands. Ice flowed out across the floor, jagged spikes of glistening cold spearing up toward him. Alex deflected one with his hand and cried out in pain as the combined cold of the ice and the magical impact left a ragged scar of frostbite on his wrist.

"You forget," Finder said, stepping forward. "Even if my magic is a pale, ghostly mirror of what it once was, I have killed far better than you, boy."

Alex threw himself aside as another wave of ice slid across the floor, only to be caught by a shockwave. Again, the force tore through his resistances without as much as a flicker of cold. Alex smashed to the ground, rolling to his knees, thinking hard through his shock and fear.

Finder was doing something—something he, Aamir, Natalie, and Jari hadn't thought of. What was it? How was he getting through to him so easily? Alex watched as the man's hands churned the air in front of him, and braced himself against another wave of energy, followed by two whizzing spears of ice.

If Finder had been able to see Alex properly, it might have been over in that instant. However, the man was blind, forced to aim wildly in the direction of his own source. Alex held the skull as far from his body as he could as he dodged and weaved through the man's magic, trying to think, trying to figure out what he was doing.

A thunderous boom sounded, and an old lord's head

spun from its statue to smash against the floor. Shards of stone spun through the air, and one glanced painfully off Alex's foot. He groaned, looking down just in time to dodge another wave of ice. Finder was coming down on him hard, his mane of hair tossing in his magical energies.

"Yes!" the old man cried. "This is how it was always meant to be! Just you and me, Breaker, until one of us is in the lake."

He spread his hands, and Alex finally saw something. A blur in the air where the man's hands had been. A little twist, and then the shockwave tore out.

In an instant, Alex understood.

Finder wasn't attacking him directly with anything other than the ice. Like the statue that had hurt Alex when it had fallen, Finder was causing disturbances in the environment, making shockwaves designed to push Alex around without any magic in them at all. While their magical source may have imparted some power, they washed straight through his resistances.

Another wave, and Alex found himself slammed against the wall, the breath erupting from his lungs as he slumped down to the floor. Finder stalked up, his tattered robes swaying in the wind, looking down at the skull. He opened his mouth, then winced, spinning back to where Natalie stood.

The girl's eyes were closed in focus. Silver light spilled from the floor all around her as sweat poured down her brow, and she clapped her hands together, the light building to a brilliant flare. Finder snarled, making his way toward her.

Alex watched in horror from where he lay. He couldn't get there in time to stop Finder from interfering with Natalie's spell. Alex bashed the skull feebly against the ground, but it was as though the thing were made of steel. He looked on as Finder stalked toward his friend, swallowing hard, trying to stumble to his feet.

He wouldn't make it. He knew he wouldn't. He slumped to one knee, feeling something cold brushing against his side from the inside of his jacket. A faint, magical pulse. The screwdriver he'd brought along for no more than simple comfort.

In a moment of desperation, Alex reached down, tore the little device out of his pocket, and hurled it as hard as he could at the back of Finder's head.

Impossibly, it worked. Finder, sensing its presence, spun, one hand coming up, a look of puzzlement crossing his face as he batted the small device away with a flux of power.

That moment, however, was all Alex needed. He jumped at Finder, his anti-magic void sucking at the air around him, hungry for magic.

"*Alex!*"

Natalie's scream was accompanied by an eruption of power that circled both Alex and Finder's heads. Natalie stood, one hand outstretched, the intricate silver circle at her feet seeming to carve itself into Alex's eyes.

"Give me the skull!" she yelled.

Alex spun, bowling the skull across the floor toward her. Finder reached for it, his mouth twisting in a snarl, but Alex lashed out with a foot, spearing into the ghost's essence with his anti-magic.

Natalie let out a yell as she seized the skull and drove it down into the silvery light at her feet. With a crunch, it smashed apart upon the marble. Alex watched, stunned, as Finder's head splintered, then disintegrated into a cloud of gray mist, the ghost staggering back a step.

But Finder still had one last attack in him. He reached forward, his hands touching the air, and Alex thought he saw the twist of magic forming there. A shockwave. He didn't need to look at Natalie's tight face, the sweat dousing her brow, to know she wouldn't be able to withstand much more, and at this short a range, Alex didn't know if he could either.

Mustering the last of his energy, he formed a splinter of void and stabbed it straight into the center of the little knot of magic.

"Ah," said a disembodied voice.

The magic popped, and then vanished. For a moment, everybody stood perfectly still. The ghost, his hands still raised to form his spell. Alex, his chest heaving, the needle of grayish nothing flickering at his fingertips. Natalie, her face drawn, her knees shaking.

"So this is how the world ends," Finder said softly.

Holes began to appear all over the ghost's body, bursting open as he slowly lost the ability to keep his form together. He reached for Alex, who recoiled instinctively, but it was as though Finder's hands were shackled. They shuddered, then snapped back, drawn toward the dilapidated statue upon his altar.

With a crackle of magical energy, the air where the ghost stood seemed to splinter, leaving a visible wound in the fabric of the world. A wave of force roiled out from the place, smashing the statues of the crypt against the walls and sending stones tumbling down over the skulls on their neat pieces of white cloth.

Then everything was still.

Alex was dimly aware of a soft noise as Natalie fell to the ground. He turned, staring with wild eyes at where the girl lay upon the torn stone, eyes closed, cold sweat prickling through her clothes. Fearing the worst, Alex scrambled to her side, dropping to both knees, and reached out to shake her.

"Hey, Natalie."

She didn't respond. Was she even breathing?

"Natalie."

One eye opened slowly, a grin breaking out over her pale lips.

"Got him," she croaked. "Told you I could do it."

Alex let out a relieved laugh.

"Yeah," he said. "You did."

The room around them was in ruins. Statues lay shattered and broken, bits of bone and marble scattered all over floor. The long strands of gray ivy hung limp now, seeming almost dead in the wake of Finder's passing. Alex and Natalie huddled together amid the wreckage, taking a moment to catch their breath.

"Aamir," Natalie said eventually. "We must check on the duel."

Alex bit his lip. "But we're already there, remember? We can't show up twice."

Natalie shoved her way to her feet, and Alex caught her as she tottered unsteadily to one side.

"Then we will have to make sure nobody sees us. We'll hide or something. I don't know…but I can't stay here."

Alex, anxious to see how Aamir was faring, thought he understood. He tugged Natalie's arm over his shoulder, his body aching, and the two of them limped their way from the crypt. Alex's side continued to stab with pain, but nothing felt terribly out of place. All the same, he grimaced as he walked.

The sunlight of the gardens was almost blinding after the shifting shadows and darkness of the crypt. They both paused as they emerged, letting out twin sighs of relief that the rest of the world was, somehow, still there. The horizon beyond the wall showed hills, speckled with bell towers.

"Where was the duel?" Natalie asked. She sounded tired beyond all reach of rest, but her eyes were hard. She hung heavily on Alex's shoulder, gripping him tight.

"Main lawn," said Alex, remembering the words of the second-year earlier that morning. It was almost impossible to believe that a scarce couple hours had passed. They had probably only been in the crypt for fifteen minutes.

Fifteen minutes. Alex tried to imagine how long his longest duels with Aamir had gone. Eight minutes? Ten? Combat was a short, violent thing. Aamir could be…The duel could have finished already. He wrapped his arm tightly around his exhausted companion.

"We need to get going."

CHAPTER 39

ALEX HAD EXPECTED TO HEAR A TUMULT OF NOISE as they approached the main lawn of Spellshadow Manor, the very place where Finder and the Head had met on that fateful day all those years ago. However, the grounds were strangely silent. Natalie and Alex apprehensively eyed the gathered crowd as they stuck to the shadows along the wall.

Their clones were standing at the back of the crowd. Clone-Alex was staring back toward the manor, while clone-Natalie was watching whatever was happening on the lawn. On an instinct, Alex ducked out from the shadows to wave at himself, and the clone spotted the gesture, a smile spreading over his features.

The image reached out, tapped clone-Natalie's shoulder, and both trotted away from the crowd to join their originals. The clones were identical, save for the real Alex and Natalie's injuries. The crowd of watchers didn't even notice the two going.

"Hello," said clone-Alex, in Jari's voice.

Natalie eyed it distrustfully. "Hello," she answered.

"We were supposed to wait for you," said her clone, also in Jari's voice. "Wait for you, and then allow you to replace us when you arrived."

Alex nodded gratefully. "We'll be doing just that, then."

He almost yelped as his clone gave an all-too-familiar smile, then burst into a little puff of light. Natalie's clone softly exhaled, then followed suit. In an instant, both had vanished.

Natalie stared at the glimmering residue that was all that remained of their doubles.

"Did that disturb you as much as it disturbed me?" she asked, her mouth twisted.

"Almost definitely," muttered Alex, tugging her forward. "Come on. It looks like it isn't over yet."

They found Jari waiting for them at the crowd's edge, his face gray and his hands shaking. He didn't speak as they approached, just gestured them in. The little crowd of the forty or so students of Spellshadow Manor parted for them, letting them go to the front.

A large white box had been drawn onto the wild, twisted grass. The stones and debris had not been cleared, and the iconic gray vines still wove through the battlefield, glistening with the previous night's snow.

Aamir lay upon the ground, his back against the base of a shattered statue, his chest heaving up and down. Before him, looking as though he was out for an afternoon stroll, stood Professor Derhin.

The man was dressed in a long robe that reminded Alex of the classic images of wizards he had seen in his childhood, vials of alchemical liquids hung across his chest in a bandolier. He wore a wide-brimmed hat that hung low, hiding his eyes, and heavy leather boots that glowed with a quiet magic.

Alex was about to comment on the ridiculous getup when Derhin shifted, and a blazing line of lightning tore the air, striking the ground beside Aamir with a splintering crash. Alex blinked, and then he understood.

In the long robe, Aamir couldn't see Derhin's hands. With the low hat, he couldn't use his eyes to determine where the man was aiming. Aamir, in his long gray jacket, was offered none of the same protection. He made a gesture, but Derhin sidestepped it before it was even completed, giving the impression that the spell fell wide.

"He's making an example of him," Jari said, his voice cracking with panic. "I knew he would be strong, but this…this isn't fair. This isn't a duel; it's an execution."

Another shift of Derhin's cloak was all the warning Aamir got before two more bolts of lightning ripped the air asunder, sending a roll of thunder through the hushed crowd of students. The earth on one side of Aamir erupted, but the second bolt sliced his cheek, and Aamir screamed as a red cut appeared on his face, little lines of electricity crackling over his body.

With a stab of fear, Alex understood why Aamir and Natalie had only ever fought over a bottle. With Spellbreaker blood, Alex would only have been chilled by that spell. Aamir, however, was almost incapacitated, his fingers convulsing as his spine went rigid.

Derhin took a predatory step forward, easily sidestepping a blast of fire that whipped from Aamir's hands.

"This is the fate of those who disobey the system of Spellshadow Manor," Professor Derhin announced, tipping his hat back to stare Aamir directly in the eyes before turning his gaze on the assembled students. "This is what happens to those who think they know better than their superiors."

Aamir slammed his hand into the dirt at his side, and the stone at Derhin's feet exploded. The man leapt aside, his body unnaturally light, landing atop the remains of a nearby statue. He looked down at Aamir, then made a sharp gesture that Alex wasn't familiar with. He rasped angrily, and then Aamir gasped as the air was ripped from his lungs. He struggled, one hand clutching at his throat, the other limp at his side.

Had Natalie not been injured, Alex would have been unable to keep both his friends from the battlefield. As it was, he managed to get a hand on Jari's wrist just before the boy launched himself into the fray. His eyes burned cold, bloody murder, his skin clammy to the touch. At Alex's grasp, he turned an angry glare on his friend.

"Don't stop me," he hissed. "I am not watching while that monster kills my friend!"

"And I'm not watching while he kills you," Alex said. He could barely choke the words out of his mouth.

Jari's eyes were wet with tears as he looked back. Derhin drifted lazily down from his stand, landing in front of Aamir, who continued to struggle in the grass.

"Poor fool," said Derhin. "Poor, sad, weak—"

He cut off. Aamir had spun, and, with what seemed to be the last of his energy, grabbed a nearby strand of the graying ivy and whipped it at the professor. Derhin's cloak rustled as he made a gesture, but his magic burst around the hurled vine. As though it were hungry for magic, the end of the creeper spun around his ankle and held fast.

Aamir sucked in a breath and pulled. Derhin let out a cry of anger as he toppled to the ground, his hat flying off. He reached to the bottles at his chest, pulling one free as Aamir staggered to his feet, ripping out the cork and downing the contents.

The ivy grasping his side glowed, as if with inner fire,

then burst. Sprays of plant matter flew through the air as the professor's hands came up, magic forming upon them.

But Aamir could see them now. Flat on his back, the man was forced to bring his hands up out of his cloak's protective embrace to cast his magic, and Aamir reached forward, his hands like claws, and grabbed the professor's magic before throwing it aside. Aamir raised a hand, and Derhin's eyes snapped to the young student's fingers, looking for the telltale sign that would reveal the magic and allow him to overcome it.

What hit him, however, was a fist.

Derhin cried out as Aamir's hand sank into his face, smacking the man's head back against the grass. He raised a hand, but Aamir slapped it aside, pinning it with his boot to ensure that it couldn't form any more signs, then delivered a second blow to the professor's face, aiming for the older man's eyes. Derhin let out a shriek, kicking, but for all the professor's magic, Aamir was physically stronger. Derhin let out a grunt as another blow pitched his jaw sideways to the grass, and Aamir's hand rose again.

"That will be quite enough."

Every head turned as the dry voice split the air, and a hush fell over the crowd as it parted for a lean figure who made his slow way over the lawn. The Head seemed larger than he had when Alex had seen him in the Manor's memories. He stood taller, his frame still willow-thin, his delicate fingers seeming to stroke the air like they were dipping into water. But his heavy boots no longer fit well, and he walked with a limp. Thin white hair spilled from under his hood, drifting back from his form like mist at his passing.

Aamir did not rise from his position atop Derhin as the master of the school approached, but he did lower his fist, his head dipping in deference. The Head nodded in return, his gaze sweeping to Derhin.

"Avery," he said, his voice low with disappointment.

Derhin began to struggle, and Aamir stepped away to allow the man to rise to his knees, his head bowing toward the Head.

"Sir," he said, his voice nasal as one hand strayed to his bloodied nose. "The boy cheated. He used crass, physical blows to win, and also abused the natural and overpowering magic that you have placed into the manor itself. Surely you can see that I am the superior teacher, far better qualified to—"

The Head held up a hand, and the stammering professor grew quiet, his eyes gazing up at the old man. Alex's eyes flicked uncertainly between them.

"You lost," said the Head slowly. "You know better than most that what I require of my professors is not sheer magical prowess, but guile. The ability to overcome. The strength to do what is necessary."

Derhin was shaking now, his hands balling into fists at his sides, his skin pale.

"Sir, I have demonstrated those qualities," he said. "More than anyone, I have demonstrated them. Allow me to duel one of the other professors, if you truly wish to accept the boy as a teacher."

"Avery," the Head said again with a sad shake of his head. "I remember when you first came here. So bright. So clever. You had half your class under your thumb in a month. You had half the staff under it by the next. You even secured your friend a position within the faculty."

Derhin nodded eagerly. "Alexander Lintz," he said. "I helped him through his trials."

So that was their connection, the reason Lintz seemed to feel indebted to Derhin. Alex's eyes widened in understanding.

"And yet, here you kneel," the Head went on. "And now even you must receive this final lesson: all things end, child."

Professor Derhin, dressed in his wizard's robes, really did look like nothing more than a child. A student who had been caught breaking the rules, and now bent his knees and his head in fear of the cane. Alex felt what was almost a flutter of sympathy for the man.

However, as he heard the Head's words, Derhin stiffened, his eyes flashing. Blood dripped off his nose to patter upon the grass.

"All things, sir?" he said, his voice sharp with derision.

The Head said nothing. The wind stirred his thin white

hair, pulling it gently back, his hands motionless at his sides.

Derhin moved in a blur. His hand spun out, his fingers splaying as he let out a cry of fury. To Alex's surprise, he did not attack the Head, but turned his anger on Aamir. Jari went rigid with fury at Alex's side, his hand darting up, the sign of lightning forming upon his fingers, but before the boy could do anything, the Head acted.

The whole world *bent*. The magic which had been rushing toward Aamir's shocked face spun up into the sky, then seemed to implode, winking out as if it had never existed. Derhin turned his eyes on the Head, cracking his neck. His voice, when he spoke, had dropped. It sounded wet, a ripping, bloody sound, and Alex cringed inwardly at the danger it held.

"And what about you, sir?" he said. "Do *you* ever end?"

Red light began spilling out of Derhin like crimson fog, pooling into an angry sea of power around him as his grin turned vicious. The Head did not move, regarding the welling magic, but Jari let out a gasp.

"We need to get out of here," he urged.

The other students had already begun to back away, the more senior grabbing their fellows by the sleeves and dragging them closer to the manor. Alex watched as Aamir looked at the growing power and began backing away too.

"What is happening?" Natalie asked, raising a hand to shield her eyes against a thrum of scarlet light that whipped around Derhin.

"Life magic," Alex breathed.

There are two types of magic in a person, Professor Lintz had explained. *One comes from your essence, and we call this magic. Life magic, on the other hand, comes from your soul itself. To tap into it, even once, causes irreparable damage to a person's very existence.*

Derhin let out a scream of pain, his hands flying to his head, his mouth falling open. A soft, bronze light began gathering around the Head in response, and where the two magics met, the air sizzled with power.

"Alex."

Alex turned to see Jari's frantic eyes.

"We *need* to go!"

Alex could not help looking back, watching in awe as Derhin unfolded from his kneeling posture, his back straightening, his feet drifting up off the ground as the dirt and stone ruptured under him. He made no gestures of his hands, but his eyes had turned a soft, glowing amber as he stared at the Head.

Dimly, Alex could hear Jari yelling, could see Natalie's pale face.

Then, the sky vanished in a calamity of bloody light.

CHAPTER 40

THE EARTH RIPPED ITSELF TO PIECES IN FRONT OF Professor Derhin, and Alex could see something manifesting—the gold and crimson form of a giant beast he could not put a name to moving through the sea of magic. Its claw-like hands savaged the dirt, the walls, the ivy. It seemed bent on destroying the manor, escaping at any cost.

Alex shouted, reaching into the void, not sure what he was searching for. His lost friends. The anguished professor. The safety of the Head's magic. He felt each there, as if in the chaos they had blended into a single entity. He felt the angry, thrashing coils of Derhin's panic.

He felt Natalie's fear and determination. He felt Jari and Aamir reaching for one another. And he felt an ancient power, deep as space and full of quiet sadness.

A bolt of amber cleaved through the storm, sending ripples of rusty light crackling over the clouds. Derhin's magic grew brighter, more fearful, savaging the confines of the manor in a desperate attempt to get away. It reached for the gate with one colossal hand, and the Head's magic flickered down in a rush.

Alex watched as the Head emerged from within his power, his hood low, his robes flapping, his hands moving in short, languid motions. With a swipe, he pulverized the great beast's magical arm. With another, he blasted a hole in the sea of red. And with a third, he ended the confrontation.

The world came back in a rush, and Alex gasped. The blue sky, the brisk winter breeze, the students, still standing where they had been moments before. Not one of them was harmed, but Alex stared in awe at where great swaths of the ivy had been torn from the wall, leaving deep, smoking gashes in the masonry. He was still staring at the damage when he heard the weeping begin.

"Please," Professor Derhin was pleading pathetically, "please, I'm sorry. I can still be useful, you know I can be."

Alex turned and found the professor crumpled upon the ground. His arms and legs were shaking violently, and his eyes looked dull and glassy. Blood trickled down from one cheek, but the professor made no move to wipe it from his face. He was staring up at where the Head stood over him.

The old man's face was invisible, and he stood in a stance that was at once authoritative and relaxed. His long-fingered hands hung slack at his sides.

"Your uses are at an end, Avery," he said.

Derhin winced away from the Head. "Please," he breathed. "Please, don't do this. You don't have to do this." Alex felt a little sick at the scene, his gut twisting with anticipation. Surely the Head wouldn't…

The Head shook his head.

"I do."

He turned, facing the crowd with gleaming eyes. "Renmark. Esmerelda."

The two professors stepped forward, faces pale, but a third form accompanied them. Lintz's heavy features shook as he planted his feet, sweat beading upon his brow.

The Head looked at him, then nodded. Alex frowned as what he could see of the Head's mouth twisted with sorrow.

"I'll do it," Lintz said in a husky voice.

Derhin's eyes widened with shock. "Alexander," he said.

Lintz looked to Esmerelda, who gave a stiff nod, and the two of them marched forward, each seizing Derhin by an arm. The man seemed too stunned to fight back. He looked between his two captors, his expression blank and uncomprehending.

"Alexander," he repeated. "What are you doing?"

Lintz didn't respond. Slowly, he began to drag the once professor toward the manor.

"We did so much together," Derhin pleaded. "We practiced together. We planned together. We were going to escape together."

Lintz said nothing, his eyes lowered.

"Alexander!" Derhin cried, one hand finally snapping up to scrabble at the big man's hand. "You can't do this!"

"Hush," Esmerelda said, her voice chiding. "Can't you see he's doing this for you?"

Derhin's eyes snapped to Alex and Natalie as he was dragged past them.

"You did this," he hissed, his heels digging in against the inexorable force of his colleagues. His face was not angry, however. It was set with resignation, and a sudden mirth bubbled out over it. His voice rose up to break into a laugh. "You helped Aamir train! But you'll never get out of this place."

Alex stared at the man's back as he was hauled away, his limbs going limp, his laughter the only sound on the cold air.

"Aamir."

Alex turned sharply at the voice. The Head stood just beside him, facing Jari and Aamir, who stood next to each other. Aamir stepped forward, and Alex thought he saw a shadow pass over Jari's face.

"Sir," Aamir said, kneeling as Derhin had.

With Derhin's laughter still hanging on the air, the Head began to speak.

"You have demonstrated a great deal of courage and capability," he said, his voice thick and soft all at once. "Are you willing to pass those qualities on to your students?"

Aamir's head sank in assent. "I am."

"Will you teach them to the best of your abilities, and raise them into capable credits to the magical race?"

"I will."

"Are you ready to make sacrifices for the greater good?"

Aamir hesitated, but in the end, he nodded. Without fully comprehending why, Alex's heart sank.

"I am."

Derhin's bubbling laughter cut off abruptly as the door to the manor snapped shut behind him, and the Head held out a hand.

"Then rise, Professor Nagi of Spellshadow, and come with me. There is much you must know. Much you must understand."

Aamir reached out, taking the Head's withered hand, and rose to his feet. He was a tall young man, but somehow the Head dwarfed him as he drew the boy to his feet, then turned and made his limping way back toward the manor.

As Aamir made to follow, Jari stepped forward.

"Be safe," was all he whispered, reaching out to give

Aamir's shoulder a squeeze.

Aamir glanced over with a smile, then looked to Alex and Natalie.

"How'd it go?"

At Alex's side, Natalie flashed a quick thumbs-up, and Aamir gave a short nod. The Head had paused, looking back at Aamir, who hurried to catch up. The crowd of students parted as the two made their way through it, vanishing into the manor.

CHAPTER 41

AMIR DID NOT RETURN TO THE DORM THAT night. Natalie had joined Alex and Jari there, and sat on the edge of Alex's bed as Jari stared over at the empty, neatly made sheets and freshly fluffed pillows of Aamir's sleeping space. Nobody quite wanted to sit there. It felt like a sacred place.

"I feel like I should be happier," Jari said, his head low.

Natalie made a soft noise of agreement.

"I mean, he won," Jari said, laughing humorlessly. "Did you see him punch Derhin? I swear, he's wanted to do that for about a year now. Must have at least felt a little bit good."

Nobody spoke.

"Where do you suppose the Head took Derhin?"

An image fluttered into Alex's mind, of a small room with chains and a bladeless knife beside a ledger. He closed his eyes a moment, trying to rid himself of the thought.

"No clue," he replied.

"When do you think Aamir will be back?" Natalie asked.

"In the morning, I'm sure," Alex said.

Jari nodded, his face lightening a little.

"In the morning."

But Aamir did not return in the morning. When the students filed into the room meant for Professor Derhin's class, they found it empty. When fifteen minutes had passed and no professor had arrived, most of the students let themselves out, wandering back to their other projects. Alex just sat there, staring at the empty desk.

"My curse disappeared."

Alex looked up to see that Natalie had taken Aamir's old seat beside him.

Alex grunted. "Guess that means Derhin is gone."

Natalie's face darkened. "I guess so."

Four orbs of fire blossomed into being all around her, spinning in a tight circle to orbit her hand. She sighed.

"I wonder when Aamir will be back," she said.

Alex stared at where Jari still sat, his eyes on the door

like a dog waiting for its owner to come home.

"Soon, I hope," was all he could say.

Days passed. Jari's grief grew to a soft, simmering sorrow. It even reached the point where Ellabell came over to him, putting an uncertain hand on his shoulder in a reassuring pat. Perhaps more alarming still, Jari only nodded in gratitude at the gesture, then looked back down at his desk.

The absence of Jari's smiles hit Alex harder than he would have expected, harder than he liked to admit. More and more he found himself wandering to the library, attempting to distract himself with the *Historica Magica*. He found, however, that he couldn't focus on the book. The words fell together in a gloomy blur, and after a time he would just shut the book and look out the window.

Nobody seemed to notice Finder's absence. Alex figured they would have a few days yet before the Head took note of the old ghost's disappearance, and then things were going to get interesting. His body still ached with the pains of the battle, but something told him it was only the beginning.

Natalie seemed to think much the same. She sat in her usual chair, gazing out the massive glass wall of the library.

"Did you hear what he said?" she asked, two days after the duel.

"Mm?"

"Derhin."

"Which part?"

Natalie was silent for a long time. "The part about how he and Lintz were supposed to escape together."

Alex nodded. He had been churning that around in his mind ever since, the fact that even the professors craved freedom. That even they weren't safe.

Natalie licked her lips, running her fingers through her hair. "I just. I mean." She looked over at Alex. "I had not thought of it like that. He was so much the enemy that I hadn't even considered that…"

"…that he might be like us?" Alex finished.

Natalie nodded, her lips twisting. "Yes."

They stared out the window together, watching a horizon of endlessly shifting waves, whitecaps frothing the water amid swirls of rain and sleet.

"How is your research?" Natalie asked.

Alex looked down at the *Historica,* then shrugged.

"Grim." How could he explain the loneliness, the powerlessness that accompanied reading over and over that your ancestors had all been murdered? That you were the last of your kind? According to the book, there was nobody left to instruct him, to guide him. There weren't even any books they had left behind, no treasure trove of advice to follow. Of survival skills.

Natalie sighed, and Alex said nothing more.

Aamir's absence seemed to have driven a wedge into every aspect of their life. The empty classes. The awkward silences that were meant to be filled by the young man's dry, academic remarks. The hole where his wry smile was supposed to be burned hot in all their hearts.

The three of them continued to attend the empty class, even after their peers abandoned it for more useful pursuits. They sat in the sea of tables and empty chairs, talking, trying to fill a space that seemed determined to fill itself with absence.

Alex was thumbing through the *Historica* when he finally found it. Jari and Natalie were chatting, and he was watching the interaction, his finger running smoothly over the pages until one caught. He looked down, and saw something sticking out between the pages of the book. A small, withered thing, dry with age, and folded into a tiny square. It must have been pressed between the pages, lodged there all this time.

He took it out, unfolding it curiously, and was surprised to find that it was the page of another book. However, while most of the books he had found at the manor were fine print, some even inked by hand in a delicate, precise script, this page looked as though it held the ravings of a madman. The writing was cursive, but seemed to follow no lines or pattern. Large, looping letters covered one another, some crossed out, others stuffed into margins. Alex tilted the page, trying to decipher it. Bit by bit, he pulled meaning out of the page.

Of our havens, it read, *nine remained. However, they*

are lost lost LOST. Winterlight's halls are dark now. Sungrove House's trees have been mulched. One by one, we lose everything. One by one by one by one by—

The trend continued, the words spiraling around and in upon themselves, filling up the blank space of the page. Alex thought that the information was at an end when he found several more notes.

Of our havens, nine remained. Of those nine, we now have four. I record them here for the sake of any who might find this journal. If you are magical, seek these places. Kingstone Keep. Falleaf House. Stillwater House. Spellshadow Manor.

Alex stared. Suddenly, his heart was in his throat, lurching to and fro. Stillwater House was the sister school that had been mentioned earlier in the year as the place where disobedient students were sent; was it possible that it was a real place? Were there others out there, like them?

The page, however, wasn't done.

Seek these places, and do not leave them, said the script, and it seemed that the writer had grown tired. The words were shaking, thin, unsteady things. *If you wish to live, cower within their walls as I have done. Cower, and await the Glutton's communion. We are all meat, and he is the mouth.*

The handle of the door turned.

Alex jumped. He'd been so caught up in the page that he had completely lost track of his surroundings. Jari and

Natalie, who had been chatting, looked at the door to the classroom as it opened a crack.

Aamir slid in through the gap, his eyes flicking around the room, then settling on his friends with familiar warmth. He wore long professor's robes, but his face hadn't changed. Jari let out a cry, bounding to his feet and all but throwing himself at the older boy, who caught him in a tight embrace and smiled.

"You're late," Jari muttered into Aamir's shoulder.

"There was a lot to learn," Aamir replied.

Natalie rose to her feet, walking over to Aamir and giving him a quick hug from the side.

"Welcome back," she said.

Aamir nodded at her. "It is good to be back."

In his chair, Alex quickly folded the page into quarters, then slipped it into his pocket. The action was almost unconscious; later he wouldn't be able to say why he did it. It was an instinct, born of much time spent looking of his shoulder. He stood, walking to where Aamir was now trying to dislodge Jari from his waist.

"Your first class has rather poor attendance," Alex remarked.

Aamir sighed, looking at the rows of empty chairs. "I guess it's only to be expected," he said.

The two watched each other for a long moment, and Alex thought he saw wariness in the other boy's eyes. A cautious, distrustful look that had never been there before.

"What did you learn?" Alex asked.

And Aamir's eyes slid away.

"Mostly we talked about the governance of the school," he replied, finally managing to pull Jari away from his chest. "How classes are run, how to evaluate projects, how best to help the students. You know, boring stuff."

Natalie's smile flickered, her eyes tingeing with confusion.

"You must have learned *something* about this place?" she queried.

Aamir smiled apologetically, but once again the expression didn't quite make it to his eyes, which continued to look anywhere but at his friends.

"The Head was rather sparing with the details," he said. "I will say this, however. I do not think he is as evil as we have thought."

Alex felt his face go blank. "What? He's keeping us prisoner," he said. "He makes people disappear."

A ripple of pain flowed over Aamir's face, and he bit his lip. He shoved his hands into his pockets and stared up at the ceiling.

"I think it might be more complicated than that," Aamir replied.

Frustration bubbled up in Alex's gut, and he could see the same suspicious expression blossoming onto Natalie's face.

"Aamir," Alex began, "what—"

He let out a yelp of pain as Jari stepped on his toe. He glowered at the smaller boy, who smiled beatifically back at him.

"Let him be," Jari said. "Aamir—sorry, *Professor Nagi* has had a long couple of days."

The gratitude in Aamir's expression as he looked toward Jari was vibrant, and Alex felt momentarily guilty. Of course Aamir was going through a lot. He had been in a duel to the death not a week ago, and since then had been stolen away by the most powerful wizard on the estate to do who knew what until being shoved back into a group of inquisitive friends.

"Sorry," Alex conceded.

Natalie, however, seemed unimpressed. "We don't exactly have the luxury of time."

Aamir winced, and Jari's back straightened. Before Jari could speak, however, Aamir held up a hand. As he did so, his sleeve fell down to reveal a small golden line wrapping around his wrist.

"I'm telling you all I can," he said.

Alex stared at the mark on the boy's skin, and his mouth went dry as he remembered the spearing blades of ice that had erupted from the place where he had severed the last such thing. Aamir's brown eyes slid to meet Alex's at last, and Alex could see something deep within his friend. It was something he had seen before, on the faces of the other professors.

Fear.

"I will do my best to keep you safe," Aamir promised. "I will do everything in my power to protect you. Do not forget that."

Alex stared at the boy, and again he recalled Derhin, staring up at Professor Lintz.

We were going to escape together.

He took a step back as Aamir sighed, his eyes wandering over them.

"I should get on with the lesson," he said. "It's stupid, but I am required to still teach these stances. Sit wherever."

He turned away, walking to the front of the room as his friends sat down in a line in the front row. Aamir's back slouched a little as he began to write down the notes for a new magical stance, his precise handwriting quickly covering the board. He was efficient, and direct in a way that Derhin had never been, and it was easy to see that he had been thinking about ways to teach for a long time, since far before the idea to actually take a teacher's position had occurred to him. He taught with a fluid grace, his jaw set, his eyes hot with worry.

Watching him, Alex could feel a shiver running down his spine. They were back together—they had won. Overwhelming victory on all fronts. Derhin thrown down, Finder destroyed. Natalie's curse removed. As Aamir chalked another line on the board, then turned to demonstrate a subtle hand position before elaborating on the types of magic it would be useful for performing, Alex found himself wondering why it felt like they had lost.

It was cold in the little room. Magic pressed against Alex from all sides, wrapping about him, poking at him like great teeth, gently kneading him until he was ready for consumption.

If you wish to live, cower within these walls.

Alex thought of the great gates, wreathed in impenetrable ivy, impossible to open or close for anyone other than a chosen few.

Cower, and await the Glutton's communion.

Walls. Great, imposing walls that kept everything in.

We walk in dreams, the Head had said. *It was only a matter of time before a nightmare followed us back.*

Great, imposing walls that kept everything out.

Another chill ran down Alex's spine. He hadn't figured it out yet. He knew he didn't have all the information. Still, he thought of the crushed remains of Finder's skull, and wondered if they had made a terrible mistake.

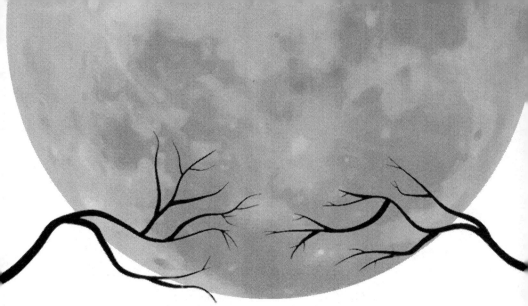

EPILOGUE

ON THE ROOF OF THE MANOR, ELIAS POURED himself from one shadow to the next. His magical body elongated and warped, sliding into the mossy cracks between the old slates of clay, deftly avoiding starlight as he made his way over to a chimney and spilled down into it. He dribbled along soot-stained brick, dripping down into a long-dead hearth.

If he had been able to feel, he might have experienced something like triumph. The previous week's plans had gone off beautifully. At long last, Malachi had been put to rest, and the school's supply of young wizards would dry up with him. It wasn't checkmate, not yet, but he had taken the Head's queen, and now he was eyeing the king with his black eyes. Yes, if he'd been able to feel, he might have experienced triumph in that moment.

However, Elias wasn't able to feel. Not triumph, not love, not hate. He had only the tattered remnants of a personality, carved into his very being in a final, desperate act by a terrified man. He had a purpose, and like a clock driving its hands perpetually toward the next minute, that cause drove him.

Elias emerged into a hallway, watching students talking in hushed voices, their arms folded and their eyes suspicious. He clung to the ceiling, curled tight into the shadow of a light fixture, magical tendrils webbing out along the seams of bricks to find his next hiding place. The students, he thought, never changed. They were as they had been, all those years ago. Scared, studious, and ignorant. It was how the Head liked them.

It was how he had been.

Elias pulled himself languorously into his next shadow, pausing as Alex, the young Spellbreaker, strode past him. Now there was an anomaly. By all accounts, the boy shouldn't have been here. His presence was bizarre. But like a desperate man handed a sword in his moment of need, Elias was not one to complain. The boy was an incredible weapon. Effective almost to a fault. The only problem with him was his morality. That might get in the way before long, Elias knew. If the boy knew the whole truth, it was impossible to say what he might do.

Beside him was the girl. Natalie, Elias thought she was called, but he didn't put much stock by her. She was ordinary. Talented, yes, but he had seen talent before. Had it not been for her association with the Breaker, Elias wouldn't have even bothered to take notice of her. She was a pawn.

Elias slipped through a lock, crossing through the mechanics' lab. Students sat, bent over their tables with loupes in hand, staring down at minuscule magic machinations that clicked and whirred under their carefully applied picks. A quick trip through the vents and Elias was in the alchemy lab, multicolored smoke clouding against the ceiling, strange smells and sounds rippling off the walls as students in long coats added to their mixtures with trepidation on their faces.

The small blond boy was here. Elias thought he was Greek, but he didn't have a name for him. He was the new professor's friend. He was stirring a violently green mixture with an absent expression on his face, a half-smile quirking his lips. Another pawn.

Elias considered the new professor as he slid back out into the hallway, darting between the quick little shadows of raindrops. The boy, Nagi, seemed smart and resistant, but he had a love for tradition that worried Elias. He might become a friend or an enemy. Either way, he was no pawn. He would be valuable in the conflict to come.

As Elias drew nearer the Head's wing, the shadows grew heavier, and he let himself slide off the wall, congealing into the familiar form of a young man with a shock of black hair. He ran his fingers through it in a gesture that was more unconscious than useful. He had a lot of habits like that. Small, forgotten ticks of a person who used to be.

He turned his head to look at things, even though his eyes had nothing to do with the location of his head. He moved his hands to bring about his magic, even though he himself *was* the magic. Some part of him, some deep, central part, remembered. It remembered skin. It remembered blood. It remembered life.

But it was only a memory.

Elias nearly hissed as he came around a corner and found himself blocked by a small avalanche of gray ivy. The stuff was poison to his existence. Touching it would create pain such as he had rarely known, an unbinding of his essence. He slid away from it and found another path.

He strode down the hallway, his feet slipping into the shadows beneath them and making no noise at all. He was darkness. He was shadow. He was…

Who was he?

His mind, broken apart and pieced back together time and time again, strained. He thought he could recall something. Something distant, something burned into the very depth of his essence.

He remembered skin. He remembered the cold bite

of manacles on his wrists as he struggled uselessly. He remembered the damp, dewy touch of the ivy as it hung heavy on his shoulders.

He recalled the scene. There had been three people. The Head had been there, along with a young man Elias knew to be himself, and another boy in shining glasses. That spectacled boy had...*hurt* Elias. He had chosen him, and seen him cast down. Had there been a fight? Elias didn't remember.

In the hallway, Elias lost his form, collapsing as a shadow to the ground, curling into a corner and waiting to regroup as he shuddered with thoughts. Why had they been there? What had happened to his skin?

He dove deeper into the memory. The Head was doing something, writing a note down on the table. The young man he knew to be himself—what was his name?—was watching the Head with sad, determined eyes. The spectacled boy said something. Something useless. Something unimportant.

The Head turned, gently lifting the handle of a knife. It was a familiar and terrible object. A silver blade formed upon the empty hilt, spilling out like mercury upon a tabletop. The young man's mouth went dry, his lips opening to unleash so many pleading cries and whimpers. He looked away. The stupid young man. He had ruined *every-thing* for himself. He had been so close.

Anger filled him, and he thrashed in his bonds, mouth

open, spit dripping from his lips. The Head walked closer, the knife in one hand, and reached out.

It was like someone had pushed a wedge into the young man's heart. The air went out of him. The very core of his being fluttered, wavered, evaporated. The young man watched in horror as the Head pulled a strand of red magic out of him, wrapping it around one finger over and over again. The Head was so gentle. So precise and gentle and cruel.

The young man strained, his head lolling, seeing the spectacled boy not looking, and now Elias recalled the boy's name. Avery Derhin. The one who had become a teacher, had challenged him. Known he was an easy target. Cast him down as Elias had done to his master, once.

And how it *hurt.* The ache of his essence peeling from his very being was an exultation of pain. It made him giddy, made him laugh, feeling the lightness of his body, the fire in his breast, the hurt, the hurt, the overwhelming *hurt.*

His hands were moving. Forming signs he had told his students never to use, focusing his energy into all the right shapes. His arms were bound above his head, and his motions were far from perfect, but his mind was an anvil against which he tempered his will, and the spell took form. Derhin's eyes widened. He said something. The Head gave Elias a sharp look with his piercing eyes.

And then, Elias was a shadow.

395

In the hallway, Elias tried to pant, but he had no lungs. He tried to stand, but he had no legs. He was magic, and he was lifeless. He was formless. He was nothing, and yet he was Elias. The memory he had been hiding within slowly melted, crumbling down around him like ice before a flame. He kept moving.

The gardens of the manor were in fine disarray today. The snags and brush cast wicked swaths of shadow for Elias to tread between, and he practically zipped across the grass, the blades not even trembling at his passing. He was not many things anymore, but he was fast.

The cemetery was in shadow. The sun had slipped behind the manor, and Elias noted with approval that the little golden line that blocked off the catacombs had been broken, leaving nothing but a tangled wreckage of ice.

The Breaker was coming into his own. If Elias could just give him the right information, he would be the perfect dagger.

Slipping over the snow and grass, Elias came to a headstone. There had never been a name there, but as he pressed his shadowy form into the stone, he could feel it all the same.

Elias Olkrum.

"Ah," Elias panted, a heat blazing through him. He contorted into the form of a man, kneeling on the grass, his hands balled into fists as he heaved with pain. His name reignited his power. It gave him strength.

Beside his grave was another. It was newer, but no less blank. If he didn't visit the little stand of headstones every day, he might not have even noticed it appear, but he did, and it had.

The image of a boy with glasses, staring at Elias as he thrashed in his chains, flickered through his mind.

In a flash, Elias was back in that room. His wrists chafed against the cold manacles. The magic burned at his fingertips. The Head held his silvery knife while Avery Derhin took a step back, his eyes wide.

The Head was a powerful magician, but an old man. He'd swiped the dagger down toward the crimson thread he'd pulled from Elias's chest, but he hadn't been fast enough. Elias had let out a hiss, his eyes open, his mouth moving in a single command as a shadow had poured from his fingertips which had formed the sign of anima. Elias the shadow had been born, and had flown across the room, sliding from shade to dark. Then the Head's eyes had stared coldly as he'd slashed with the blade, and the little red cord emerging from the human Elias's chest had been severed neatly at the base. The Head had stood there, and as shadow-Elias had fled, he'd seen the man sliding the life magic into a little black bottle. In his chains, hung from the ceiling, Elias had shuddered once, and then gone still.

And so, shadow-Elias had watched human-Elias die.

He'd fled out into the hallways. His memories had fallen apart. His emotions had died with his life.

His entire existence had begun to revolve around a single, simple mantra. The words that had been burned into him by his dying breath.

Elias got to his feet in front of his grave and looked up at the tall walls. Slowly, he let his form dissolve, sinking back into the shapeless mass of darkness.

He knew he wasn't a man anymore. The Breaker had called him 'homunculus'; perhaps that was correct. Elias didn't even have the capacity to care.

What he knew was that he had been killed. His last words burned inside him, the only thing that mattered, the command to be carried out at all costs.

Destroy this place.

Without a sound, Elias vanished back into the manor.

Dear Reader,

Whether you're a fan of my Shade series, The Gender Game, or brand new to my books, I want to thank you for your time in taking a chance on this book. I haven't worked on a story quite like it before, so it's been a new experience for me—and I hope I managed to entertain you!

As for Book 2 of the Spellshadow series, it's called The Breaker, and releases April 30th, 2017.

Visit: www.BellaForrest.net for more information.

Until next time,
Bella x

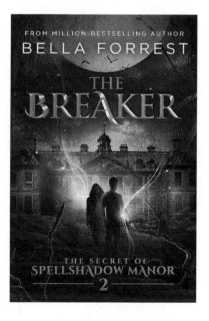

ALSO BY BELLA FORREST

THE GENDER GAME

The Gender Game
The Gender Secret (Book 2)
The Gender Lie (Book 3)
The Gender War (Book 4)
The Gender Fall (Book 5)

A SHADE OF VAMPIRE SERIES

Series 1: Derek & Sofia's story
A Shade of Vampire (Book 1)
A Shade of Blood (Book 2)
A Castle of Sand (Book 3)
A Shadow of Light (Book 4)
A Blaze of Sun (Book 5)
A Gate of Night (Book 6)
A Break of Day (Book 7)

Series 4: A Clan of Novaks

A Clan of Novaks (Book 25)

A World of New (Book 26)

A Web of Lies (Book 27)

A Touch of Truth (Book 28)

An Hour of Need (Book 29)

A Game of Risk (Book 30)

A Twist of Fates (Book 31)

A Day of Glory (Book 32)

Series 5: A Dawn of Guardians

A Dawn of Guardians (Book 33)

A Sword of Chance (Book 34)

A Race of Trials (Book 35)

A King of Shadow (Book 36)

An Empire of Stones (Book 37)

A Power of Old (Book 38)

A Rip of Realms (Book 39)

A Throne of Fire (Book 40)

A Tide of War (Book 41)

A SHADE OF DRAGON TRILOGY
A Shade of Dragon 1
A Shade of Dragon 2
A Shade of Dragon 3

A SHADE OF KIEV TRILOGY
A Shade of Kiev 1
A Shade of Kiev 2
A Shade of Kiev 3

DETECTIVE ERIN BOND (Adult thriller/mystery)
Lights, Camera, Gone
Write, Edit, Kill

BEAUTIFUL MONSTER DUOLOGY
Beautiful Monster 1
Beautiful Monster 2

For an updated list of Bella's books, please visit her website:
www.BellaForrest.net

Join Bella's VIP email list and she'll personally send you an
email reminder as soon as her next book is out:
www.MoreBellaForrest.com